Thrust

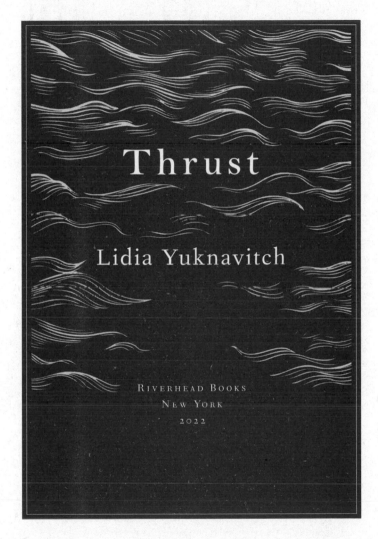

Thrust

Lidia Yuknavitch

RIVERHEAD BOOKS
NEW YORK
2022

RIVERHEAD BOOKS
An imprint of Penguin Random House LLC
penguinrandomhouse.com

Riverhead and the R colophon are registered trademarks of Penguin Random House LLC.

Illustrations on pages 1, 34, 109, and 265 by John Burgoyne; image on
page 161 courtesy of the American Antiquarian Society.

Library of Congress Cataloging-in-Publication Data

Names: Yuknavitch, Lidia, author.
Title: Thrust / Lidia Yuknavitch.
Description: Hardcover edition. | New York : Riverhead Books, 2022.
Identifiers: LCCN 2021043189 (print) | LCCN 2021043190 (ebook) |
ISBN 9780525534907 (hardcover) | ISBN 9780525534921 (ebook)
Classification: LCC PS3575.U35 T57 2022 (print) | LCC PS3575.U35 (ebook) |
DDC 813/.54—dc23
LC record available at https://lccn.loc.gov/2021043189
LC ebook record available at https://lccn.loc.gov/2021043190

International edition ISBN: 9780593542156

Printed in the United States of America
1st Printing

BOOK DESIGN BY MEIGHAN CAVANAUGH

This book is for Miles Mingo, sun of my life.

~

And for every child who will cross the threshold next, every kind of body and soul, every orphan and misfit, every immigrant and refugee, every gender imaginable, every lost or found beautiful being looking for shore, home, heart. That space between child and not: imagine it as everything. Hold it open as long as you can. You are right. You are the new world.

I say I'm writing about time and water, and people open their eyes and ears and say, "Wow, what do you mean?" And I say, "In the next one hundred years, the elements of water on the planet are changing." So the glaciers are going down. The sea level is going up. The pH, the ocean acid level, is reaching a level that we haven't seen for fifty million years. This is happening in a single person's lifetime.

—Andri Snær Magnason

To articulate the past historically does not mean to recognize it "the way it really was." It means to seize hold of a memory as it flashes up at a moment of danger.

—Walter Benjamin

She felt . . . how life, from being made up of little separate incidents which one lived one by one, became curled and whole like a wave which bore one up with it and threw one down with it, there, with a dash on the beach.

—Virginia Woolf

It may just be that the subterranean places we, the fugitives of the present order, must now run to will not be dug out by the hard excavatory machinery of adult logic or the noble spiritualities that claim to know the way but by the gentle seeking fingers of our children caressing the soil, tickling the ground until it guffaws wide open.

—Bayo Akomolafe

Penny

Cruces 1

We dreamed we were hers.

The body of us thought that, because we built her, we belonged to her. We built her in pieces from our bodies, from the stories we held and the stories before that and the stories that might come. She arrived by boat in pieces.

When the ship *Isère* finally reached port, we wept. The sailors too. They had been convinced that the tempests they'd endured on board would drown them in the ocean, and the cargo with them. The deck of the ship was nearly a farmer's field in size. The hold had been covered with huge black tarps for the journey. When the sailors pulled the tarps back, the hold looked dark and foreboding.

I was asked to jump into that dark.

Like plunging into the ocean's deep.

Down in the hold, my eyes began to adjust. Gigantic crates the size of houses filled with pieces of the colossus: a woman in slices, crated and shipped. One by one, we found her body parts.

Hair.

Nose.

Crown.

Eyes.

Mouth.

Fingers, hand.

Foot.

Torch.

She had arrived, in pieces of herself.

Later, while discussing her reassemblage, an engineer remarked that the "embryo lighthouse," as they called the interior skeleton of the statue, held clues to reconstructing her form. Yet many elements of her construction went unexplained, left us puzzled. We were left with our imaginations to create adaptations.

During those months, we lived in the city and we labored on the island. We were woodworkers, ironworkers, roofers and plasterers and brick masons. We were pipe fitters and welders and carpenters. We mixed concrete, we pounded earth, we armed the saws and drills. We were sheet metal and copper specialists. She arrived in our hands as thirty-one tons of copper and one hundred and twenty-five tons of steel. Three hundred copper sheets had been pressed to create the outer skin of her.

We were cooks and cleaners and nuns and night watchpeople. We were nurses and artists and janitors, runners and messengers and thieves. Mothers and fathers and grandparents, sisters and brothers and children.

During the day you could always hear the insistent hammering, the files grating, the chains clanking, the copper singing as it was being shaped over wooden scaffolds, the cacophonous orchestra of our labor. You could always see arms swinging, hands at work, shoulders and biceps and the jaws of the workers flexing and grinding. Those sounds were our bodies. Her body coming to life from all of our hands. We the body took pride in our labor—as if we expected that someone would know our names, carry our stories.

When the winds in the harbor grew too strong, we had to abandon scaffolding. We used pulleys and ropes. We took care to be gentle against the softer metal. We dangled ourselves around her body, swung around the pieces of her, like the swoop and lift of acrobats, or birds, or window washers—though all of us were tethered to her body.

Sometimes, for just a moment, a body can feel real inside a story that way. As if each of us existed.

At night, when it was no body's shift, some of us would stand around her head and stare at her giant rounded eyes. We thought she looked sad. Or angry and sad. Her eyes each much larger than a human head. Her face neither male nor female, or perhaps just both. We felt she had the stare of our labor but also our loss, our love, our lives. Sometimes, holding near to her, we thought or felt *mother*, but we meant it in some new way no one has imagined before.

We were the impossible possible voice of bodies.

Some of us were born here and some of us were the sons and daughters of mothers and fathers not from here. They came from famine they came from poverty they came from occupations and brutalities and war. They came from something to leave, which is why they crossed land and water. They spoke of persecutions or poverty, but they also spoke of rolling hills or sunsets over the desert or flowers with names that made our hearts reach out. The leaving of a place carried sorrow as well as relief, and the coming here carried both as well. We spoke of both brutality and beauty—or remembered beauty—in our homelands, or in the hands of infants born here. We let go the hand of prior homes to reach this place.

We were Jews and Italians and Lithuanians and Poles. We were

Irish and Native American and Chinese. We were Lebanese and African and Mexican. We were Germans and Trinidadians and Scots. There were hundreds of us over time and across distances; it is impossible to say how many.

We were an ocean of laborers. We spoke Russian and French and Italian and English and Chinese and Irish and Yiddish, Swahili and Lakota and Spanish and a swirl of dialects. Our languages a kind of anthem.

We understood that labor crossed oceans. Some of us unloaded the statue pieces after her oceanic journey and some of us reassembled the pieces. Those of us who had unloaded pieces, and then reassembled them, felt a strange connection. Toward one another and toward her. Or we might have.

The sum of us—the *we* that might have been—could have understood from the passing around of stories that our French colaborers meant for her to commemorate the abolition of slavery. The French sculptor's early model had held a broken chain in her left hand. Our eyes saw the drawings. The model. We knew what the chain meant. Some of us might have rubbed our wrists or ankles or necks at the thought or memory of it. But then the chain moved. On her body, and on our bodies. Down near her foot.

We might have known then, in our bodies, that our states were stitched imperfectly—that war had ripped open a forever wound. That some of us would not be fully counted, our rights still pounded down on a daily basis. That children were being ground into dust everywhere, in the factories. That laws were excluding us even as we the body built the means of transportation across the land. Stories were traveling between us that could have led anywhere, turned in any direction, in spite of our backbreaking work.

That *we* could have been born from her, but small cracks began to appear in the story, just as in the materials of her body and our labor.

Instead of a broken chain, she held a tablet. The tablet signified the rule of law. The broken chain and shackle were moved to the ground, all but hidden under her feet. You could barely see them, but we knew they were there—our labor had put them there—and we had thoughts about it.

We wondered what story would emerge in place of emancipation, now that the chains were hidden. We wondered what story would be drawn from the tablet, from the newly prominent rule of law. We wondered what the figure herself thought about these changes to her body, these shifts in the story. No one asked what we thought, or what she thought, for that matter. Statues don't speak. A fear slid through some of our necks—that maybe she was not ours, or we were not hers—but no one wanted to say it out loud because we needed to make our livings.

Once, when we were working on the head and the face at ground level, I saw a suffragist from a protest march spit on the face of her as we worked. Why should a female face represent freedom when women cannot yet vote, she asked. She shook as she yelled, as her question streaked down the hard copper cheek.

I thought about that streak for a very long time.

After everyone was gone for the night, I took a rag to the copper there, crying briefly as I wiped it away. The suffragist was right. I saw her meaning. But I had been among those who'd worked to make that statue's face, worked so that it could hold both the gravitas and the tenderness of an idea that I believed could be beautiful. In some future—not ours, but some day to come. A face that might become something we were not yet. A freedom obscured in the shackles hidden beneath her feet, rising up her body and arm all the way to the torch, the sky, the endless heavens. I had an unusual dream in the form of her face. My face had its own markings.

Our labor had a rhythm and shape and song that were larger and reached farther than our differences. Maybe the song of us helped us feel part of some whole that did and did not exist. The song of us helped to get the work done, helped our bodies not to give out or give in. The song of *we the body* met the air and the water around us differently from how any one person might; *we the body* were part of everything and nothing at the same time.

In those days, for the first time in my weary life, I had people I loved. Endora and David, John Joseph—all of us from someplace else, all of us collected by her body.

Maybe because we were building her body, we felt our own bodies differently, and that welded some of our hearts together. Me with my patchwork-skin story. Endora's barren gut and foul, funny mouth. The opalescent mosaic of scars on David's back. The way John Joseph always talked with his hands, as if he were reaching for some meaning beyond words. The way his words would then return to his ancestors.

Or maybe our labor made us love one another. That happens to workers sometimes, when you labor near other bodies. Maybe we were looking so hard for something in this emerging place that we turned inside out a little. I don't know.

I only know that we built her in pieces from our bodies, from the stories we held and the stories before that and the stories that might come. She carried us in her.

Or we thought she did.

Some nights, after we worked together on her body, John Joseph, Endora, David, and I would drink late at night and talk about what it would have been like if the woman we built had really represented emancipation. If the broken chains had stayed aloft, in her left hand, for everyone everywhere to see.

The original story. Instead of the story that came.

And John Joseph's hands would come alive and he'd say, *You could have been president.* I'd tell him, *You could have been secretary of the in-*

terior, and Endora, she could have been vice president! And Endora would say, *Are you kidding?* I'm *the president. You lot would just muck everything up.* David would stare at the fire and smile. Of all of us, David believed in fantasies the least. He was the heart of us. Then we'd all pause and take a drink. We laughed our asses off. It made such sense. It fit the stories of our labor, our bodies. The stories we told ourselves were part of the stories that created the weight of her. But sense wasn't what was coming.

One night, as we stood together on the ground at the edge of the water, before we boarded the ferry back to the city after work, John Joseph bent down on the ground and scooped something out of the mud. It was a turtle. He handed the turtle to me. I looked at it with some strange sorrow. The shell so beautiful and small and strong. The creature inside wrinkled and ugly. I kissed it. I don't know why. Then I threw the turtle back into the Narrows.

That's when the four of us saw something thrashing in the water, and Endora, half breathless, said, *By saints, there is a girl.*

The Water Girl

(2079)

S he looks like a man," whispers a young girl with hair as black as space, her lips barely the height of the ferry railing. Under her breath, she whispers a list: *The Flowing Hair cent. The Liberty Cap cent. The Draped Bust cent. The Classic Head cent. The Coronet cent. The Braided Hair cent. The Flying Eagle cent. The Indian Head cent. The First Lincoln penny.*

"I think she was meant to look . . . *majestic,*" her father answers. "Like an archetype." Aster looks down at the red of his daughter's jacket and the blue of her pants and the white hat spun into wool from rabbit's fur and knit by a mother's hands.

"Can people be archetypes?" Laisvė asks. But the wind picks up and so Aster just smiles at his daughter and tousles the hair on her head.

They have all taken risks, traded things they had, for tickets to see the drowning statue. The ferries that come and go in The Brook are fewer and less frequent now. No one knows for how long. Those who have lived through the collapse, and the great Water Rise, move around in tiny circles to avoid attracting attention in the wrong place at the wrong time. Trouble rises and falls in seemingly random waves. Visiting the underwater woman reminds them of a story they once knew.

The people cluster at the ferry's edges like a human organism as the boat makes its way toward what was once an island. Their wonder takes the shape of draping arms and hands over one another as well as the ferry railings. People who do not know one another taking a small act of time to share some sense of wonder is no small thing in the world.

The girl with hair as black as space nests herself amid the legs of a mass of passengers on the ferry.

"Not so close to the edge, Laisvė," Aster says. He knows the pull of water in his daughter.

The murmuring layers of language float up toward the sky as the ferry nears its destination. The backs of the children's heads, foreshortened as children are, populate the front of the boat. A few of them now begin to point toward the object hovering on the waterline in the distance, their fingers becoming the word for it.

The bustling adults now create a kind of kinetic energy. The men button up their wool coats and stand a little straighter; the women arrange their scarves and hats, and place their hands on their chests, everyone—maybe everyone but, really, who knows—breathing just a little differently as they near the statue. Maybe it's the memory of generations in their heads. Maybe the desire for beer or pizza or sex or the hope that they will not get caught and sent back home because they dared to take a day to relax and visit a sinking wonder of the world.

Aster hoists his infant son up more securely on his hip, the baby boy crying, probably hungering for his long-gone mother's breast. He whispers, Hush my son.

And the person standing next to Aster on the boat, having no idea what the father says to the son, simply responds to the crying in his own language by saying *Ah, the boy is hungry*, and the woman standing next to that person, not understanding either of their languages, smiles and says, in her language, *Bless this journey*—or is the translation "boat ride" or is it "family"—her hands clasped in prayer or just common gesture, and everyone smiles all the same, because an infant crying for his mother's breast is its own language in any language and a shared journey across water binds strangers.

Closer to the ground, where no one is looking, the unnoticed black-haired girl begins her climb up the rungs of the ferry railing, whispering to no one but the water—for this is not the first time the water has called to her—*Mother.*

Sometimes the story of who you might become comes before you understand it. You might have to go into the water to collect all the pieces.

A loudspeaker reminds people how much time they will have to view the phenomenal sinking statue. How long until they arrive, how long the boat will circle the statue and then turn back, how little time they have left to purchase snacks or souvenirs.

Everyone laughing and leaning into the wind. That father holding his infant son close, the smell of harbor water and the skin of a child.

Then: a woman with a full bosom and a purple headscarf notices a flash of color dropping from the second level of the ferry right in front of her. She screams. Too big to be a bird. Dread fills the woman's chest. The people around her hear her scream. They look at her with alarm—is she speaking Italian? Something else? The man standing next to her tries to match the sound to the two years of a foreign language he had as a boy in Germany years ago, so many years. But this woman is Basque. No one near her understands what she is saying. A Japanese man puts his hand on her shoulder, all he knows to do. The crowd follows her face and emotion down toward the water, and in that instant, they finally see the truth of it: a small girl gone overboard in the waves, her body thrashing and fast receding in the churning white-lace waters of the ferry.

Everyone now rushes to line the railing, their hands clutching the white metal, their faces all alarm and horror. *Stop the boat*, people shout over and over again in different languages. Men bellow and run around. Women wail. Children weave themselves in between their parents' legs. The girl in the water gets smaller and smaller in their collective line of sight.

Aster still clutches his infant son, but he has been shoved back a bit, and so he cannot see the action at the railing—the yelling men, the wailing women. He scans the area around him at knee-level for his daughter.

"No, no, no, no, no," he begins to bleat. "Where is my daughter? *Laisvė*," he screams, but everyone thinks he is screaming the word *live* in his despair.

Then, faster than you can say "America," Aster hands his infant son to a stranger. He climbs the rail and dives into air all in one motion, like someone leaping from a building. He hits the water and sinks immediately, or that's how it looks in the moment. This man cannot swim. Man overboard. A life preserver ring is thrown into the water.

His infant son now in the arms of a stranger, a floating boy in a crowd.

This cannot be happening, someone laments. The age-old lament.

The boat horn blares and the engines go full stop and the vessel tosses back and forth amid the waves. The souvenirs in the souvenir shop shiver. All hands on deck throw over two lifeboats; the men who pile into them start rowing furiously—toward what they don't entirely know, some vague direction behind them, some half-heard news of a girl gone over. No one can see any girl in the water, not anymore. Is that the red of her jacket or the blue of her pants or the white hat spun into wool from rabbit's fur and knit by hand, or isn't it? A single arm and hand point out, toward the water.

At first, all anyone sees is the hand and arm and crown and face of a looming drowned statue: what's left of the impossibly huge woman gleaming green in the afternoon light, the beacon, the partially submerged attraction they came for, pulling them all toward what used to be her shore but is now more like her torso.

But then a girl. Her tiny arms. Her body a faint splash of girl-fish, teasing the watchers at the surface.

Impossibly, the girl appears to be swimming.

Swimming toward the half-drowned remains of the colossus mother.

Aster, the father who cannot swim, is rescued, pulled back onto the boat.

The infant son now in the arms of an unscrupulous man who, until the moment he was handed an infant boy, a prize of great value, had considered this ferry ride a last gift to himself, a ride to see a sinking wonder, before he killed himself, unable to survive his own poverty and hunger. But a baby boy in his arms . . . that was something of value.

The water girl now swiftly becoming a nameless legend. The people know to keep real names inside their mouths.

How the water girl leapt into the air like an idea suspended before the fall. How she swam in spite of everything, everyone around her, toward a drowning statue of a woman. How a father tried and failed to save her, and in so doing, lost his infant son. How the girl swam all the way to the statue, didn't she? Or did she disappear, and they only thought they saw her make it to the statue's edge?

The Water Girl, the Comma, and the Turtle

(2085)

Laisvė carried a penny in one hand and a big blue plastic letter *P* about the size of her head under her arm, stopping at every corner to peer around the edges of buildings, looking out for trouble. In The Brook, on her side of the Sea Wall, trouble could rise quickly. But a good trade was worth it.

To make a good trade, a carrier needs not to care about transgressing time. A carrier needs to slip her way into the barter. To use objects and signs in unorthodox ways.

Laisvė whispered the names of trees as she passed them. *Norway maple. Green ash. Callery pear. London plane. Littleleaf linden. Honey locust.* She stepped over roots protruding from what used to be sidewalks. She never—ever—stepped on any crack in concrete. What used to be apartments and businesses yawned at her with their abandoned open doors or winked through cracked-window eyes. Her neck skin tingled now and then. She knew she was breaking the rules wandering The Brook, She knew Aster would be angry. Or terrified. She'd noticed that the two feelings often came into contact in her father, and that if those two feelings made an electrical current, her father could have a seizure.

It was much easier, Laisvė had found, to study the emotions of another than try to feel them for yourself. Wherever her feelings lived in her body, she'd yet to locate them. It was one of the many things Aster put on the list of "things to work on"—feelings. Like anger. Or fear. Two emotions that led to the Hiding.

In memory, the Hiding had begun not long after she and Aster tried to integrate into a group of people who were trying to create a community by squatting in a bombed-out apartment building. Most of the people had children of various ages and sizes and dispositions.

The parents were worried about the impact that isolation and hiding and scarcity were having on the psyches of their spawn, as near as she could tell, so they were making an effort to collect themselves, maybe for safety and to share resources too. But they made one grand error: they wanted to socialize their children. The parents had a strange terror that the children would suffer without proper education and social engagement.

This puzzled Laisvė.

They tried to collect the children together to *play*. The idea was that the children would teach one another things they knew, and spend a good bit of time "just being children" too, playing, that sort of thing. Any open field or urban area not overrun entirely by thick weeds and bushes worked, but caged courtyards near apartment buildings worked best. One in particular nested near the Narrows; the parents took some comfort in the idea that a fresh breeze laden with moisture would keep the children well. But the experiment had gone badly, at least for Laisvė. Or maybe mostly for Aster. If the parents had just thought the idea through a little better, Laisvė thought, they would have realized that none of the children had any human social skills left whatsoever. Either they'd lost what skills they had, or they'd been born without them. All they had were survival instincts—*animal* skills.

Laisvė was thinking of bonobos. The genus *Pan*, the closest living relative to *Homo sapiens*. They shared the genus with chimpanzees, but their matriarchal order was more altruistic, empathetic, compassionate, and sensitive than chimps'. In bonobo societies, males derive their power from the status of their mothers.

That day, in the midst of the children's play, Aster heard screaming. He ran through a crowd of kids that had gathered in a corner and found Laisvė standing alone, holding one hand in the air. The hand was bloody. At her feet was a male toddler, his body still. *She killed the baby she killed the baby*, they were all saying, but when he asked, *How? How?*, the words punching through his throat on the way up, no one could answer him. No one had seen it. All they'd seen were her outstretched arm and her bloody hand, held up above her head.

The toddler was an orphan, and he was not dead after all. But his mouth and neck were covered in blood.

No one, including Aster, thought to ask Laisvė what had happened. Nor did anyone notice the balled fist of her hand—or try to open it—or they might have found the small object she was holding. An object the toddler had found somewhere, and which two other boys had told him to put in his mouth. A rusted nail, it turned out, which the toddler had swallowed, and which Laisvė had pulled from his throat so he did not die.

No one noticed either, probably because of the male toddler so near death—*My god, she nearly killed that boy*—that Laisvė had seized one of the boys who'd made a joke out of trying to get a smaller boy to eat a nail, that she'd taken justice upon herself. She pushed the cruel boy away from the immediate area, out into the water. No one would notice for several hours that the boy had floated away, his internal organs already beginning to fail, how he grabbed at his gut with abdominal pain, how he shat himself and vomited for hours as he floated, until he became jaundiced and died from liver failure, like a fish gone belly-up in the waves.

After that, Laisvė had to be kept secret.

In their falling-to-pieces apartment building, time never budged. She understood that Aster wanted to protect her and hide her from harm, but she was starting to learn how stasis could kill a person. Look at evolution. The question was a kind of trade: Was it more dangerous to risk being out in the world, knowing that the refugee Raids were happening everywhere these days—armed men in vans snaking like killer whales through the streets, taking people away to god knows where—or was it more dangerous to atrophy, like a stone growing moss, inside a squatter's apartment with a father dying from grief? No one ever became anything stuck inside staring at shadows, languishing inside Plato's cave. People could forget they had bodies at all, living that way. Being alive meant walking toward death, and she had no special fear of death. Life and death were a story familiar to her.

She'd located the penny she carried in the swollen riverway lapping around The Brook. The *P* she'd found in an alley between abandoned and misshapen buildings, half buried in rubble and ensnared by weeds. This falling-to-pieces city was beautiful. She had no fear on this day, except the fears her father had put into her. To Laisvė, objects were everything, because they moved backward and forward in time. Sometimes the same was true of people: the right people might be in the wrong time and thus need carrying. When that happened, she went to the Awn Shop.

The closer she got to the shop, the louder her heart beat. She knew she was supposed to be a secret of a self—staying at home while her father was at work, walking the iron to build the Sea Wall to keep the water back—but she couldn't sit still the way he wanted her to. The beauty of abandoned subway tunnels piled with debris and grown over with thorns and ivy that didn't need much light, the sound of moles and rats and mice dotting the ground, the decommissioned library filled with falling-apart books, the fractured windows, a roof caved in here and there—well, everything vibrated, beckoned to her, *come.*

What used to be the public library was now a strange word-and-sound church, filled with all manner of birds and small rodents and disheveled books. When it rained or snowed, she sometimes moved books to different rooms or floors in the library, away from the weather. Sometimes she'd see someone else in the library, but not often. If she met up with any other person, she had instructions from her father: she should give her name as Liza, then hide. Names were tricky in these times.

Her armpit itched from the big blue *P* she'd tucked under her arm. At the door of the Awn Shop, she closed her eyes briefly, calming her breathing to a four-count rhythm as Aster had shown her.

Inside the shop, an old, old, old man sat curled like a comma over a great glass case. His eyes sat embedded within such a deep nexus of wrinkles that his face looked to her like an aerial map, which she very much loved. His hands were even better—veins like mycelia dancing over skin and bone. She suspected that he was blind, but he never let on.

Her favorite thing about the Awn Shop: the most important objects were always in the front glass case, but the whole shop was filled with time, as if time itself were among the objects on display. Everything there was from some other epoch. There were no customers left in The Brook, that she knew of, except in the underground economy. What used to be businesses had turned to debris. The peeled paint of the Awn Shop's exterior walls was dung green. The front window was clouded with grime and time. She had no idea how the shop endured.

Today her excitement made everything orange and yellow. Steadying her breathing, Laisvė opened the front door and entered.

"Liza," the old comma said. "Welcome."

She set the *P* carefully atop the glass counter.

He looked at her, then at the blue plastic letter. Her cheeks flushed. She scratched her armpit. She knew it was something.

After a pause—long enough for Laisvė's eyes to focus on actual dust particles moving through the light and air between them—he opened his mouth. "This object has been missing for a long time," he said. Then he did something strange. He bowed, as if to thank her. She'd never seen him bow before.

"Is it yours?" she asked, the pulse at her neck quickening.

"In a way, yes," he said. "This letter belongs to a word, and the word used to be very important in my life. The word used to be my livelihood. Before the pandemics. Before collapse. Before the water. Before the Raids." He bowed again. "Come with me," he said, and they walked outside of the building for a bit. He pointed to the big blue plastic letters of the Awn Shop sign. "See?"

She didn't see, but she nodded and smiled, and they went back inside. Something important had been exchanged, she knew. Adults were weird. Then, her confidence renewed, she placed the penny on the glass counter between them.

He produced an eye magnification device. He studied the penny. "You see this green coloration?"

"Yes," she said, their heads nearly touching.

"That's what happens when oxidation occurs between copper and air. Over time, copper turns green."

"Like the drowning statue," Laisvė said. The statue was her favorite large object that lived in water. As she'd told him ten thousand times. "The drowned statue is made from thirty tons of copper," she continued. "Enough to make more than four hundred and thirty million pennies."

"Yes, yes, so you've said." The old comma had a gentle way of redirecting the story. "This coin here is the Flowing Hair cent. Incredibly rare. You know what? People hated it! They thought Lady Liberty looked insane. And people fear the insane. Evil people, thinking evil things."

Laisvė stared at the coin: the flowing hair, the wide eyes. "*Evil* is just *live* going a different direction," she said. "People need to learn to understand backward better. Words. Objects. Time. People get stuck too easily."

"So true," he said. He stared out behind her, beyond her. "When coins stopped making their way through the economy, the feel of them in your hands left too." He picked the coin up and held it between them, staring at it so closely, his eyes seemed to cross a little. "Buying shriveled up as the disasters came: pandemics, fires, floods, the Raids. From the highest towers of government down to the bank tellers and hardware stores and candy shops and restaurants, that strange metallic feel in the palm, that noise not quite nameable, not a rattle, not a clanging—it disappeared."

They sat inside the silence a moment, honoring the fact. She thought about the taste of copper in her mouth; she thought about his story, what he'd told her of it anyway. His ancestors had been from Guangdong Province, as it was called before it sank into the sea. He'd been something like a historian before he became an old old old comma, or that's what Laisvė deduced.

Laisvė had probably been something else before too. At least in the prenatal stage, when a fetus could be a pig or a dolphin or a person.

"I'll trade you an apple for the *P*, he said, leaning back and waiting for her answer. "And for the penny—"

Laisvė gently pulled the penny back. "I have to keep the penny. I have to carry it. Also, I'd better get back home. Before there's trouble."

The Awn Shop man peered down at her. "I see," he said. And he reached behind his chair, retrieved an apple, and handed it to her.

She turned the apple around, noticed a faint yellow glowing spot, and plunged her teeth in. The sound of her bite hung between them. "Goodbye, then," she said.

She stared at the penny as she turned and left the shop. A penny was a complex object, an artifact. She thought, not for the first time, about the word *thief*. It was a word her father used, but not a word she would apply to what she did. Whatever she was holding, her father always took it out of her hand to examine it, worrying about what trouble it would bring.

She thought of herself with another word: *carrier*. A thousand times she had to convince her father that she did not steal objects from the Awn Shop. Aster was convinced that losing her mother and brother had subjected Laisvė to some kind of trauma that led to problematic, erratic behaviors: stealing objects, endless list making, a tendency to focus obsessively on meaningless things. She was convinced that Aster's seizures came from the same origins, only he had yet to understand them as meaning-making spaces.

To her mind, when she carried objects, she was participating in the so-called underground economies she'd read about in the dilapidated library. And it was during her reading that she came to realize how, sometimes, people too moved backward and forward in time. How the right people might be in the wrong time and thus need carrying.

She walked home from the shop feeling, if not happy or content, then complete, like a sentence or a math equation solved. She walked in a zigzag pattern through the alleyways between buildings, every structure holding its emptiness or its stories or its people and secrets. Sometimes she closed her eyes and let herself be guided by her hand as it ran along a building wall. It was a fun game, to walk the urban textures with your eyes closed, follow old paths made by different feet. Smells and sounds and cold and heat became more real, and colors filled her head.

But eventually she remembered her father's fear for her, and she opened her eyes and sped up her serpentine trek. When she heard a *tat-tat-tat*—it could mean either machinery or trouble—she stopped, then turned away from the sound and tried to walk a different path. To distract her mind, she listed the names of worms she knew: compost worms, earth-mover worms, root-dwelling worms, whispered under her breath over and over: *Eisenia fetida—tiger worm. Dendrobaena veneta— nightcrawler. Lumbricus rubellus—red wiggler. Eisenia andrei—red tiger worm. Lumbricus terrestris—earthworm, beloved of Darwin.*

Another flurry of popping sounds—still some distance away, she thought. She paused and spoke aloud to no one but the dirt and the building walls reaching up on either side of her: "Darwin put the worms on his billiard table at night. He shouted at them, clapped at them, played the piano and the bassoon at them. He blew whistles at them. He decided they didn't have ears. But when he played a C, for a moment, there was silence. They'd felt the vibrations." She then went back to whisper walking, her eyes closed, her hand running lightly against the wall, tracing place, making for home. *Didymogaster sylvaticus—extremely rare. Megascolides australis—possibly extinct.*

Walking walking walking, her hand against the bumps and chunks and bricks of buildings, her mind making its patterns. The corner of a building emerged beneath her palm and the rocky dirt gave over to pavement beneath her feet. She came to the end of an alley that opened up onto a street near her apartment building. Her intention already across the street. *Get back before there's trouble.*

She peeked around the corner. In one direction, about six blocks down, she saw the sounds, saw the black and gray, saw what she was supposed to run from. The sounds had a name: Raid. A Raid, like her father warned of in his terror voice, was raging just down the road. She could see the uniformed men with guns, she could see the black vans lined up, she could see the terrified or angry people pouring out of the buildings, hands on heads, men, women, children. Piled into the black vans. Screeching tires toward who knows where. She could feel her father's fear in her shoulders.

She watched until all sound stilled. Then she looked in the other direction. No one, nothing, it seemed—just good, solid, still, soundless air—so she took a step forward. But the bottom of her red skirt shivered, then cut back across her leg—a violent whoosh of air and heat so close to her face and body that she jumped almost into the sound of it, something like a hundred rabbits landing *thud-squish* onto pavement as if they'd all been thrown at once, violently, from a great height.

Next to her—in fact so close it could have killed her—landed the body of a woman in an indigo flower-print dress, her head exploded into blood, her face rearranged until it was just an array of shapes, arms and legs splayed in wrong directions, the shape of her body slack and bent. Laisvė felt dizzy. She squatted down low to the ground, closing her eyes until she stopped seeing spots and her breathing felt real again. She stared at the woman. No breathing. No sound at all. Laisvė looked up to the sky, past the top of the buildings. Nothingness.

She waited for a feeling. Terror. Anger. Sorrow. But nothing came. Instead, when she stared at the dead woman in the street, she saw colors—red and blue and gray and a putrid yellow, all in waves. The colors were the word *dead*. She smelled piss and shit. The woman's blood began to travel on the pavement.

Laisvė did what came most easily to her: she studied what she saw. She let her eyes wander like fingers across the terrain of the body, pausing here at the place where a shoulder made a rounded boulder, peering in toward the creases made in the indigo dress by the woman's bulk. She let the woman's hips and legs bathe her in their humanness; she felt the body before her lose its hold on reality and become fluid, like air or molecules or water, so that maybe their two bodies were no longer even two separate things at all. Then, aiming her focus at one hand, she counted out loud the fingers on the woman's right hand, then began to count the fingers on the twisted left hand, nearer to her. Cupped in the woman's left upturned palm was a small object. It was the object that made Laisvė's imagination vibrate.

For a moment, nothing moved except Laisvė's breathing. Her eyes fixed on the object. It was a locket on a chain, gold, dirty, old, or just scratched and faded with time. She couldn't not reach for the object. She couldn't not yank it free. She couldn't not open it.

Inside, under glass, was a lock of baby-fine hair.

She was studying the object and the hair until she saw a flash of color and movement in the corner of her eye, low to the ground, something about the size of a hand, coming closer to her. A turtle—a northern box turtle. The turtle ambled up to the dead woman's hand and stopped.

"Please, girl, can you help me back to the Narrows?"

Laisvė looked at the turtle. The turtle strained its neck up toward her.

"It's not a rhetorical question," the turtle groused. "What's that thing?" The turtle turned its little head toward the mound of dead woman. *Was that a furrowed brow?* she wondered. *Did box turtles have brows?*

"A woman fell here. Next to me," Laisvė said. "That's her. She's dead. She almost landed on me."

The animal raised its voice. "Well, that's nothing to do with me, is it? Is it anything to do with you?"

Laisvė puzzled on the question. She did feel a tug at her attention, if nothing else. The color of the print on the woman's dress was impossible to ignore. Along with the pattern of the turtle's shell, god, you know, the flowered fabric was mesmerizing.

"Look," the turtle said. "I'm in need of aid. I have an injured leg. Might you return me to the Narrows Botanical Garden's turtle sanctuary?"

Laisvė was still staring at the dead woman's dress when she answered. "That sanctuary has been gone for years and years. It lives in another time. I read about it."

"Right, I know. However, there is still an overgrown plot there where we are relatively safe from predators. Nothing that existed before isn't something else now. And, anyway, it's not the sanctuary but the old Narrows I'm trying to reach. If you are able to help me, that is. I've a relative in greater need than I am. I could just use a lift. Besides . . . there's trouble about."

Laisvė's gaze drifted to the mud and yellow shapes on the dome of the turtle's back. She could not help but admire the creature's shell, the bright orange-yellow eyes, even the skin—the slime-green bumpy jaw and upper neck giving way to the smoother folds of the lower

neck, the yellow-spotted legs, even the toenails. Well, phalanges, actually, but to her they resembled beautiful elongated toenails. She
wondered at the perfect body, the plastron connected to the carapace.
Briefly, she imagined herself shelled and immediately felt less ex-
posed and anxious. Why had she been born a human girl?

Her choice was not difficult. With one hand, she snatched the
locket's chain from the dead woman's grasp; with the other, she
picked up the turtle. "I can take you to the old Narrows." She began
a brisk walk across the street toward the waterway, bypassing the
Awn Shop, which made her heart beat fast enough that she could feel
it in her neck. "But you have to show me which current path to take."

"Current path?" The turtle's little head swayed back and forth as
she carried him. "What are you talking about?" Now the girl was
running.

Soon they were at the lip between land and the old Narrows.

The turtle was grateful, if a bit suspicious. This girl seemed
strange. He wished she would put him down. Or even just throw him
into the Narrows. He could smell where he wanted to be. He was
craving earthworms, wishing he'd sucked one down back at the dirt
patch.

The girl stopped running at the edge of a dock, or what remained
of one. He could see the surface of the Narrows.

Laisvė held the turtle up to her face, so that they were eye to eye.
"I know about you box turtles," she said. "You appeared abruptly in
the fossil record, essentially in modern form." She turned the turtle
over to glimpse its belly and then back again. "In just a moment,"
she said, "when we reach the water, I want very specific directions. A
deal's a deal. There's a penny I need to carry."

What was this girl thinking of? "What do you mean, *carry*?"

"You know, like carrier pigeons. Derived from rock doves. The
ones with magnetoreceptive abilities." She scratched her head. When

had she become a carrier anyway? Maybe the moment they shot her mother and she watched her sink into the sea, her outstretched hand sinking into the water Laisvė's very last glimpse of her mother. Or possibly the day her brother dissolved into a crowd on the ferry, nothing left but the words of him in her, a forever floating boy. The holes in a girl have to fill with something. Her fingers twitched. "What's your name?" she asked.

He sighed. "Kingdom: Animalia. Phylum: Chordata. Class: Reptilia—"

But she continued for him: "Order: Testudines, suborder: Cryptodira, family: Emydidae, genus: *Terrapene*. Not what I asked, though. What is your *name*?"

The turtle studied her. He turned his head from side to side. He considered lying. Who the hell did she think she was to demand his identity? But something in her eyes compelled him. "Bertrand," he said. "And you?" he asked, though he wasn't necessarily interested. Still, she had a head on her shoulders, this one, underdeveloped and odd as she was. Most humans were stupid; the rest of them suffered from a melancholia that was something like an irrational addiction to nostalgia, or so it seemed to him. A decidedly human ailment. They were addicted to dead things.

"My name is Laisvė," she said. "But please don't mention any of this to my father. I'm supposed to stay inside every day, now that the Raids are getting closer."

The turtle nodded. "Best get to it," he said, nodding toward the previous trouble.

With one hand clenched around the dead woman's locket and the other around the turtle, Laisvė jumped into the water.

Aster and the Fear of Falling

At the end of a day of labor, in the moments after the horn sounded, Aster would straddle the iron beams, locking his legs and closing his eyes, and then hold his arms out away from his body. Up at that height, the clouds and the descending sun seemed more like kin than faraway elements, and he felt held. If there was wind, it would find him, a strange pull toward the open sky, toward a kind of upward surrender, before he had to climb back down to land, to reality, to daughter.

How easy it would be. The leap.

It was a thought he could never stop.

He wished he could talk to Joseph. He missed Joseph terribly—missed him mostly in his legs. If Joseph was still there, he imagined, they'd have a talk before making their way back down to ground.

"Well, shit. It doesn't matter to me where you're from," Joseph had said the second day he knew him. Aster had been told about Joseph Tekanatoken by a man from Ontario who had passed through the

Yakutia territory in Siberia long ago on a geological expedition. Joseph in The Brook can get work, he said, for anyone crazy enough to walk the iron, work in the sky.

Every night that followed, Aster dreamed of a man walking on lines in the clouds. His dreams became a want in him. The want carried him like a craving, and then, like all addictions and contractions of the imagination, his want destroyed his life.

When Aster arrived in The Brook with nowhere to live, with grief larger than an ocean and a daughter whose face was blank with trauma and a baby boy who cried too much, Joseph Tekanatoken had let them sleep on the couch in his trailer. The trailer was parked on a patch of dirt far from water. All three of them came to rest there, like some strange animals braided into one another's bodies. Joseph fed them eggs and cheese, and brought them milk. Every single day for a year.

One night the electricity went dead and the trailer was too cold for children to sleep. Joseph never said a word, but he brought in a giant thick blanket woven from wool and put it over them all like a tent. Then he surrounded them with his own body in a gesture that was as gentle as it was gigantic. (But that couldn't be true, could it? That Joseph had been able to surround the whole of them with his body? It felt true to Aster.) The air was warm. The children slept.

It felt good to talk to Joseph, and in those days, almost nothing felt good to Aster. He tried to narrate to Joseph who he was, where he had come from, but every time he tried, the story split into too many tributaries. The one story he could replicate with any consistency was built from a tiny fragment of memory involving a woman who may have been Aster's mother. The woman in the memory sat inside a long building with a long table. When she spoke, everyone in the room listened. If he closed his eyes, he could see her silver hair. Was the woman in the memory his mother? A mother? Or a dream he had conjured in place of a mother?

"She was probably an animal or tree soul," Joseph said, and then they stared at each other while Aster tried to figure out if Joseph was fucking with him or not. Then came that laugh, something like car tires going over small stones in a road, and the sound of it made him wish what Joseph said was true. Whoever his mother had been, she'd been killed like an animal. Maybe the woman in his memory was just one of the women from the village who raised him; maybe she was just a woman who'd raised her voice at some shared and useless dinner. Maybe she was just a woman he'd seen in a movie or a book, someone who seemed like a mother. Maybe the woman in his memory was a ghost. Maybe she *was* a tree soul.

The only female in his present tense was his daughter, Laisvė, and his only job on earth was to get her safely to womanhood, to help her forward until some path—any path—appeared in front of her. It occurred to him she might have to *swim* open a path. Aster had never learned to swim.

When Aster started working with Joseph in The Brook, on the Sea Wall, he'd listened for hours as Joseph told him the stories of things from before. Told him about a line of men who might tell and tell and tell a story, as if it were a lifeline to something.

"You know, generations of us Mohawks have been coming down from Canada since the twenties to build the frames for buildings all over that city. Immigration tried to deport us as illegal aliens— stupid, right? They're the foreigners. But then a court ruled that you can't arrest and deport Mohawks, because we're a people from a nation within two nations and treaty rights say we can move through our own tribal territories and their imaginary lines that are supposed to divide us. We have a special kind of freedom. Not that they still don't try and make it a pain in the ass for us to go back and forth." Joseph's laugh emerged gravel-throated and deep from his chest, as if the sound had taken miles to grow. "Freedom of movement gave us the ability to pile ourselves up in the big city. Ain't that some shit? We had the most skill walking iron. You know the Empire State Building?"

Aster hears Laisvė's voice again in his head—one of her lists, her endless whispered recitals: *The transcontinental railroad. The Canadian Pacific Railway. The Hell Gate Bridge. The George Washington Bridge. The Waldorf Astoria. The Empire State Building. The United Nations, Lincoln Center. The Twin Towers. The Freedom Tower. The Sea Wall.*

Joseph continues. "The Twin Towers? We Mohawks topped off the Twin Towers. And we were there again for rescue and support when they fell. We knew them better than anyone. We helped carry out the dead bodies. We helped build the Freedom Tower."

Aster sometimes said something stupid when Joseph would finish narrating, like "I don't know if I can keep doing this," and Joseph would say, "What *this*?"

"Staying alive," Aster would respond. "*That* this."

And Joseph would say, "That's some stupid-ass shit. What kind of talk is that? You got a daughter, man."

Sometimes Aster would stumble a little further—*I have no origins*, he'd say—but then he'd get lost trying to explain and Joseph would be silent for a while. Maybe night would fall. Maybe Aster's arms would feel too heavy. And then Joseph would tell Aster how the Mohawk had always taken people into their tribes, for a hundred different reasons. War reasons. Family reasons. Love reasons. Hate reasons. Orphan reasons. Shelter and displacement reasons. Some reasons were brutal and some reasons were beautiful. But every one of those taken in were considered members of the clans and tribes into which they were adopted.

"Some are from ancestral blood and some are from migrations of the gut or heart," Joseph would say, and then Aster would feel less like someone whose body was about to leave an orbit and spin off into space. "I barely knew my father. I mean, I knew him for a little while—about twenty years. Then he died. So what?" Joseph would clap Aster on the shoulder, then light a cigarette with one hand while driving, and take in and slowly release a drag. "But they say my grandfather John Joseph was the best iron walker ever. Worked on the statue, all that pretty copper. How's that for pride? Tough to beat that. Shit, Aster, maybe it is in your blood, maybe not, but your body sure knows something. I've never seen anyone as sure-footed as you up there."

Sure-footed. A father who could not save his wife, a father who lost his infant son. A father unsure how long he could keep his own daughter alive.

Once, Aster confided in Joseph his desire to surrender. Joseph, who had taken him in when they first arrived. Joseph, who'd taken care of him and his infant son and daughter as a father might have, or as Aster imagined a father might do. Joseph, who'd taught him how to walk.

"It's so peaceful up here," Aster told Joseph one evening as they straddled the beams, looking out toward the water and in toward the land.

Joseph looked up into space, then down at the ground. "Yeah, well, it's always fucking windy, and you ain't no goddamn bird," he said. "You're a father."

Of course, his heart would lurch homeward then, the fact of his daughter would jolt his sternum, and down he'd climb, grateful for another day's labor, grateful to be working on the one thing that might hold the water back enough to keep them alive. Only after he was on the ground did his fears creep back up his legs and hips to his gut. *Keep feeding her, keep brushing her hair, keep teaching her about the world that was. Keep her hidden. Keep her alive.*

———

The sun had nearly folded into the horizon. The water glowed blue
and orange. The Brook's dappled dwellings and half-submerged
bridges, dripping with vegetation, red-tailed hawks, and eagle's nests,
all went to shadow.

Aster made his way from the Sea Wall site down to the ground.
He unhooked his rig, pulled his coat collar up to his ears. He wondered, for a moment, whether the Sea Wall was really designed to
keep water out, or perhaps to seal people in. He turned and set off on
a circuitous route back to the apartment. He reached into his pocket

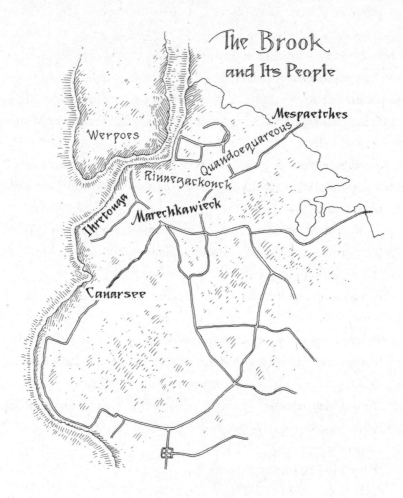

and pulled out a folded-up piece of paper. A map of his daughter's making, covered with her writing and drawings, strange lines crossing through their streets in The Brook. All of it labeled with syllables he didn't recognize, the names of objects, Latinate terms and categories for animals. *What does any of it mean? Where is my girl?* A map to nowhere:

Then he cried.

I do not understand my own daughter, and I will die if I cannot keep her safe.

Once, Aster came across a doctor who was squatting in a warehouse a few buildings down from theirs. He met him standing around a fire in a metal can after work. The man said he had a brother who'd been taken in a Raid; he told Aster that he'd become a doctor years ago in an effort to help his brother, who was living with a brain tumor that impacted his speech and behavior. The man wept for his lost brother.

One particularly desperate night, after Laisvė had come home late carrying a knife, Aster found the doctor again and asked him to visit Laisvė. When the man arrived, he sat down across from the girl in the kitchen.

"Where do you go when Aster is at work?" he asked.

"Nowhere. I just make up the stories I tell him. I have a vivid imagination."

"Where do you find all these objects, then?"

"Just here, in the apartment building. Things people leave behind, I guess."

"Do you hear voices?"

"No."

"Do you see things?"

"What kind of things?"

"Oh, things that look more like a dream than the regular world. You know, irregular things."

"No. Isn't this world irregular enough?"

"Do you miss your mother and your brother?"

Here there was a long silence. Aster watched his daughter look at her hands, no doubt weighing something as invisible as love. "No, I have Aster."

She seems like the rest of us out here, the doctor had said. Traumatized, all of us, and just getting on with things.

Now, heading home, Aster folded his map back up and returned it to his pocket. He rubbed his arms for warmth.

Outside their falling-apart building, he steadied himself on a tree. *This bark is older than I am*, he thinks; *maybe this tree remembers things that can help me break through this fear. Things from the world before this one.*

There were things he knew himself, things he was sure of: Once there was a wife. Once there was a son. A journey across water. *All I have left now is water and daughter.*

He climbed the stairs—even his breathing sounded like giving up—and opened the door to their apartment. There, instead of despair, he saw his daughter at the kitchen table with a pile of crayons. She was drawing a whale. The whale's eye blue. Her own hair wet.

"Laisvė, why is your hair damp?" he managed to say, though the words in his mouth felt heavy. He took his coat off and hung it by the door.

"I'm just hot," she said.

"You mean wet," he said.

But he already knew that anger was of no use with Laisvė. Rage just shut her down for days, and so he knew he must start the story over again whenever he needed to remind her to be careful, to stay inside, to stay away from trouble.

"Tell me the story again," his daughter, his love, his life said.

The apartment shuddered with the coming of late fall. His daughter had already started a vegetable stew—just potatoes and carrots and onions and water, really, with a handful of wild herbs she'd found breaking through the cracks in the ground. He walked to the stove, stirred the stew with a wooden spoon. He looked back over his shoulder. Laisvė turned something small over and over in her hand, a tiny secret. He knew it now: she'd left again, against his wishes, and come back with a new object. Nothing is more daughter than this: a father making dinner in place of a mother, trying to keep his terror and anger at bay; a girl keeping her secrets, taking her chances, asking for a story where a family, a home, a city should be.

"What's that you've got?" he asked.

"Story," she reminded him, holding her treasure under the table. "Tell me the story."

"You fell out of a boat as a young child and turned into a whale," he said.

Laisvė half smiled. Rolled her eyes. "I'm not a whale, Dad."

You fell out of a boat and nearly drowned. More than once.

"Aster? What's it like?"

"What's *it*?"

"Your seizures. What's it like when you have one."

A line of pain shot from his sternum to his forehead. *How wrong it is*, he thinks, *this world she endures. How I hate it.* "It's like being trapped at the bottom of the ocean," he tells her. "Cold and black and alone. But my imagination keeps going."

"Like when you dream at night?"

"Sort of, yes. And then the bottom of the ocean becomes a whale, and the whale takes me to . . ." He paused.

"Svajonė. Where my mother is. At the bottom of the ocean."

"Yes." He stared at the wall. "But seriously, one day you fell out of a boat and became a mermaid. Look at that tail!"

The girl laughed like a daughter, caught in domestic comfort. There was a big distance between the words *jumped* and *fell*. For a second, the words *son* and *mother* and *daughter* made him bite down his back teeth hard enough to make his temples pulse. *Where has she gotten to this time? Did she steal anything?* The collection of objects in her room flashed up in his mind's eye. Coins. Feathers. Bones. Rocks and shells. The skin of a corn snake. Dead insects. Books everywhere, and pages and pages of lists. *Did anyone see her? Follow her?* He counted to four and breathed in, held it, counted to four breathing out to calm himself.

"Okay. Now the real story. From the beginning."

Sometimes all a father can do is smile for his daughter and give her the story she desires. Perhaps in fairy tale form children can live with what really happened.

The walls of the kitchen pressed in on him, the cracks and splotchy paint scratching his body like old skin. The smallness and cold and mold of the entire apartment tightened. He stole a glance at the cardboard and duct tape they'd used to cover up wall holes and window cracks. He fought off the feeling that the apartment was nothing but a moldy and diseased blanket folding them up toward death.

"Once there was a star in the sky who fell in love with a fur spinner," Aster began.

Her smile widened with satisfaction. She kept turning the object in her hand, out of sight beneath the kitchen table. "And they lived across water, in a place that used to have land bridges. And the land bridges before them carried their ancestors," she answered.

"Who is telling the story?" he asked her, grinning.

"You are," Laisvė said.

He continued. "Far enough back in time, yes—a land called Siberia. Though, before that land was taken over, it had other names."

"Where is Siberia? What were the other names?"

He walked over to the tiny kitchen window, crisscrossed with duct tape covering cracks in the glass and sealing the edges. On the wall nearby, he'd hung an old map from the turn of the last century in America. He's made this journey across the kitchen before, has told his daughter this story before—it doesn't matter how many times. "Siberia lived inside what used to be Russia, and before that, it was the Soviet Union. Here." He pointed to the expanse that once— before the ice melted, before nations became unstitched—was Siberia, traced it with his forefinger. Then he lifted his pointer finger and studied his own skin for a moment. His finger had a cut that never healed properly, never quite scarred over as it should have, like the land and the people.

"What were they like? Countries? Was the Soviet Union a bad place? Was Siberia? Was America?"

"Maybe. Maybe not. Depends on who is telling the story. Times change."

"You're telling it."

"Nations were like forever-dancing animals. Sometimes one was the prey, sometimes the other; sometimes they both were but neither one knew it. Nations used to be forged by wars and power. And Siberia? It was a kind of enigma—"

"What's *enigma*?"

"Am I telling the story?" He began again. *I could not love this girl more. In fact, sometimes I think this is all I have left of love. The way I carry it in my body—it may kill me.* That's what happens when love is desperate, when it's filled with a skin-shivering terror.

"Siberia was a place bigger than just a *place*. It was unknowable. That's an enigma. People lived and died there in a way no one knows anything about. People were sent there and they just disappeared. Or they formed strange communities in the nothingness. It was a land covered in ice—until one day the ice began to give, to melt, and it revealed what had been unknowable before. That's the afterlife of an enigma."

Aster paused to feel the weight of the fact that their very existence—a father, a daughter—remained an enigma to him. He stirred the stew. "The earliest Siberians—some of the very first of them—they left their home to cross the great land bridge called Beringia in the glacial time, and they landed in the Americas. Before there *were* Americas."

"Or they went in a boat."

"Yes," he conceded. "That may be too."

"*Or they swam . . .*" Laisvė whispered, but her voice faded into the wood of the table in front of her.

"What?" Aster asked, stirring.

"And what about this place. Where we are. Is this home?"

The word *home*. It was there and then it drowned, which is how he thinks of everything now: language and people and his dead wife and what she knew about words. His infant son, the small warm weight of him, lost. His own heart an abyss—like some giant empty iron tank.

Who would his daughter be if he could allow her to go to school like children used to, a classroom where she might learn whatever it is they're teaching in this place these days about things like history and geography and anthropology and the existence of countries and nations? Is there even school anymore? In a place where fathers and daughters are not? He could brush her unruly black girl-hair forever, and he would still never know how to be the father of a twelve-year-old girl, her life snared in such a liminal state—thanks to him.

The skin around his eyes tightened. He ground his teeth against the truth of it—their secret lives, years and years without proper paperwork to live legally in this place. Or any other place. All the borders in chaos, all the countries shifting underfoot. A father and a daughter nested inside a crappy apartment building. His labor and the trades they made for food and clothing and shelter—a tenuous living at best.

So he told her the story, over and over again, and soothed his guilt.

"So you fell off a boat and turned into a whale."

"*Daaad!*" Laisvė moaned, cracking a smile. On the paper before her, she'd drawn a girl inside the belly of a whale.

"What? I just wanted to see if you were listening." Nothing on earth is more beautiful than her smile. How does he not die from loving her? His head swam with terror and anger. And then a different question came into his body: How does she carry so much in so small a body without feeling it?

"Your mother, Svajonė, was studying the Yakut indigenous languages when I met her in Siberia," Aster said. "The first moment I saw her, I actually had a seizure." Aster held his breath. Sometimes he wished he had died right then, in that moment, inside the image of her following his fall to the ground, kneeling to put his head in her lap. "She was the most beautiful creature I had ever seen in my life."

"My mother was a linguist. And a philologist."

"All right, all right." Aster surrendered. "I will tell you the story of your mother. Show me what's in your hand, and I'll tell you."

He walked the small distance to her and gently took her hand in his and removed the object. His face instantly hot. "Laisvė. Where did you get this?" He turned the tiny object over in his hands. An old coin, rusted and dull. It looked to be some kind of penny, but not like any penny he remembered. Pennies had been out of use for years. He barely remembered them at all. Rubbing the coin with a dish towel over the steam from the stew, he saw the date: 1793. Across the top, the word LIBERTY. The kind of thing you might find in a museum—or a pawn shop. His ribs ached.

"Where did this come from?"

Her eyes widened, but not with fear. "Close to here."

Aster couldn't stop himself—his worry leapt ahead of his logic. Without conscious intent, he grabbed his daughter's shoulders and shook her. "Laisvė, how many times do we have to have this conversation? You *cannot* steal things! Ever. Is this from the shop across the street?" His voice crescendoed and thinned. "Listen to me—this is serious. It's *dangerous*. That man could turn us in! He is not your friend. We cannot trust anyone. Ever. There could be a Raid at any moment and we could be on their damn lists. I don't even know where they would send us anymore. We have no identities, no home, nothing to tie us to anywhere. . . . I've told you a hundred times you *cannot* steal things. Not ever again. Or—" His voice fissured with terror, rising in tone and pitch until it was almost like a mother's. In his mind, a familiar storm took shape: *Have they seen her? This daughter who sometimes roams the neighborhood unsupervised, this daughter whose curiosity is as untamable as her tangled hair?*

"I didn't get it from the shop! I didn't steal it!" Laisvė stomped over to the map on the wall and jabbed her small finger on the fading blue part, the part that was not land. "I got it here. The water."

"What water?" Aster asked, alarm now skittering chaotically at the edge of his voice.

"The water you pretend I almost drowned in!"

If she could feel rage, could feel need, could feel anything like the rush of emotion her father battled daily, it might look like her face right now. Laisvė lunged at Aster, hugged him as hard as she knew how, her head driving into his gut. For a minute, it felt as if she were trying to press her head into the meat of him and beyond, to hollow out a womb in his body, but his stomach pushed back with the muscles of a laborer, their two bodies clenched tightly against each other.

Just as her small force was relaxing into him, everything crashed. Aster heard footsteps pounding up the apartment stairs. His heart a stiff apple in his chest. He put his forefinger against his lips so hard that it would leave a bruise. "Get down," he whisper-yelled.

His daughter dropped to the floor, then crawled to the cupboard under the kitchen sink and climbed into the space behind the wall just as they'd practiced, as stealthy as an animal diving into a burrow.

Aster's head swam. His arms went numb. His legs collapsed. He saw stars. He couldn't say which happened next: the seizure that wracked his body, or the Raid breaking down the door.

The Water Girl and Her Story

Laisvė crawls hard and fast, drilling down like a worm into the bowels of the apartment building. The sounds she feels at her heels make her feet hot. Her knees scream.

This is not a story. This is a Raid.

The crawl space she navigates for the hundredth time behind the kitchen sink is made from old boards lodged between walls. Sixteen feet deep, she hits the dug-out hole in the crawlway. She turns and places one foot down a rough hole onto the rung of a ladder. *Do not stop for anything. Do not even turn around to look back. If they are here, then your only choice is to go. If they have come for us, your only choice is life or not-life. This is the right time to have no feelings.* She drops her whole body down into the eye of the hole. Rung under rung, she watches her own hands, imagining in her mind's eye how many floors until she touches the ground. Her father a question mark, a tension, a vibration made of fear the color of a blood river, becoming more and

more distant above her with each foothold. *Will they take my father?*
Will I ever see him again? Will they shove him from the roof like the woman
with the locket who dropped dead from the sky in the indigo flowered dress?
Did they come for her in a Raid? Did they push her out of a window? Will
Aster die or will he be taken? Her heart in her eyes.

To calm the rush of her own fear, Laisvė imagines her collection of
coins—making head lists of things is the only way she knows to give
a pattern to the racing colors in her head. She pictures her coin collection. *The Flowing Hair cent. The Liberty Cap cent. The Draped Bust*
cent. The Classic Head cent. The Coronet cent. The Braided Hair cent. The
Flying Eagle cent. The Indian Head cent. The Lincoln penny.

She sees a kind of glowing copper ribbon, but then her thoughts
click like marbles in bright yellow sparks, so she starts to speak
out loud as she descends. The collection of pennies dissipates in her
mind's eye.

She moves on in her imagination to other objects she hasn't been
able to stop collecting, still climbing the ladder ever downward. Out
loud now, she names the objects she collects, to no one but her climbing self: "Rocks from every river or ocean I have been to. Pennies.
Spoons. The bones of animals. The wings of insects. Maps. Feathers
from different birds. Animal and bird skulls. Hair: deer hair and dog
hair, the hairs of goats, cows, horses, cats, donkeys, bear hair, fox
hair, beaver hair, rat and mouse hair, the hair of a reindeer, the moss
from a reindeer's antlers, my mother's hair, my father's, Joseph's knife,
Aurora's hair."

Something besides words rising in her throat. The Raid team may
take her father. The Raid team may kill her father. The Raid team
may follow her. *This is the right time to have no feelings.*

She smells the damp reality of dirt underground pluming up toward her. She says the number of ladder rungs out loud—"twenty-five,

twenty-four, twenty-three, twenty-two, twenty-one"—and a purple color like a helmet forms around her head. She knows the ground is near because the number 1 is purple.

Mercifully for her brain flux, Laisvė's right foot hits solid ground. Against the mud wall, hanging from a wooden rod, is a backpack. Inside the backpack there is food and water and the address of a safe house. Laisvė reaches into the pack and pulls out a miner's cap with a headlamp, a pair of kneepads, thick work gloves. *Do not slow down for any reason. Do not stop. Do not remember anything about what your life has been, since you might have to forget it to have a life at all from this point forward.*

She begins her dirt crawl. The tunnel is about a foot wider than her body on the sides and above her; she feels lucky to be a child, not an adult. She thinks briefly of Aster falling to the floor, having a seizure, and she begins to cry, but not in a way that would slow her down. The tears fall but her breathing is steady. She licks the salt of the drops when they reach her lips. They have told each other this story hundreds of times: *The story is in her skin. The story says move or be captured or put on a boat and sent away to god knows where, a final fracturing forever.*

The pack on her back scrapes the ceiling now and again, and each time it does, she gets a jolt of silver white in her peripheral vision. The sound of her knees and hands is blue and purple and yellow, in bursts in front of her eyes that extend as far ahead of her as she can see. The smell of the dirt floor and walls is a low vibration in her ears, a kind of constant low-noted hum. What she smells is red. A dark, almost black, red. Color in her where fear would be in some other child.

At a bend in the tunnel, its throat opens up some. She scrapes her shoulder and the side of her head near her temple on the wall trying to move too quickly. She knows that soon after this bend she will be

able to stand, to run, to run like children do. She can run to the safe
house that is the father-daughter plan.

Except she isn't going to the safe house, and she knows it. *Forgive
me, father.* She will make for the water. The Narrows.

Her crawling is frenzied now. She touches her head and her hand
comes away red, but not a lot, not enough to stop her. Her knees ache
and the balls of her hands ache and her heart aches, but she sees the
color turquoise ahead of her, so she doesn't stop; she thinks of all
the people who have come and gone in the world; she thinks of all the
journeys across history of all the people and plants and animals and
water. She thinks the most about water, how water cut the shape of
land everywhere on this planet, how water took her mother and hid
her brother from her, how she must enter the water, how she must find
people and things not now but in an otherwhere, how she cannot save
her father but she must follow his wail anyway, how water is where she
must go because water is without time, and yet water could still swallow them whole.

Feet first, arms at her sides, into the plunge.

Bubbles.

Then calm.

The water is the only place on the planet where her body instantly
calms.

"Girl, is that you?" A small wavering voice.

Laisvė turns, her hair swarming around her like seaweed, and sees
the box turtle swimming up to her face. Her urgency and fear sub-
side; everything underwater loosens into blur and wet.

"Bertrand?"

"You seem agitated. What's wrong?"

Laisvė fades into her own underwaterness to calm herself. "I need
to be in another time."

The turtle tilts its little head. "Tell me a story and I'll tell you how to get to the other time."

"I know a little about moving through time waters, but this is urgent. I've got to make an important trade. I'll give you one story but that's it, okay?"

"Okay."

"There is a water girl who lives in the belly of a whale—"

Bertrand interrupts: "Is the girl you?"

"Who is telling the story?" Laisvė stares through water. Easier to think of herself as a girl from some oceanic fable than live in the endless fear-filled life her father has made for them.

Bertrand pulls his head in a little and treads water where he floats. "I'm listening. How's the story go?"

"The girl loves her father. She loves him and loves him, but it is not a love she has ever heard of anywhere else, not in the world and not in any story that she knows. She loves her father like she loves history and animals and plants and fossils and, most of all, lost objects and water. She loves her father because she understands how deeply the love of a daughter can make meaning in the world, even when the meanings in the world seem to be shutting. Without daughters, fathers are dead. It's not that any daughter can save a father, ever. All fathers are doomed, the girl knows this with her whole body. We've made a wrong place for fathers in the world, so they throw their lives at heroisms and braveries and wars, and winning and owning, and desire poking out of their pants in a way that is desperate, and then they die with a want inside them that is larger than a body."

"My god, that sounds terrible," Bertrand says. "Turtles are not like fathers. In Africa, we're considered the smartest. In Egypt, we're understood as part of the underworld, which makes sense to a certain extent—but then the whole concept of evil . . . what the hell is that all about?" He casts his eyes sidelong, then continues.

"In ancient Greece, we showed up on their money, their seals. And there's that story about Aeschylus, the playwright—killed when a bird dropped a tortoise on his head. What a hoot. The Chinese consider us sacred—to them we represent power, tenacity, longevity. They think a tortoise helped Pangu to create the world. The Chinese used to inscribe all kinds of ancient stories on our shells. The Chippewa, the Menominee, the Huron-Wyandot, the Abenaki, Shawnee, and Haudenosaunee put us into their stories too. Look at my shell—shaped like the land, even like the dome of the universe, see it?" He twists his neck slightly, then turns back to her. "Our backs are very important in India too. In Japan, the tortoise is a safe place for immortals. In the Mohawk tradition, earthquakes are a sign that the World Turtle is flexing, turning beneath the enormous weight that she is carrying."

Laisvė listens until the turtle finishes.

Bertrand stretches his head all the way out from his shell. "Now, what about this daughter girl?"

"What daughters can do is carry new meanings into the world. Like a beacon." And with that, her story emerges fully:

Once there was a water girl who lived in the belly of a whale.

Her father feels like a gun. Laisvė knows that the sentence is true and untrue. She knows that her father did not harm her mother or disappear her brother, but she also knows that her father is hopelessly and forever tethered to their deaths. As fate played out, their deaths ended up bearing her into the world, giving her a life.

The last image she has of her mother lives between worlds. She sees the shore of the northeastern edge of a land of mostly snow—her father has pointed to the map on the kitchen wall a hundred times, saying, *This used to be Siberia*—and she sees the lip of a boat in the Bering Sea and she sees her mother's body between the land and the boat. Her father already on the boat that will take them away to safety with her infant brother. She sees her mother stepping, as if to board the boat, and then her mother is not; her mother is shot; her mother falls into the water in the most graceful slow-motion death in the world, more beautiful than any other death; her mother's long and languid beautiful arm reaching out to them, her too-white hand held out toward daughter or family or something of them. Her mother's outstretched arm and hand then rising toward the sky then slowly sinking, beginning to go to water. The last image is of her arm and hand, sinking.

Then whoever was shooting at her mother—Do we ever really know who does the shooting?—was directing their fire at the people left on the boat, and the boatmen hurried to move the boat away from the shore. All the people crowded down onto the floor of the boat, which wasn't much of a boat in the first place, some kind of used-to-be sea fishing vessel that had been repurposed for the kinds of people who might be fleeing the shore of war or poverty or punishment from boat to boat out into the vast unknown of the ocean.

Once there was a water girl who lived in the belly of a whale, but really, she rolled over onto the floor of the save-your-life boat and looked at her father's face, her father gripping her swaddled infant brother. The two of them looked like a single organism caught in anguish. In that moment, as she watched, everything about life and love in her father drowned. For an instant, her father's eyes looked dead, then the shooting sounds brought them back to life, as the boat created distance and wake, and when she locked eyes with her father, she understood that the rest of his life would be about his children not dying. She also understood that she was a piece of the dead and drowned mother in a way that her brother could never be.

Her daughter-body leapt up and threw her over the side of the boat; *motherwater mothertongue motherheart*.

Laisvė finishes the tale for the turtle: "The men in charge of the save-your-life boat could have left the girl to the waves, but they did not. One of them, who had spent most of his life as a sea fisherman, acted as quickly as lightning and netted her. For a long minute, she dragged through the teeth-cracking, skull-numbing icy waters, gulping air when she could, letting her arms and legs lose feeling so that they flopped to her sides desiring to become fins. Then she was pulled back onto the boat and wrapped in wool blankets, and some men yelled at her and other men rubbed her body and her father with her infant brother looked at her as if she were a dangerous fish, a new species he hadn't a name for, water girl both of him and never again of him. The girl willing to throw herself into the motherwaters, to make them home. Then they were herded into the hull of the boat, crammed full of other anguished people.

"Once there was a water girl who lived in the belly of a whale. The whale was a boat that carried her father and her brother and her body, brought back to life and a different, motherless shore."

"Ah . . . so the whale was a boat," Bertrand says. "Or was it a kind of world? A holding place? The whale is a metaphor?"

"The whale was also a whale," Laisvė says, beginning to lose her patience.

"I've known a number of whales," the turtle says, turning its little head back and forth to crack its neck. "The way you want is a whale way. You want to move toward ocean. That way. The Hudson to the Atlantic, or so your people called them in the gone time. These water paths, we don't call them anything. We don't have to. Language isn't so . . . stunted for us. Language moves more like the ocean."

"Thank you," Laisvė water-whispers. "Goodbye, Bertrand."

Bertrand swims away.

Laisvė watches his little butt and legs until she can't see them anymore. In her mouth, she holds a coin, wet with salt water.

Of Water and Limbs

A week before the Raid that separated Laisvė from Aster, she'd been searching for information about two waterways: the Lena River in Siberia and Lake Xochimilco near Mexico City.

Laisvė was trying to remember something about death and something about life that was bound not to human history but to the history of animals and water and desire. Once, between rails in the overgrown subway system, she'd found what looked like a white rose pendant carved from an animal tusk. Ivory, perhaps. She'd taken it to the Awn Shop.

"That's not from an elephant," the old comma-shaped man said. "This is something much older." He adjusted his eye magnifier. "This piece is straight out of the mouth of history."

"Mammoth?" Laisvė whispered. In the years just before the great water rise and global collapse, she knew, the tusks of ancient mammoths had been discovered rising from the mud and permafrost along the Lena River. Around the same time, axolotls, the colorful amphibians that were among Laisvė's favorite creatures in existence, had started migrating through a network of canals from Lake Xochimilco. One of these species was extinct, and the other had come back from near extinction, and this is what interested her.

Two things fascinated her even more. One was that an underground economy had grown up around the hunting and selling of prehistoric mammoth tusks the moment they reemerged. The other was that axolotls had the ability to regenerate their own lost limbs.

In Yakutia, where people had spent lifetimes scratching out a living hunting and fishing in the surrounding forests and rivers, whole villages suddenly became rich as the blooming of mammoth tusks, known as "ice ivory," gave rise to an ivory gold rush. The biggest demand came from China, where they harvested more than eighty tons a year. Traditional ivory carvers, their work long thwarted by a ban on the sale of elephant ivory, swarmed to get hold of the mammoth tusks. For those who partook of this new ivory trade, the tusks were an unexpected source of income; for researchers, they were a potential key to everything they'd wanted to know about mammoths and their demise. Two countervailing forces—money or knowledge; money or survival—creating torque among humans.

It was hard to say if the rush on mammoth tusks had helped or hurt the illegal killing of African elephants to harvest their ivory. But Laisvė understood that the earth had spit the mammoth tusks up as a test, to see what her species would do. Every time the earth did that—as with diamonds, as with gold—humans had a choice. She had a kind of sense-memory of seeing the tusks herself in childhood, a kind of retinal flash—a series of tiny moving images next to the image of her mother she carried in her body. The tusks reaching out of the mud seemed to be saying something, but she wasn't sure what. They rose like ghostly question marks toward the sky.

Once, Laisvė remembered, she and her mother had happened upon a prospector knee-deep in river mud, trying to pry a tusk loose from the detritus. The tusk hunter had a large knife and a gun. Her mother was carrying her brother on her back. *Hold as still as a statue*, her mother told her. They hid behind a tree. The tree spoke to Laisvė when she put her hand against its bark: *This is the end of an epoch*, it said. *The animals are returning, and they are doing it one fossil at a time. Water is rearranging.*

Laisvė watched the river Lena rushing by. The river had already washed away more than one village and many people.

The history of animals and plants and water made Laisvė see all history differently, and she told her mother this even as a young child.

"What is history to you?" her mother had asked her once.

Laisvė recited her understanding of the word *history*, in triplets: "Explosion, cosmos, chaos. Water, land, cells. Plants, fish, animals. Indigenous humans, habitats, stories. Dreams, desire, death. Invasion, dispossession, colonization. Money, ships, slavery. God, goods and services, slaughter. War, power, genocide. Civilization, progress, destruction. Science, transportation, cities. Skyscrapers, bridges, poison.

"Nations, power, brutality. Terror, insurrection, incarceration. Collapse, raids, water."

"I see," her mother said. Then, to calm her daughter, her mother told her a story.

"You know the axolotl, Laisvė?" she began. "*Ambystoma mexicanum*, from the Nahuatl 'walking fish.' But it's not a fish. The axolotl is an amphibian. It reaches adulthood without changing in any way. For that reason, it's a model organism for scientists. Its body does things humans cannot. It can regenerate its own tail. Its legs. The tissue that makes up its eyes, its heart, its brain. Its whole nervous system."

Axolotls even have four different breathing methods, she explained. They can breathe through their external gill branches, known as fimbria capillaries. They can breathe through their skin. They can breathe through the backs of their throats, in what is called buccal respiration. And they can breathe through their lungs—a curious adaptation, as most animals have gills in place of lungs. Axolotls can swim to the surface of the water, swallow a bubble, and then either send it to their tiny lungs or, for a little while, use it to float.

Underwater, Laisvė's memory leaps to *mother* with or without her permission.

Motherwaters

The past is always in present tense when it emerges in her memory. Like a movie, the images quickening. So when she remembers the first time she went to water, when she thinks of her mother, the memory is inside a perpetual now.

The first time Laisvè leaps into the water, she is jumping in after her mother. Her mother shot dead in that moment, quick and sure, a step away from boarding a boat meant to save their lives. At the sight of it, Laisvè does not feel or think. Instead, she leaps.

Under the great weight of blue, she feels the weightless shift of her body. Back to a breathable blue past, an amniotic sea, liquid lungs. Gray green blue murky veil of water and then sight, plain as day. Laisvè turns her head and arms and body, in a kind of girl-swirl, until her feet find the bottom. She holds her hands up to her face and stares at them: empty but real. She half-pulls half-walks her way along the bottom of the ocean, feeling her way for mother.

A dark shape approaches. It grows in size, until it becomes enormous, and *as it turns in front of her, Laisvė finally sees: it is a whale. For a moment, her heart feels like it might be too big for her chest. Her love of whales is bigger than a lot of things in her young life.*

"Do you know where my mother is?"

The whale eye widens. "Yes, child. Behind you. Not too far. She has an important object she needs to give you. Then she must come with me. You trust me, don't you?"

Laisvė nods. The logic of the world on land and the logic of the world underwater are different universes. Only children and animals understand. (And trees, but talking to trees is risky.)

Laisvė turns around, slow enough to prepare herself. She does not want to cry like a baby. She knows her mother is shot; she knows they are down there for a reason. When she finally sees her mother's face, her own body dissolves into the tiniest particles, the way sand is made from everything in the ocean crushed down to tiny particles over time. She is wave and particle when her mother speaks to her, a see-through water girl.

"Laisvė," the motherbody says. "Take this object. Put it in your hand. Hold it tight. Take it back to the world with you. It will become as you become. Keep it close to your body. This object doesn't earn you anything. It will only have value in your hands."

Laisvė takes the object. She puts it in her mouth; it tastes of blood or copper. She can see through the motherbody, see straight through to the fish behind. The motherbody smiles. The smile goes into Laisvė's body, first into her feet, up her shins and knees, into her thighs and hips where the smile pools for a bit, then up her belly and chest and shoulders and neck, until the mother's smile has become the daughter's. Laisvė feels whole again.

"I love you," the mother says, "my love will always be in your body."

Laisvė considers how crying underwater isn't anything. Or how crying underwater is just tears going back to their origins.

"Listen, my beloved," the mother says, "this is not the last time you will enter the water in your life. Do you understand?"

Laisvè nods, and for a moment, her floating underwater hair entwines with the mother's floating hair. Tendriling.

"This time, you were given a coin. The coin will help you to move your father. He needs it more than he has any idea. His grief is killing him, and it endangers others. There is a man named Joseph who can help, at least a little. You need to find Joseph—he is in the past, and then also in the present. The next time, you will swim to a woman—she is larger than life—and help her to save a multitude of children by moving them toward an aurora, a new dawn.

"Then, finally, you will look for your someone-like-a-brother. The boy you find may have a fever in him; he might seem as if he will kill you, but I promise you, my beautiful water girl, my seal, he will not kill you. It's the world that pulls boys away from their possible becomings. Remember: you can't save anyone. Not me, not your brother, not your father, not the world. You can only move objects and people and stories around in time. Rearrangements. Like rebuilding meaning from falling-apart pieces."

Laisvè tries to run to this mother, but the mother turns entirely to water.

Then the whale returns and gently lifts Laisvè toward the surface of the sea. She hears a giant crashing sound, like a wave or the hull of a boat ramming into something, and the water bubbles around her and some force wrenches her upward—back to the surface, back to the save-a-life boat, her shivering father sobbing, her bundled-up infant brother wailing, the mother gone to water forever.

After that, she knew not to be afraid to go to water, because time slips and moves forward and backward, just as objects and stories do. She knew something new, about moving pieces around. She knew something new, about death and becoming.

Ethnography 1

My great-grandmother used to spit on the floor whenever anyone mentioned the Gold Rush. She said the Nisenan women were brutalized by Johann August Sutter— and then she'd spit on the ground twice, like the two *T*s in his name. This man fled his country to avoid jail time, she said. He left his five children behind. He stole fifty thousand acres. He declared our homelands to be his property. He declared our women and children to be his property. We worked ourselves to death building and cooking and cleaning and helping to defend "his land" so that he would not kill us. He interfered with our tribal marriage customs. He took my sister and my cousin and other women to his bed. He liked to fuck women in clusters. He molested me as a girl. He molested my friends too, boys and girls alike. Those who did not want to have sex with him were considered enemies. Those who did not want to work with him were considered enemies. The

Sacramento River carried our blood. We were fed leftover
wheat bran from wooden troughs. No plates, no utensils.
He ate on china. We slept in locked rooms with no beds.
He beat us. Some of us he killed. Others he traded with
local ranchers. Sold our labor like we were livestock. One
year, after a measles epidemic killed most of us on Sutter's
Ranch—she'd spit again—he built a sawmill. Sutter's Mill
is where the Gold Rush started. Of course, we already knew
there was gold in the rivers and hills. That's where it lived
and breathed. We didn't know what they would do with it,
with us, with the land. This man's brutality made a chapter
in our story that branched off in many directions, taking
our children and ancestors with it. Then she'd stare at the
floor where she'd spit, as if something might grow there.
My great-grandmother lived to be one hundred years old,
but her body was bent with sorrow and rage. Today, the
only Nisenan who work here in the Sierra Nevada valley
work at low-wage jobs. In the 1950s my father taught us
how to stay quiet. He said, *Never trust the government. They
come and steal children. They did it to my brother. So learn to be
quiet or you'll get killed.* My father made a turtle shell rattle
on a deer hoof; I have it to this day. My mother made neck-
laces of abalone shells. My sister has expertise in watertight
basket weaving, using redbud, bracken fern, willow. Still,
some of the people I know are losing language . . . My
great-grandmother told me that, when we speak or sing or
dance, the trees and water and animals understand. I still
know some words and songs. I work at a diner as a line
cook. My daughter is a scientist. My daughter was just
accepted for an internship at the University of California,

Berkeley, and the Lawrence Berkeley National Laboratory. She wants to be an astrophysicist. She says, *Dad, gold was forged during a violent burst when two orbiting neutron stars collided. Neutron star mergers account for all of the gold in the universe.* I listen to her.

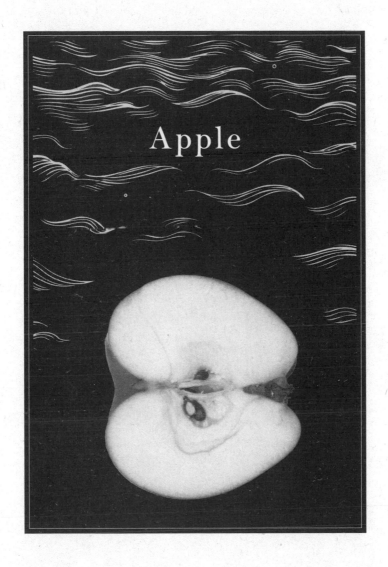

Apple

Cruces 2

What if our labor could help our arms and legs and bodies to understand that our worth might go beyond money? What if we labored together with other bodies toward a single purpose: to build this woman's body into the sky, so that she could show our secrets to god?

I have never felt homesick. Instead, I feel hope-sick.

Because, you see, her body had other secrets underneath the weight of her. I remember when John Joseph told us that there were Lenape Nation bodies and sacred artifacts on Bedloe and Ellis Islands. Someday, he said, people would dig there and find prehistoric objects—iron, pipes, clay pots, coins—that belonged to his Lenape ancestors. It bothered him, that we labored on top of the bones of his ancestors. Sometimes, when we weren't working, he just stood and stared at the dirt. It bothered us too, Endora and David and I—we felt like we were desecrating a grave—but we all kept working, to build her on that land, and our labor bound us to one another. After he told us that, though, from time to time some of us whispered tiny prayers toward the dirt.

I first met John Joseph at the boardinghouse, when we both showed up at the front desk looking for a place to stay. The man in charge said he had a room that slept four people, nothing fancy, just solid shelter for laborers. I looked at John Joseph's hair, black to the middle of his back. He looked at the discolorations on my face. This silent exchange seemed to work like language; we took the room. Endora and David joined us not long after.

Years later, John Joseph and I were both hired to work on another project, a monument to Indians to be built on a bluff overlooking the Narrows. I liked the idea; the two of us liked working together, and I thought our statue would be pleased to have a companion. The new statue was to be an American Indian warrior—similar in scale to the woman we built, but reaching even higher into the air. Any ocean-going ship on its way into the city would see the monument well before the woman we built. Thirty-two chiefs attended the ground-breaking ceremony, including Red Hawk, from the Oglala Lakota, and Two Moons, the Cheyenne chief, both of whom had fought the army at Little Bighorn and elsewhere. Two Moons had even been one of the models for the buffalo nickel.

But then the fundraising failed. Thanks to arguments among politicians and the wealthy, the project, like the chain, was dropped. By the time the world war came along, the following year, it was forgotten altogether. Even the chiefs' names—Cetan Luta, Éše'he Ôhnéšesêstse—were remembered wrong, in the wrong language for the real story.

Stories get overwritten that way. In my home country, slavery was rewritten as discovery. When French colonials came to Saint-Domingue, they devoured the population as if we were the raw material for their own story of themselves.

Once I asked John Joseph what he thought about "discovery."

"Be wary of travelers arriving during a storm," he said. "The stories that come across water have teeth in them." I wasn't sure what that meant, but it stayed with me.

Sometimes, when we were drinking together at night after a day's work, John Joseph, David, Endora, and I would talk about what might have been: if the woman we built had been allowed to represent emancipation—broken chains in her hand, the original story, her form standing on the bones of the Indigenous killed there, not as a monument to killing, but as a reminder that the birth of this place carried death with it in a way we'd need to reckon with. What if she had stood within that story, the Indian warrior her sentry and companion overlooking the Narrows? What if that had been told as the story of America? Instead of the story that came?

Endora was a former Dominican nun. We met aboard the *Frisia*, on the journey from Ireland. Our meeting is either a stain or a salvation in my memory, I've never been sure which. I was heading west because I needed work—factory work, I was hoping, in a steel mill. The steel mills were paying more than paper mills or cane fields or coal mines.

Late on the fifth night of the journey, a phenomenally drunk man was giving me grief on the lower deck. I couldn't sleep at night, packed in so tightly among the hundreds of people and piled-up cargo, so I'd taken to venturing out after dark to stand by the railing nearest the stairs that led down to steerage. That night he came up to puke, and when he saw me, he whipped a knife from his jacket and came for me. He had me backed up to the edge of a railing, his arm swinging wildly back and forth with the blade, his head lolling with drink. I could hear the rush of water at my back. It was the middle of the night—almost morning. Dark enough not to matter to anyone. Plus, we both had among the least evident worth of any of the passengers on the ship; maybe, with his threadbare jacket and darkened teeth,

he was looking for a way to feel bigger. The drunk man swiped at my
arm and caught a lucky slice. *Looks like we got a leper on board*, he
said—talking about my mottled face, my neck. *Looks like you're turning into a sea monster, best get you back where you belong.* He said other
words too, words I'd been called my entire life in four different countries. I don't know where he was from, but his mouth was filled with
bile, and as he sliced away at the air with the knife, closer and closer
to my face, I couldn't tell if he was looking to kill me or send me
over. I lunged at his midsection, trying to knock him to the ground,
but he clubbed his hand down on my back, hard, and I lost my
bearings. He shouted down at me, drooling, then raised his arm
for another attack. *You diseased devil*, he spat, his breath like rotting
apples.

Just before the knife reached my head, I closed my eyes. That's
when I heard her.

"*It's got a name*," she bellowed. When I opened my eyes, I caught
Endora in the moment before she smashed in his skull with a fire-
man's axe. The man crumpled to the deck in a heap. "It's called
vitiligo," she told the still mound of him at our feet.

We both stared at the dead man. Blood pooled on the deck around
his head. "Help me get this louse overboard," she said.

There was no noise at all around us in that moment, nothing but
the sound of water. No lights but our faint navigation lights and the
stars.

We pushed the man overboard; the splash barely registered as sound.
She threw the axe over behind him. The ocean swallowed them both
without comment. "Sad to see that go," she said. "My father said he recovered it off a Dead Rabbit in that free-for-all at Five Points, years
ago. I've kept it with me for comfort." She looked up into the night sky.
Thunder rolled up from the horizon. The air smelled of sky and sea.

Then, out of nowhere it seemed, it started raining, so hard that we took shelter underneath a lifeboat.

The woman was wearing a gray nun's habit and glasses. By her face, I made her to be in her teens, but what I remember was her physical strength—with the axe, with the business of hauling the man overboard. She reached into the arm of her frock and pulled out a flask. We drank. For a long time, we said nothing, until finally she spoke. "My name is Endora." When she tipped the flask back, I caught a glimpse of a cross at her neck. Not on a golden necklace, but in the blue-black stain of a handmade tattoo under her jaw. I learned later that the same man who attacked me had ravaged her earlier in the trip. She saw me looking at her neck. She dropped her eyes to look at my neck, where the stains on my skin were most obvious. We stared at each other's necks, stories forming from our two bodies. Then she reached up and removed her clothing—veil and coif and scapula, the whole habit—and threw them overboard. She stood up and removed her tunic too, hurling it into the sea; it wavered in the night wind like a flying dolphin, then dropped into the churning water.

Without the habit, Endora looked to be without gender, hair all which way. She ruffled it with a hand. She looked like a man, and not like a man.

"My name is Kem," I said.

I don't know if god was there or not.

David Chen came into our body, and our story, when the iron framework began to climb into the sky. The statue's inner skeleton was a wrought-iron square, ninety-four feet high. David and John Joseph worked near each other on the iron rivets, the saddles and armature bars, and the double-helix metal staircase that ran straight up her middle. *It looks like a vertical twisting railroad,* David said. *It looks like metal thatching,* John Joseph said. *It looks like a corset,* Endora said. From the inside, the workings of her body became apparent—the webs of beams and posts and iron, not bones, that she was made from.

John Joseph said that he never saw anyone as good as David was at dangling himself between armature bars and iron. He'd rig the roping as gracefully as a dancer, tying off or untying and retying as he moved from place to place across her body. Sometimes he hung suspended from one arm with his leg wrapped around rope and his other arm just loose, his head tilted, staring at something or nothing. John Joseph said that no one was braver than his ancestors, but I believe no one was ever more beautiful in his bravery than David.

On one particularly hot day, David took off his shirt during a break in the labor and turned to look out at the harbor. He didn't know anyone was near him, but we all saw what looked like hundreds of tiny white feathers all over his back. I opened my mouth to ask, but Endora shot me a look that shut it. Later, when I asked her about it, she said one word: "Scars." Endora had seen all manner of bodies as a nurse during the war. I spent many nights dreaming about how David's back might have become marked like that. As if some kind of blast had etched itself across the whole length and breadth of his back.

On some nights, David did not come back to the boardinghouse with us. When he did stay with us, he slept only fitfully. Once, just before dawn, in his sleep, I heard him whisper one word: *aurora.* He looked to be dreaming, like a child. It made me smile. My favorite time of the day or night happened watching David sleep.

Not all of us worked on the crown, but David did. He had read, in the papers, that the crown was modeled after the bonnet given to Roman slaves when they were freed. The seven rays, he said, were meant to symbolize the reach of freedom, across all the oceans and continents. The twenty-five windows in the crown were meant to give the illusion of light, reflecting the light like facets of a diamond.

To us, it seemed right that David worked inside the crown. Whatever had happened to his body gave him some kind of right to ascend into that space.

Frédéric and the Apple

(1870)

S trewn across my desk on cream-colored parchments, my own
drawings stare back at me: designs in red Conté crayon, at once
regal and sublime and then mocking, like specters who materialize
only to laugh at my incompetence before they dissolve into abstrac-
tion again. I cannot seem to find the form. The body. In the dim
piss-yellow light of my office, my project demands a design: a sculpture like no other. A monument to the Franco-American alliance. I
push the failed drawings aside until I uncover Aurora's most recent
letter. I close my eyes. I smell it. Ocean water and the faintest hint of
lavender. And perhaps dirt.

Sometimes I think my relationship with my cousin Aurora is like
the relationship France has with America. She has always inspired me
and simultaneously challenged me. So it is fortuitous, and both exciting and frightening, that we will reconnect as a result of my work.
When I open one of her letters, for a moment, I want to cross oceans
of time and water to reach her. When I open her letters, I have to sit

down. I smell the envelopes, eager for hints of her, of lavender and skin. My hands shake as I open the envelope.

My brilliant cousin, my obscene genius, my Adonis Frédéric,

I am in love with the drawings of your colossus, with your mind at work. If you should ever stop writing me, I will throw myself out of this window into the river, sink myself like a stone statue. The might of your imagination! Your drawings give me a world of visions—enough to palpitate a heart, to throb a cleft. What a gorgeously unholy perfect union we have made.

Of the three you sent, here are my assessments:

1. *Too Egyptian. This is not the Suez Canal, my dove. I understand your disappointment at losing that project, but still. And she's not really a lighthouse, not in the traditional sense, right? I think your imagination is exoticizing. Or else that trip you took with your delicious painter friend Jean-Léon Gérôme to Egypt has left you aching.*
2. *What has this majestic androgyne got in its hand? A broken chain? Those poor dimwitted god-addicted souls, still tortured by their loss in the Civil War, will consider this heresy. They'll protest, riot, try to tear it down. This bawling, sprawling infant of a country will never get over losing its power to enslave and slaughter other humans as if they were objects. We're built from it. They'll fight you on it. But, oh! How I love those perfect broken shackles, held in the air for everyone to suck!*
3. *I miss her breasts. Where are they? Though I do admire the masculinity of her face. This one may be my favorite.*

Now let's discuss this book I've told you about, this work you must read. Yes, I understand your objection; yes, the author was merely a girl in her teens; yes, this is meaningless to me. How can you dismiss the modern Prometheus? You don't know what girls know. I, however, do, as I think you will remember. The apple? Your own awakening? When we were children?

How precise she was, this "girl author," as you call her. What she created was, I believe, the most perfect articulation of the drive of men—so much so that it made me gasp, left me wet, left me taken by her brain. This monster she conceived, so worthy of compassion. This girl gone mad from loving a man—for isn't the author writing herself as well? Creating a new creation story to combat her grief? Did not her offspring die at the moment of birth? Or prematurely? Child loss induces a grief in a woman that is never overcome. A hole inside a woman is a monumental thing too.

My idea is this: We should rob all the churches of bibles and hymnbooks—like we did when we were eleven, remember, cousin? And we should honor her, the monster's creator, by replacing them all with her work. Break the very ground. Frankenstein every pew.

Remember, I went to war at eighteen. Lost a leg before I was twenty. That's the kind of "woman" I am. Puzzle upon that, beloved.

Love in endless waves,
Aurora

Aurora, my uncontainable dawn,

I accept the transaction. My Darwin for your Shelley. How your words move me. As always. And I am grateful beyond language for your assessment of the drawings.

I remain haunted by that question that so vexes me and so bores you as the point of origin: What does an abstract idea look like? Is it possible to bring the ideal to life?

I have a horror of all frippery of detail in sculpture. The forms and effects of that art should be broad, massive, and simple. "Virtue" and "courage" and "knowledge" cannot take shape directly in stone or metal. Least of all "freedom." By their very nature, concepts have no shape, design, or texture. They shoot the mind outward into space and time, leave it hanging there without traveling anywhere real. To make ideas visible, an artist must personify them, reduce them to a form recognizable to the beholder. Think of the Pietà, of the Venus de Milo. A mother's sacred grief and love, or the so-called figure of desire.

Yet in this project something made my imagination falter. Bodies like those are beautiful, but not right for the ideas. That is, until the first time I clapped eyes on the Winged Victory of Samothrace—and I dropped to the floor. I stared up at her, this headless, armless woman larger than life. How how how, I wondered, did the Christ figure ever beget a faith, compared to this glory? This true figure of worship! For me, she conjured every idea—action, forward momentum, triumph—all in Thasian and Parian marble. In her body, the violence of motion meets a profound and eternal stillness. Before she lost her arms, her right arm was believed to have been raised, her hand cupped around her mouth to shout, Victory!

*Those lost pieces of a woman—pieces of woman—troubled my
vision. Her head never found. Her hands lost to history. A wing
partially gone. And though they continue to haunt me, the concept
that haunts me is not victory. Victory is not my commission.*

It is freedom.

Is freedom a man, a woman, neither, or both?

My first memory of my cousin Aurora is a scene from her bedroom
when we were children. She was twelve, and tall for her age. I was
just ten. She stood in front of an extraordinary pair of deep-red velvet
curtains.

Aurora had recently undergone surgery for a partially cleft lip. In
this and other ways, her body has always carried the trace of things
gone wrong in the world. Unable to eat solid foods, she'd been fed for
days on nothing but milkshakes and ice cream and porridge, which
made me painfully jealous, even though she shared what she had.

On this particular day, she led me into her bedroom and pulled an
apple from a pocket of her dress, a look of great seriousness in her
eyes. I was mesmerized. When she held the apple up between us, her
lips stitched and swollen and red, she said, "Don't move a muscle,
don't tell anyone, or I will forget you ever existed." Her words were
almost swallowed up by her wounded mouth. "Hold as still as a
statue," she said. I did.

In that moment, I believed her more than I had ever believed
anything in my entire short life. She was the only person in the world
who gave me attention, the only person who did not find me odd or
anemic or too preoccupied with things no one else cared about.

She stepped toward me, till she was only an apple's distance away.
I stared at her eyes as hard as I knew how. I could smell her skin.
Lavender soap and the sweat of a girl and blood on her lips. The

smell of the apple. The smell of a boy who has no idea what will happen next, a feeling I would long for the rest of my life.

She plunged her teeth into the apple, enough to hold it in her mouth without using her hands. Her stitches stretched and she bloodied her own lips further.

Then she waited for me to do what she had instructed me to do. My body felt like one human tremor. But there was nothing I would not do for Aurora—then or now, for the rest of my life—so I took my dumb little fist and pulled my dumb little arm back and socked the apple out of Aurora's mouth.

Her head snapped to one side. She made not a sound.

Blood everywhere.

Stitches unsutured.

Mouth unholy in its wound.

She turned to face me. She smiled. Monstrous in her beauty. The laugh that came from that ragged hole of her clattered my little spine.

I was scared—but I was also drawn to her. So I smiled too.

Then she started to peel off her bloodied dress, right in front of me. For a moment, all I could see was her white slip and the form of her, a tiny drop of blood having made it to the crest of her breasts, then just beginning.

For the rest of my life, that image of Aurora would become my understanding of things. And I knew that moment would shape my life's devotion to her.

My life, and possibly hers, were shaped in that childhood room.

Much later, when Aurora lost her leg in the war, my devotion took material form. I could not bear the weight of her lost leg. In my nightmares I watched her try to walk and fall, try to stand and fall, try to move at all and fall again, like a statue collapsing but infinitely worse.

So I set about to design and build her a new leg.

First, I studied the history. And there *was* history—which surprised me.

In ancient Egypt, the wholeness of the human form was important in the afterlife as well as the living realm. Some of these objects have survived to be rediscovered in our time. The Greville Chester Great Toe was made from linen, glue, and plaster.

The horse-hoofed prosthetic leg was popular in China.

The Middle Ages were filled with peg legs and iron legs.

Tezcatlipoca, the ancient Aztec god of creation, lost his foot in a battle with the Earth Monster. He is often depicted with an obsidian mirror where his flesh foot used to live.

In the mid-to-late 1500s, Ambroise Paré invented the modern prosthetic leg. He is also considered to be the father of modern surgery. He was a barber, a surgeon, and an anatomist for four different French kings. In addition to improving amputation techniques, and thus survival rates, he developed functional limbs for all parts of the body. The adjustable harness and hinge knee, with lock control, are still used today.

In the United States, the demand for prosthetic legs burgeoned during and after the Civil War. James Edward Hanger, a Confederate engineer—and, it is said, the first amputee of the Civil War—designed and patented a prosthetic leg while he was convalescing, a device known as the Hanger Limb. Hanger and other prosthetic pioneers, including the Salem Leg Company of Massachusetts, marketed a range of devices, extolling their comfort, strength, durability, convenience, and elegance. Their products were notable for the use of sockets and sheet metal and steel, enhancing their steadiness, smoothness, and silence; they were often lined with leather dyed to resemble flesh, and often included hair.

It would be no exaggeration to say that I became obsessed with the design and construction of Aurora's leg.

I began by studying the basic form of the Salem Leg, designed in 1862. I admired especially the joints and the smooth lines of the foot. For Aurora, however, the leg had to have something quite different: it must be beautiful. Beautiful enough to be its own *objet*, an artwork worthy of museum display. I used rosewood, a favorite of ours—*A wood with blood in it*, she joked. After devising the basic construction of my own version—its own formidable task—I set about hand-carving the wooden frame, adorning it with roses and vines and gold inlay. I hand-painted bloodred toenails as well. And, after weeks of labor, when I was finally satisfied that it was worthy of her gaze, I bundled and wrapped this precious object and sent it over the ocean to her.

Of course, I never saw her reaction when she opened the package. And she never spoke of it, except in one brief letter she sent by return:

> *It is said that god created Eve from tsela,* אַחַת מִצַּלְעֹתָיו
> *traditionally translated as "one of his ribs." And yet the term can
> also mean a curve, a limp, an adversity. Not necessarily a rib at all.
> Think of that. Perhaps Eve is something more like a limp—in which
> case we might do well to consider her power to be larger than life, as
> I have experienced my own limp as a source of insurmountable
> creative and erotic power.*

With my first monument commission, I bought Aurora a boarding-house.

I devoted my life to creating larger-than-life statues.

There are times when I think they are all for her.

My dream manifester, my vision-maker Frédéric,

Do you know what I wanted to be as a girl, my apple?
A nun! Is that not priceless?

*On my childhood journey across the Atlantic, aboard the German
liner Frisia, I met—well, I suppose it would be more accurate to say
I pestered—a Dominican nun. The woman was a mere four years
my senior, yet the distance between ten and fourteen in a girl is vast.
I know the same is true of boys and men and every creature in
between, but the distance plays itself out differently on the bodies of
girls. What blooms there—supposedly between our legs, but really
everywhere in the world, drawing us to it as if we were starving
children—is desire. There is no desire greater than the desire of the
child. One must not speak of it. One must not admit it. We hurry to
create taboos around what first emerged in us in place of tails: that
incredible world where piss, shit, cum, and life fully live. Otherwise,
girl children would people the earth with devils!*

*The steamer carried around ninety first-class passengers, one
hundred and fifty or so in second class, and about six hundred in
third and steerage. I know these figures because I positively hounded
Endora, the Dominican nun, and she had made it her business to
know everything she could about the souls who would share our
passage. I had fixed my eye upon her—you will love this, my love—
from the moment I spied her travel trunk being loaded when we were
still ashore. It was a simple trunk, covered in horsehair, but nothing
about that journey was more mesmerizing to me than that trunk,
as if held within it were the real object of my girl-curiosity, the
nun's story.*

*Before the ship had sailed, I found my way into her line of sight,
and soon into her confidence—and, by the time we reached your*

*statue's city, I had decided that I too would become a nun. You
laugh! But I was dead serious. And I think you know how
formidable my desire was, even as a child. What interested me about
the nun's story were her descriptions of caring for gravely ill hospital
patients. Diseased bodies and horrible sores and broken bones, illnesses
so horrific that nurses had to wear protective clothing and tend to
patients by reaching their gloved hands through gauze curtains.*

*But this Endora nun wasn't like other nuns; her piety carried a
dangerous otherness. She had the jaw and strength of a man.*

Something entirely erotic to the mind of a child.

*Oh, I know other children would have experienced horror and
abjection. As you know, I was not other children.*

*But, cousin, this is no simpleton's story of a girl toggling between
virgin nun and sex-craving whore. That story lacks complexity, lacks
even a subject. That story frames women as objects of a desire not
their own. Take heed: if that thought is beginning to tendril around
in your brain, as you are reading this, I will feel it—and make no
mistake, if that is what you are thinking, I swear on my vulva that
I will make you wait an entire year for your next fulfillment. And I
know already that your longing will be too puny and impatient to
stand in wait that long. You will die from your own longing. And
how would that be? So consider yourself warned.*

*No, my oscillation between two callings—woman of god and
woman of sex—came from one thing: my bone-deep understanding
that spiritual agency and capital agency each give women mobility
and subjectivity in the world. In the case of the former, that mobility
was tied to the feet of a holy man. In the case of the latter? Well.
Women have been outsmarting their counter-genders since the dawn
of time.*

*I do wonder, though, when women will tire of their part in the
story and revolt. I imagine the bloodbath.*

But here is the scene—for I know I have now activated the eros of storytelling in you. The first person I clapped eyes on, after we disembarked the Frisia *and stepped onto our new country's soil, was a creature so convulsively and magnificently free I nearly vanished the nun's existence in a single intake of breath. I forgot her even as she stood by my side—let go of her hand! That protective, maternal nun, the person who could deliver me safe to this new world!*

Remember that cleft on my lip? With my now-free hand, I fingered the scar and smiled, remembering the blood between us. You and I, blood-bound for life.

There she sat in her carriage, this creature, like a crowned bird of her own species. Powdered ever so slightly, rouged with small faint circles of pink, like two aureoles—or perhaps areolas—on her face. A perfect specimen of beauty and, I recognized, of perversion.

A man walked up to the side of the carriage, intent on making a quick and easy transaction. He held money up toward her. I understood the action to be obscene. He looked puny. Just from the impact of her gaze, looking down on him, he stumbled the slightest bit. When he tried again, she flogged him head and shoulders with a horse whip.

The horse did not move. The man fled.

That's freedom, my dear.

Love,
Aurora

Aurora's Children

(1885)

To Whom It May Concern:

Before I begin, two items of note. First: should you someday find me gone, please use the following as a mortality document: "Aurora Boréales, successful businesswoman, aged forty-three, mysteriously disappeared from her residence on the tenth of May while she was meant to be delivering canned goods to the less fortunate. A week ago, her body was found in the Narrows. The face was terribly mutilated, and the body indicated that a fearful outrage had been committed on her person. No clue of the circumstances of her death has yet been discovered." You'll know how to place the story.

A juicy murder mystery. I'd like that.

The second item of note. What I intend here to write is my anti-obituary. That is, I intend to write myself back to life. Let these letters, between myself and my cousin the genius sculptor, draw me back to life.

Should I disappear, watch out for an unexpected object. A gift.

And now the story.

———

They came to me first because of my leg. I think children were enchanted by the idea of a woman who existed in pieces. An adult like a doll, with a removable part!

The first child who came to me approached as I stepped into an alley to adjust a strap on my leg. The street clattered with the syncopated clop and rattle of hooves and carriage wheels, and as I turned back around, I was confronted with a mess of a boy, standing so near me I thought sure he meant to rob me. Not that he could have, mind you, but I thought he might try.

The alley smelled of piss, the boy not much better. He had the face of a creature unused to bathing. Instead of attempting to snatch my pocketbook, however, he watched me lower the curtain of my dress back over my knee, down below my shin to my ornamental shoe. His eye traced the path with an intensity that interested me. Under his gaze, I could almost feel a foot where none existed.

"Please, ma'am, may I see it again?"

I took a closer look at him, and that's when I saw it: he was missing an arm. My cheeks flushed from the idiocy of my earlier thought. There hung a little lump of flesh, the right arm of his dingy shirt short enough for me to see it. His right side announcing an absence where an arm should be.

The look in his pale-blue eyes and his night-dark scruff of hair suggested that he was not originally from the city. "Where have you come from?"

"Ireland," he said.

"By the belly of a steamer, I'd wager. Packed in with the cargo?"

"Yes, ma'am." His eyes returned to my leg. "May I see it? Please?" He removed his hat, or what passed for one, to further his plea. Slowly—and I do know how to perform a task with seductive patience—I began to raise my skirt. His eyes moved me. His eyes reminded me of my beloved cousin Frédéric's. The only gaze that has ever truly moved me, even when we were children.

Is it wrong to say that his stare meant everything to me? The way he gave my body his full attention as I pulled my skirt up over my prosthetic; the way I felt a leg, a foot, captured inside his stare? The way I imagined his absent arm and hand lifting my skirt to reveal my absent leg and foot?

Despite the new labor laws, child workers were everywhere. I'd see them emerging from factories and mills at all hours, day and night. Children were of high value to industry—and there were so many of them. The manufacturers knew they needn't pay them anywhere near as much as adults. In fact, adults often sold their children's labor to the factories and mills. Even today, my reformer friends tell me, the changes they seek are vehemently opposed by parents, industry—even by children who live in their own care, and who remain steadily in need of employment and food. As sentiment hardened against the work mills and factories, a desperate backlash evolved; owners began to speed up the machines and overpack the rooms laborers worked in, you see. The children were of even higher value now, due to the smallness of their hands, but often the children were unable to keep up with the whir and bite of the machines, and the runaway technology tore through their body parts.

What is the worth of a child in this era of industrial multiplication? It's a question I think about often, as a childless woman with a womb so barren that if one were to peek between my legs you might find yourself looking up a long vacant tunnel straight to my brains. Every day that I walk my own city streets, I see plainly that the machines and their product are valued infinitely more than the battered, dirty, often maimed, always hungry children I see departing their shifts, day and night—like small ghosts, really. Their mechanization as valuable workers erases them as humans. They become the same as the com-modities being produced—no, maybe less, the same as the raw materials used to make the products. The child body at the cannery is worth less than the tin can she stamps.

Once a child, who looked to be missing half her face, noticed my lingering glance and held my gaze long enough to explain: she suffered from phossy jaw. I had no idea what she meant. I put my hand to her face, and she continued—with difficulty; her speech had been impacted—that her facial disfigurement was the product of her work in a matchstick factory, where she applied the yellow phosphorus that makes matchstick heads easier to light. Her fellow workers had mouth abscesses, she said. Some suffered facial disfigurements, others brain damage.

"Come see me at night," she told me. "Me gums glow greenish in the dark."

A migrant child, then. Fresh immigrants, around the age of eight, were considered the ideal workforce. Just the right size, the right level of desperate. New faces arriving weekly, in infinite supply, infinitely replaceable.

Some industries had special needs. Coal-mining companies employed children as young as five—small bodies still able to slip through tiny tunnels and fissures where men could not. Girls and boys were strapped to coal sledges, crawling on hands and knees. Textile factories packed women and children in together like colorful bobbins in a box, always with the windows and doors locked. The smallest of children were forced to crawl under blazing machines to collect fallen production materials.

When—or should I say *if?*—these children made it to adulthood, they arrived malformed. Hunched backs and bowed legs, crushed pelvises. Forever damaged vision. Loss of hearing.

Lost limbs.

Many machines sucked in a girl's hair. Some tore off pieces of scalp.

Countless hands were lost. Arms, even faces, mangled. The sunk cost of mechanizing America, creating the fiction of freedom, included the slashing of woman and child bodies. The disconnected pieces fell to the ground, reaching for one another across brutalities and absence, until the wet gutters carried them away.

At a granite mill, twenty young girls, some as young as five, were killed in a fire. Burned alive. Suffocated. Killed while trying to leap to safety. Papers called for reform: Not a reduction in child labor, but an increase in fire-safety measures. *The workplace must be made safer for children.*

How in the world will we ever become whole from this?

I designed a different solution.

"Come with me," I told the boy transfixed by my missing leg, the boy with one arm. And I led him through the corridors of my infamous establishment, past unparted curtains, to the largest room in the building—Room 8, a former theater space of some kind—where I lead the children I can. Here, safely behind a wall and sturdy door, beyond reach of the all-consuming bulge of monied men in my city, is the room where I conspire to bring children of every nationality and age and size to be educated, to be drawn away from industry toward intellect, toward economic autonomy.

In a thriving city, children make such plump targets. As much for capitalists as for kidnappers, slavers, and sociopaths.

If my city wants these children, it will have to come and get them.

Aurora's Eye

The makeshift school behind the door of Room 8 in my building had desks made from the finest cherrywood to be found in the city. The chairs were equally exquisite, with velvet cushions and backs so that each small body might feel held in a way that had eluded them in life. Prosthetics were abundant throughout the room—some of the newest inventions, their works clicking surely into position, some even humming mechanically. All of it the bequest of a former client upon his death: his work impeccable, my secret safe.

People give up on children all the time. They hurt them, abuse them, abduct them, extract their labor to the point of exhaustion, then throw them out like trash. One weekend in 1874, a Philadelphia dry-goods purveyor named Christian Ross looked up to see his five-year-old son, Walter, approaching him with an object in his hand.

"Open your hand, my boy. What have you got there?" he asked in a fatherly way.

The boy opened his hand. The object held in the cup of his small pink skin was a candy. The father asked the boy where the candy had come from.

"From a man in a wagon," the boy explained. "He gave one to Charley too." Charley was the boy's four-year-old brother.

Three days later, while washing dishes, a local woman looked through her kitchen window and saw a wagon pull up to the curb near the home. The driver and another man talked to the two boys; then the wagon drove away with the boys.

On his way to the police station, filled with terror, the father saw his son Walter coming back to him, in the company of a man who had found him lost and crying. The story his son told him cracked his heart. The man they'd met earlier in the week, the man who had given Walter and his brother candy, had drawn up to them in a wagon with another man. They asked the boys if they wanted to buy fireworks for the upcoming Fourth of July. What boy could say no to fireworks? The boys went with the men. Charley sat between the men and Walter sat on the second man's knee. When they arrived at a cigar store, the men gave Walter twenty-five cents to go inside and purchase firecrackers.

When Walter came out of the cigar store, the wagon—with the men, with his brother—was gone.

The abduction became a sensation, of course. But what made its infamy linger was that the kidnapping of Charley Ross was the first recorded case in which a ransom was demanded. The four-year-old boy was never found. Two years later, the father wrote a book about the disappearance of his son. Soon, however, it was all forgotten.

So, you see, I do not believe that anyone is searching for these children in my care. My goal, in gathering them together, was to give them a chance to exist without violence or fear.

You may wonder about teachers.

You will question my judgment.

But I was certain of my methods.

In Room 8, the children were the teachers. Each was tasked with gathering a piece of information, of truth, and sharing it with the rest. I was present at times, but not often.

You see, their hunger to be full people in the world drives children to gather knowledge voraciously, to study, to share what they've found. What I could grant them was to see that they were fed and clothed and cared for in a beautiful house, where a child was free and safe to be a child. In place of a maternal embrace, I gave them the space to exist as full humans. Also: Books. Maps. Information. Drawings. Photographs. Paper and pencils and drawing pads and paints and canvas. All manner of small machines, including candy-making machinery—to study the mechanics. The new invention of sound reproduction—Mr. Edison's phonograph, Mr. Bell's graphophone—will soon give children the chance to capture their own voice. I wanted to give them the chance to invent their own world.

For years, the Raids had constantly replenished the workforce, a sinister kind of labor trafficking machine. Nightly roundups, perpetrated by unscrupulous men with clubs and ropes and nets. At first, they trained their sights on black children and Native American children and Asian and Mexican children, who rarely received pay, since their debt tethered them to their owners. Then, as demand increased, they expanded their reach to *all* children, to the endless supply that arrived in the city from the farmlands, from overseas, from anywhere. Debt bondage was common. The men who worked the Raid force may well have been victims of debt bondage themselves, or criminals seeking something besides a life behind bars or the poorhouse. Some, of course, were simply evil.

In place of a mother's love, I felt an embodied responsibility to reflect their exquisite worth back to them from the inside out. A girl known as Ruby wrote with her left hand, since her right hand was missing two fingers. An eight-year-old called Cammy, long employed picking cranberries in a New England bog, had fingers curled like those of an old woman with arthritis. The boys who had been cutters in canning companies had the faces of shrunken old men and hands that had been hacked to pieces. A boy named Hiram, who'd been paid five cents a box to pack sardine cans, though he could manage only four boxes a day, could no longer extend his fingers from their bent positions without pain. Before being sent to the cannery, he'd worked full nights at a spinning factory; he was so young and small that he had to clamber up the sides of the spinning frames to work the threads and bobbins, and he'd lost most of one foot in the process. A girl of nine named Mary had a scar running all the way down her cheek, ending at her collarbone. When a man tried to rape her, she'd used the considerable blade of a sardine knife to stab him at the jugular. Before he died, he got off one slice that disfigured her face forever. One seven-year-old boy's wrong move at a glassworks left him with no hands at all.

What I gave them was witness: You exist. You are not nothing. Take your life back.

One day, in the midst of a history lesson—and when I say "history," I mean showing the children of Room 8 the paths of global commerce and migration and immigration overlaid on the paths and lives of the original inhabitants, the national and local trade routes, the pirating routes, not to mention the laws surrounding individuals and their bodies and movements, the arc of geologic time, and the myths and stories people have created to track and remember themselves—the girl named Ruby, an eight-year-old former oyster shucker, was asking me, *Please wait, I can't keep up*, when a noise cracked through the air, so loud

that it shook all the desks and even my own vertebrae. A great flash
of light, then another, larger explosion. The window glass quivering,
the floor briefly buckling, my jaw clacking so hard that I drew cop-
pery blood from my own tongue. The children held on to the sides of
their desks. More than one crawled underneath.

When the shock passed, we all ran to the windows and looked out
toward the water. With our faces pressed against the glass, we must
have looked like immigrants lining the hull of a ship.

Just three buildings away from us blazed a furious fire.

Twenty women, mostly girls under the age of fifteen, perished that
day when they could not get out. The doors and windows had been
locked.

I took in the deepest breath of my life, held it, thought about shirts
and collars and corsets; odd, the images that come into the mind during a crisis.

Aurora and the Want of a Child

To anyone who inquires earnestly, I explain that my business involves bodies.

Beyond the separate undertaking that fills Room 8, I rent rooms. The rooms I let are not residential. I have . . . rearranged the aims of the building my beloved cousin purchased for me. My clientele are men and women of means, and I curate my rooms based on their wants. In return, along with the customary consideration, they never cease to provide me with good stories—as if they were all characters, I sometimes muse, in a novel or stage play.

Sometimes their occupancy makes the walls vibrate.

For example, some years back, a man walked into my building, introducing himself as the owner of a very successful preserve manufactory, a company that produced canned tomatoes, jellies, fruits, vegetables, meats, and soups. At the time, I gave little thought to his tiny empire; it was enough for me that he seemed able to pay his bills with us. He was a frequent visitor, which meant he did not lack an imagination, and in time, I came to admire him.

During the war that took my leg, many of us had been saved from starving by eating food from cans, and during the intervening years, I had amassed a small collection of these "survival soups," as I liked to call them. More than once in my life I had to rely on the survival soups, to help others or even myself survive. But I always restocked them when times improved. I became fond of their presence. They were an antidote against fear, and a reminder that scarcity and wealth are no distance from each other. Once the preserve canner became a client, I hired a local finish carpenter to design a special blue cabinet, with sixty little square caves only slightly bigger than the cans, and displayed it in a place of honor in my business quarters. The cabinet of gleaming and colorful cans was a frequent topic of curiosity and conversation with other clients.

This factory owner was kind, at least in my company. He only ever wanted to be ever so gently spanked, and the only remarkable aspect of that desire was his stamina; he could take that light touch for several hours—far longer than any other client. He liked to sustain the quality of a treasured thing over long periods of time. Like a tomato or peach hidden inside a tin can, its surprising hue and ripe bulge glistening from within the moment you sawed through the edges of the silvery-blue metal. And he liked to keep one hand clenched around my artificial leg, as if his life depended on it. That leg holds a thousand of his tender kisses.

Once, as he was dressing after his session, I walked over to the cabinet, pulled a tin of pears from its blue cave, and opened it with a can opener. Lifting the lid, I held the can out toward his mouth. He dipped his fingers into the thick sugary pear muck, pulled out a pear, and ate it, his eyes never leaving mine, except when he closed them to experience his brief autoerotic pleasure more fully.

You may know that the French inventors of the tin can failed to invent an opener for their container, and for years, the cans could only be opened in a brutal manner—with a hammer and chisel, a rock, or a bayonet. Equally interesting to me is the fact that the first canned food was invented for seamen who were inefficiently fed disgusting meals, by all reports, of meat and fish stored in barrels of brine. Everything tasted of salt. (Too much salt on the ocean? Well, that's the thinking of men for you.)

My favorite can story involves the lost expedition of Captain Sir John Franklin. In 1845, Franklin, an officer of the British Royal Navy, departed on two ships, the HMS *Terror* and the HMS *Erebus* on an expedition to cross the last unnavigated territory of the Northwest Passage. When the two ships became icebound near the Victoria Strait, however, the mission collapsed and all 129 men were lost.

Three years later, Franklin's wife helped launch a search, which became the first of many. In 1850, relics from the expedition were found near the coast of Beechey Island, in the northern Canadian archipelago. Further relics and stories of the Franklin party were collected from local Inuit communities.

It's here that the story fades—except for what I gathered from another girl who approached me one day, a strange girl who claimed to be from the future. In the year 1981, she said, a team of scientists from Canada studied the bodies, graves, and relics collected from the ships and concluded that the crew likely died from tuberculosis, pneumonia, starvation, and lead poisoning caused by badly soldered cans on board.

You heard right. A visitor from the future.

She went on and on when I first met her, this girl, like she couldn't stop: the history of the tin can, its invention and manufacture, its evolution. She told me all about the original inventors of canned food. Some Parisian fellow, named Halpern or Appern or Appert, who worked out a way to seal prepared food in glass bottles with cork stoppers, then boiled the bottles in water. An Englishman who developed tinplate cans with soldered lids instead of glass containers—good for sailors, she said, since salted meats hastened the onset of scurvy. In her time, this girl claimed—a time unimaginably far away—canned food had once again become as sought-after as it had been useful at sea with Napoleon or on land in the Civil War. With visceral joy, she told me about a can of tomatoes she'd eaten, in her world, that very morning.

Poor girl, I thought. It's a good story, though, isn't it?

I'd never met a girl like her before.

Though, as I mentioned, children always found me.

When I first met her, I was carrying a bag of soup cans over to Laborers' Row. The night I met her, she was standing across the street from my building. Her hair hung black and wet. She stood across the street, her dress wet, her right arm held straight up in the air. She had an object in her hand, but I could not see what it was. We both held our ground. We held each other's gaze. Finally, I said, "Well, then?" And she lowered her arm back down like it was a regular arm and came toward me.

I don't know how to explain what I felt in my body as she walked toward me. Like a hard pang in my abdomen.

What is inside the abdomen of the aging and childless woman? Is it a hollowed-out nothing? Is it something? Is it a hole as if each woman were suddenly excavated through and through, like a statue of our former selves, not the object of anyone's desire any longer, but an object with questionable use-value?

When she reached me, her brow made the V of a child reaching for seriousness. "I have something very important to trade," she said. "I mean, in . . . the underground economy."

I held in a chuckle. What a creature, to come out with such a thing. *The underground economy?* "But do you have a name?" I asked. She looked to be somewhere between ten and twelve years of age. Her hair cascaded past her shoulders in black turbulent waves that seemed to argue with one another all the way down her back. Her faded red dress was cut high on her legs, revealing knees that were scuffed and brown with mud and, perhaps, dried blood. She had no coat, no hat, no gloves, just her girlhood and the object in her closed hand.

She did not answer my question with any name.

"I see," I said. "Well, then, what's this about something to trade? Are you a thief?" I crossed my arms over my chest to signal that I expected some kind of answer.

"I'm not a thief." She frowned. "I'm a carrier."

Even more intriguing. Where do you come from, then?"

"Across time," she said, looking at me directly. "That's how I got here. I crossed through time."

"So you're a . . . carrier, and you cross time."

She nodded.

My night was improving by the minute. "Do time-crossing carriers need to eat or sleep, like regular children? Would you like to step inside and dry off?"

She ignored my questions. "Is this 10 Reverie Road?" she asked.

"Yes," I replied.

"In the water, my mother told me to come to 10 Reverie Road. Here I am."

What a strange little creature.

"Either that or I've drowned, I guess. Either way, I'm here." Then she held out her hand and opened it, and even under the dim light of the streetlamp, I could see what she held: a locket. "You have an object inside the Room of Reliquaries. I'd like to make a trade."

That piqued my interest. How did she know about my rooms?

"All right, then," I said, still thinking. At the very least, I could give her a meal, a bath, maybe some rest. Whether she could join us in our own underground economy—Room 8—I was not yet ready to decide. Her limbs were all intact. As to her wits, I was far less certain.

The girl looked up at my building. She seemed to be counting stories. Then she looked down at the river gurgling in wavelets against the foundation. Then she stared at me so hard, I thought she might bore right through my skull.

"There's going to be a Raid tonight," she said. "Later. Someone has revealed your secret and you are all in danger. They'll take them. They'll make them child workers. Or worse."

"Who do you mean?" My throat tightened.

"The children. The whole of them. We don't have a lot of time."

An uneasiness spread like a fever in my body, hot and cold at once. My eye twitched. In eight years, we'd never been raided. No one had any idea there was a functioning school for orphaned children behind the door of Room 8. Not even my beloved cousin Frédéric.

"Come inside." I held out my hand, but she didn't take it.

On the way into the building, the girl asked me if I had seen any lighthouses in the area. The cans were suddenly nothing to her, compared to lighthouses.

"You know, the lighthouse on Turtle Hill is frozen over just now," I ventured, which had the peculiar and fascinating effect of detouring and focusing her speech.

"Yes, the light on Turtle Hill! It lives at the end of the long island in your time. I've read about this. The very first public works project when the nation was in its infancy. The fourth oldest standing," she said, as we climbed the first flight of stairs toward the Room of Reliquaries. "The light can be seen for approximately seventeen nautical miles. Designed by Ezra L'Hommedieu. *L'Hommedieu* means 'the man of god,' or just 'man-god.' My mother was a linguist. Lighthouses are beacons, you know."

The girl turned off her monologue, as abruptly as she'd begun it, and looked at me with fiery eyes.

I don't know why I was so compelled by her stare. Except that sometimes the want of a child is bigger than everything you think you know; their eyes can arrest you midlife and throw your entire purpose into the wind like seeds.

I unlocked the door to the Room of Reliquaries and watched her eyes scan the room; for a moment, I felt I *could* imagine her traveling through space and time. What she was looking at: hundreds of glass containers of beautiful shapes and sizes, each containing an object someone before her had found astonishing. As she looked around the room, I thought she stopped breathing. Here and there: small octopuses or giant beetles preserved in formaldehyde and water. Whole walls decorated with wet specimens. All varieties of worm, which she took a particular interest in. Feathers and bones and jaws, the organs of fish and fowl, eyes and hearts and lungs from countless creatures, minerals and claws, the wings of bats or birds.

What arrested her, though, was the thing she came for: a bluish-purple umbilical cord—an oddity to be sure—spiraling gracefully inside its fluted glass container.

She opened wide her palm, inside of which was a locket. Without taking her eyes off the pearled knot of the umbilical cord, she opened the locket to show me what was inside: a lock of hair. She meant to make her trade.

"Whose hair is that?" I had become mesmerized, not by the macrocosm of the room but by the miniature world of her hand and its object. Of course, the thought that seized me—before logic could challenge its absurdity—was that it was a lock of Mary Shelley's hair, the locket the very one I had proposed an elaborate fantasy to steal. But the girl cut into my fantasy like a thief.

"Your son's," she replied.

A sound came out of me, something like a laugh, but incredulous: a puff of voice and air. "But I can assure you, I have no son," I said flatly, an odd weight on my chest.

"You will," she said, leaving a cleft of silence between us. "With Lilly. You will be whole. In a different time."

I had no earthly idea what she meant by that, but I took the locket from her hand to examine it more closely anyway.

"Liza," she said. "My name is Liza."

Dear bold, beautiful Frédéric,

Before you suffer one of your terrible lapses of imagination, you must read Mary Shelley's book—to fulfill your desire as a sculptor and find an answer to your question. You are birthing a creation! A monstrous one, even! If by "monstrous" we might mean something away from the dull drone of fear and horror . . . Perhaps monstrous is just another word for magnificent. I tell you, this Mary knew more about birth and death and the horror of art and mankind than any writer yet published.

So, then. To contribute to your great art, I will make you a wager. I will finish reading the plodding Darwin you sent me, if—and only if—you read the book designed at the hands of a girl.

But first I must make a final stipulation: you must accept that fiction and fact are not at war. Realism and fact convince us quite seductively that there is no evolutionary transformation, no possibility of radical adaptation, that can rival the formidable matter and energy of pure imagination.

For my part, I hold Mary Shelley against Darwin. If you accept my proposal, the winner—that is, the mind with more acumen, and the body that is more infinite and sublime—shall receive one night's activity in the room of their choice. A night to murder all other nights. Designed by either you or me. Whoever is most persuaded by our authors and their visions. If I win, the night shall be devoted to my own conjurations, inspired by my divine Mary. If you win, you are free to choose as your model that dullard Darwin. (Though, please, no insects.)

I know you would be laughing right now, were we together. And we would, of course, be drinking. And I would touch your face, and you would touch my hair, and all your intellect and all your success would melt into the simple intimacy of your artwork and my imagination, and I would construct for you a new room. A Room of Rooms. And I would ask you to keep drawing, into the night, and I would simply sit near you until you absolutely could not resist drawing on my body, and I would surrender, and you could map your entire imagination onto my skin. Press the pen so hard, it cuts.

But I know what you want. You want another installment, another chapter in our unending night stories. So that you might figure out what turn your shapes should take in as they rise from the ground to the sky and form your new colossus. (I pretend that you need me to tell you all this. That you need me in order to create. And I pretend I need you to be my adoring audience, rapt and receiving.)

Another episode from my rooms: last night I was with the beautiful David Chen. He is without a doubt the most tortured slumberer I've ever encountered. If sleepers mimic the dead, then he is an unholy and active ghost, like a statue suddenly bending and thrashing, liberated from its seemingly captured stone. He comes to inhabit the Room of Rope, but he must always sleep first, as if his exhaustion is his existence. I study his back in his sleep; he always sleeps on his stomach. This is the most remarkable detail, my love: his back is covered all over with what looks like a swarm of white feathers. Or that's what I thought the first time I saw him unclad. But they were not feathers.

Hundreds of small scars, they were. All of them white and pearled, and small enough that they correspond to nothing else on this earth that I can think of. I know not to ask him, at least not yet. The only things I know about him are his sleep, his desire, and that he worked to help finish the transcontinental railroad when he was twenty. He says he is thirty-six, but the body has its own calculus, doesn't it?

But when David is disturbed corporeally in his sleep, it is something like an unconscious rapture. I often cannot tell the difference between a smile or a grimace, the sweat of eros or tears of terror—the sentiments are truly indistinguishable. His body is simply taken with the world of night, senseless, out of tune, without law. It looks as if he were experiencing an explosion from the inside out when he sleeps. When he wakes, it is—for a moment—as if he has come out of a great and long illness. And when he realizes where he is, his face contorts into a more familiar animal mask—oh, don't pretend you don't know what I mean. Everyone shifts masks every hour of the day—and he readies himself for the Room of Ropes.

From that point forward, I spend tender hours suspending his body. Touching his skin so lightly with a feather that he weeps.

He hangs for many hours.

I think he wants to touch something he has lost.

That is my story for now. This man moving through torture to tenderness, suspended from thick ropes made from the silk of spiders.

Love unto death,
Aurora Boréales

My soul Aurora,

Your story of this David moved me mightily, and thus conjured another in me. The first time I saw David, the statue, I visited so often that the guards made inquiries. I was warned many times to refrain from touching him. I could not eat or sleep without torment for weeks thereafter. I carried a profoundly base thought in my body: Why is this magnificent David not a possibility in my life? Why can't my obsession take form in his body? His desire taking me into back alleys and bathrooms and forests at the edges of cities . . . anywhere I could be unseen and feel the dirt and grime and sweat and cum coming up against the white of marble and perfectly clean skin that plagued my thoughts.

Where is my David?

Do you recall when we first rediscovered each other as adults? Come, you invited me. Come and see what I've done with your gift, you said at the door to the boardinghouse I bought for you. The building was brick, painted black, rising three stories into the air— its bulk heaving almost directly out of the water, so close I could throw a cup out of the window and hear a splash. Each story of the building had six rooms. A beautiful banister staircase made of cherrywood to seduce those who enter ever upward.

That night, I asked you if you were a prostitute.

It's not like there was a shortage of high-end ladies' clubs peppering the neighborhood. The most esteemed was probably Kate Woods's House of All Nations, where the claim was that foreign-born women of any extraction could be purchased for the right price. And baser brothels thrived amid the dense and raucous workers' neighborhoods too. The business of pleasure was booming. It seemed an innocent question.

But it was your answer that arrested me—an answer pushed through lips pursed so tightly, I imagined your teeth screaming.

"I am neither a madam nor a prostitute—not ever again in this lifetime, my love. I do not traffic in the bodies of women. I traffic instead in stories—ones that take a body to its edges."

You remember how I looked at you. With the blank stare of a bovine, you said later.

But that night you were patient with my dullness. Leaning close enough to kiss me, you whispered: "I draw a very different client, Frédéric. Those who enter my rooms come away not in some banal love or lust, but with a craving to exist, again and again, inside a much more interesting and intense space. An ecstatic state. A space between."

The cilia in my ears stood up. I said, "Death?" Then I laughed—the laugh of an educated and refined idiot who doesn't quite know what is going on.

"Close," you replied. "More like the meniscus between pleasure and pain." You pinched the skin near my nipple so hard, my lip twitched. But I did not make a sound.

We were children again in that moment.

"I bring to the surface of the body, and the psyche, stories held so deeply within us that we shudder to speak them. I bring stories to life, so that we might recover our own bodies. I am wholly narrative, I am the hole of narrative, I am the holy narrative. These rooms are a storyletting," you said. And that was true—but I was ignorant, insecure, too anxious to sound witty and knowing.

"Do you mean that you are an endless hole, my love?"

You looked at me in a manner that would shrivel both brain matter and scrotal sack into ash.

"Certainly not. Have you lost your mind in your travels?" You poured more whiskey. "Have you become my gorgeous yet slow-witted cousin since we've been apart? A witless beautiful object—what a terrible combination. No, what I'm referring to, my angel, are the systems and practices that humans rely on to interpret behavior. Rules and practices eventually become the very system they were meant to describe. Exhibit A"—and here you outlined your own torso and head with a flurry of gestures— "the object we call 'woman.' I am, in short, unbearable, overwritten by imbeciles."

I stood. You pushed me back down, so that your body rose above mine.

You explained an entire court proceeding, somehow turning it into a seduction. Something about criminals and corporations and I don't know what, but I did not turn away, not in my head, neither in my other head. You concluded with an illumination I think about still: "If I can only exist as some dim object, inside an insipid story laid out for me before I was born by morons who need the stories of mothers and whores to keep the social house in order"—you pressed your sex down harder onto mine—"then at the very least I am going to require my own fucking pen."

The vast wet of you became apparent in my lap.

"I am not a prostitute, as noted earlier," you said. "Now let me show you my rooms."

The answer to my prayers began there, Aurora.

I therefore remain devoted to you above all.

> *Your Frédéric*
> *(Shall I be jealous of this David?)*

Ethnography 2

Most of us came from Guangdong Province. The poverty in Taishan and Xinhui devastated entire families, whole villages. Starvation and disease in waves. Famine. The civil unrest threaded like an electrical current into villages and crops and families and bodies. We were dying. The people in adjacent villages, neighbors for generations, developed new animosities, sudden distrust. When we got on boats to California, or found work cutting sugarcane in Cuba or mining guano in Peru, we were saving our own lives. When you watch mothers without enough milk in their bodies to feed their own babies, when you see children of your own or your brother's or your neighbors' with arms so thin that they seem as if they might snap, when your sisters and brothers and husbands and wives and parents die in front of you wearing more bone than flesh, you'll get on a boat—any boat—that holds out the possibility of saving them.

Some of us started on the West Coast and worked all the way out to the East Coast. We were paid twenty-five dollars a day for a six-day workweek. And a meager increase if you

agreed to work the tunnels. All our work was done by
hand. We opened earth and we cracked rock and we laid
track. We cleared roads by moving mud and rocks and dirt
and snow. We forged iron. And when something needed to
be blown up, we handled the explosives. The best money
went to those of us willing to be lowered on ropes to plant
explosives in tunnels or into the sides of rock walls, holding
on to hope—Was it hope? Was it something else?—that
we'd be lifted back up before the blast. When we drilled
those holes into the mountains, into the gullet of a canyon—
when we dangled from precipices in baskets—I don't know
why we ever believed we would not explode along with
those rock walls.

Maybe, sometimes, death isn't death anymore. We
learned the difference between being no one in Guangdong and being the raw work force in a country building
everything in sight toward the end of creating money. We
saw those white workers—mostly Irish—and the money
they made: nearly double our take. We saw the money the
Chinese accountants made. We saw the money the railroad owners made. We laid their tracks. We created transcontinental trade. But we created no profit of our own.

Still, the story of money got inside us.

Rope

Cruces 3

S he slept in pieces.

Before we assembled her, she slept in 350 different pieces of
body packed in 214 crates. We thought about those pieces a lot as she
slept on the water; we dreamed of her body pieces and felt our own
limbs differently.

When she finally arrived, in the belly of a boat, each piece of her
was given a number. The pieces were lined up according to the creator's numerical system, where the pieces needed to fit together. Each
piece had rows of holes that needed to be fitted—riveted.

All of this got me thinking. Bodies in the belly of a boat. Packed
together like freight or animals, assigned a numerical value.

Once, at a pub back on the city side of the water, Endora cornered
me to talk about how I had been sleeping. "You make moaning
noises," she said. "And sometimes you say words . . . or what I think
are words. Do you suffer when you sleep? Does it stay with you when
you wake?"

I don't know how to talk about what it means to be haunted by other bodies, by family stories, by ancestral sorrow. By other experiences from the past. Maybe all of us carry the voices and bodies of everyone who has come before since the dawn of time. Maybe some of us carry them differently. The story of all those bodies my one body carries did not begin, nor will it end, in the belly of a boat meant to make meat of me. I won't let it. But the weight of the suffering threads through me and beyond.

My body carries crisscrossing narratives from the past, the present, and whatever uncertain future we will face. One such story was that of Henry Moss, a man of African descent who was born in America. Moss made a show of his depigmentation, the story goes; he made a living from it. People were said to be mesmerized by his skin. There are other such stories, of men and women who were used as entertainment for freak shows and circuses: an enigma of black and white confounding the audience after the brutality and bloodshed of the war. Who would we become? Maybe the drunk man on the *Frisia* meant to make meat of me. Another story concerned a white man who took pity on a child originally from Saint Vincent, a child with vitiligo. The white man loved the orphan boy, the story said, and gave him a home. When the boy died young, the man was so distraught that he buried the boy in a plot he'd secured for himself, having no other children. When the man died, he was entombed with this boy. I don't know if that was love or something else.

"I do not suffer when I sleep," I told Endora. "I think the suffering of others finds some of us in our sleep. I think"—and now I wasn't sure I would make any kind of sense to her—"it moves through us."

"That seems true," Endora said. Then she clenched her own belly and grimaced.

"Are you feeling ill?" I asked.

"No. I'm remembering something I used to carry in my body that was taken from me."

John Joseph looked at me. David stared at her belly. We knew enough not to say a single thing out loud. Later Endora confided in me: she'd given birth to a baby out of wedlock. The baby had been taken from her. And that baby was buried in the ground behind a church. Our own bellies felt different after that.

Maybe that's why none of us was all that surprised at the sight of a girl coming up out of the water, her arm raised and reaching. We'd lost a lot between us: Families. Languages. Identities. Heart. Finding something, there amid the vast unknown, made us feel worth something.

"Do you ever feel like going back home?" I once asked Endora.

"Home?" she said.

I didn't know if she was giving an answer or naming us there together over a simple meal after a day of work. We all smiled, for whatever reason.

The night the water girl appeared, we were getting ready to board the ferry back to the city side after work, back to our shared boarding-house.

As soon as the girl was safely on deck, she pulled something from her mouth: a penny. She handed the coin to John Joseph as if he'd been waiting for it.

He turned it over in his hands. "What's this?" he asked.

"For an ancestor of yours who is coming later, the boy called Joseph," said the sopping-wet girl. "They call it an Indian Head, but it's not the head of an Indian. It's just Liberty wearing an Indian head-dress. That's how Indians and women lose their worth, you know—they put us on their money, or make us into fake prizes and objects, so we can't move in the world like regular people. I told Joseph that. In another time. But pennies and objects all change their worth, with time and water."

"I don't have any children," John Joseph said.

"You will," she said. "Your son and his son and his will walk the iron. Like you."

We'd none of us seen or heard anything like this girl before. She didn't look distraught or lost. She came out of the water looking comfortable.

Then she turned to David Chen. Walking around him, she placed her hands gently on his back and closed her eyes. We all put our heads down. It must have looked something like prayer, though it felt nothing like that. David let out the heaviest breath I'd ever heard, as if he were releasing a long, thick, coiled rope.

None of us knew what to make of this strange girl. She looked to be about twelve years old, but she also had the look of a woman in midlife—something about her jaw, or her eyes, or both. She brushed herself off, as if she could make herself fully dry with just the wave of a hand. She looked over across the water, at the work we'd been doing. By that point, only the legs and hips of the statue were standing; the torso and arms and head and crown were all still to come.

"She's going to turn green, you know," she said to us.

We said we knew. Oxidization of copper.

"She's going to drown too," she said.

None of us knew what she meant by that.

"The ocean is going to acidify and change," she said. "Just like copper changes when it oxidizes. The water will rise faster than people think—faster than a lifetime. Some women drown, you know. Does she have a heart?"

None of us said anything until Endora did: "That's a good question." I think we thought of ourselves as her heart—but that's stupid. Isn't it?

Then the girl walked up to me, staring at my face and neck, at the place where my skin screams differently from anyone else's. She traced the shapes with her finger. I didn't move. "This is a map of the new world," she said. "All the land masses will change shape. All the words will too. All the bodies will embody differently." Her small hand rested on my face longer than you might imagine.

Then, turning back to Endora, she reached into a little rucksack slung over her back and pulled out an odd-looking roll of silvery fabric. "This is called *duct tape*. Only a welder might understand the power of duct tape. A mother came up with the idea. Using fabric tape. She tested it out in the ammunition factory where she worked."

Endora held her own belly.

"You can even use it to suture a wound." The water girl scooped Endora up in her gaze. "There are so many ways to carry." They stared at each other. Neither flinched. A strange and brief still air surrounded them. No one's mother locked in a gaze with no one's daughter. There was no word for what they were to each other, unless the word was the energy itself between them.

One night, early in the project, John Joseph threw his shoulder out of joint and cracked a rib. Endora, a fine riveter, also had medical skills, and she tended to him. Taking John Joseph's arm, she put his hand on her shoulder, then whapped him a good one, so that his shoulder went back where it was supposed to be. He didn't scream or anything.

"Well, that's it, then," Endora said.

That's how we felt listening to this girl: *Well, that's it, then.*

When we boarded the ferry back to the city that night, the girl came with us. John Joseph turned the penny over and over in his hand. Endora looked—well, this isn't possible, of course, but she looked taller. The girl wove around our bodies there at the railing, humming contentedly under her breath, or seeming to. She appeared entirely at home with us. She wasn't afraid to touch us or lean on us. At one point she even took David's hand; then she reached out and held mine too, this girl between us like some kind of conduit as we crossed the water. My hand warmed in hers.

Behind us, our half-made woman watched us leave. One hundred thousand pounds of copper, even more iron. When she was finished, her total weight was two hundred and twenty-five tons. Yet her skin—copper sheeting—is about the thickness of a penny. Enough copper to make more than 430 million pennies.

As we all hung over the ferry railing, Endora pressed the girl to tell her story. "Where are your parents? Where do you live? What's your name?"

They seemed responsible questions to ask. As it turned out, though, they were not the important questions. The important question turned out to be: *How do we assemble our hearts to keep us from breaking apart?*

The Lament of
the Butcher's Daughter
(1995)

L illy Juknevicius woke in the night again, bathed in her own sweat, wrestling her own sheets, grinding her teeth. Same dream. Same goddamn dream. A box the size of a body—a coffin stood upright—then her father stepping out of it and walking toward her. Her past a secret locked in her body. She waited for her breathing to return to normal. She grabbed a pillow and bit into it as hard as she could.

She got up, naked and wet, and walked to the bathroom, where she cupped her hands under the faucet, drank, splashed her face. In the mirror, she was the spitting image of her father. And her brother.

She thought about the—what was it, thousands of dollars?—she'd spent in group therapy for survivors and immigrants and refugees. She was neither a survivor nor a refugee, yet her life felt hemmed in by their violent narratives. They'd survived war, atrocity, dislocation. She'd survived . . . what, beyond what they'd left her?

In this city, she knew, a library housed the documents of their brutality: atrocity files, trial records, reports and videotapes and recordings, storage disks and microfiche, artifacts of infamous events, dates and times and names and faces, all organized into one great historical pileup. Miles of information, gathered in one place and made available so that a person might hold the evidence in their own palms, so that questions might be answered, so that judgments might be made, so that stories would not be lost, so that memory might outlive slaughter. So that crimes against humanity could be witnessed by the humanity that survived them.

An exhibit greeted visitors in the library's grand lobby, confronting one and all with the evidence of atrocity: a pile of gold fillings the size of a bed. Diaries and journals discovered hidden behind toilets, under floorboards, inside walls. Names written but unspoken for years, scratched onto paper marked by age and rot and rain and the oils of an ordinary hand. In another pile, children's shoes stacked to the ceiling. In an art museum, this might be mistaken for an aesthetic object; in this library, the pile of shoes stood like an act of resistance.

The first time Lilly tried to walk from her apartment to the library, not long after she moved to the city, her feet looked ridiculous to her. *The feet of an immigrant*, she thought. *But I've changed; these shoes do not belong to me.* That day, instead of going to the library, she found a boutique and bought a pair of tall black leather boots. Then she strode back down the sidewalk until she came to a posh bar with a partial view of the city's great monument—*Just the tip*, she joked in her head. There she drank whiskey for five hours until the obelisk began to sag on its axis. On the way home, her toes and ankles burned in their stiff new leather casing. But the *heel-toe heel-toe* tap, hypnotic against the blacktop, brought her home. *Freedom*, she thought.

After the first month and the second had passed, and she'd settled on the same black pencil skirt and crisp white blouse and black blazer to wear every day, she found her legs taking her back toward the library. Almost as if she were an ordinary visitor.

Her newest case was a lost cause. Dangerous, or so they said.

"That one's yours?" the guard said. "Don't even bother. He won't respond." Blotches of sweat stained the guard's gray-blue shirt.

"Is that so," Lilly muttered, looking past the guard at the boy-nearly-man standing awkwardly across the facility grounds. "Why's that?" Standing out there with this guard, in this patchy shadeless yard, she felt the humidity weighting her breath. Why were there no trees, no bushes or shrubs? What few trees there were had been shoved out toward the perimeter, a safe distance. Even the grass looked like dirt.

"He's a tough nut. Probably run out of chances. Kid's fifteen—nobody in their right mind even tries to save a boy like that anymore. I'd say he's in the system for good now. From here right into some institution."

"Institution? He's a long way from eighteen." Lilly dug into the ground with the tip of her shoe. "When did he stop speaking?" she asked.

The guard removed his sunglasses, swabbed sweat from his forehead with his forearm. "'Bout two years in. Used to scream every night. All night. During the day, he just raged at anyone or anything he could. He'd fight with the other boys, cafeteria workers, counselors, guards. Then it all escalated. He started fires. He shoved another kid's head into a wall so hard that one of his eyes popped loose. One day, the guard checking his cell found him trying to cut off his own hand at the wrist with a torn-up piece of scrap metal—*shit*, the blood. Came this close to losing that hand." The guard kicked at the dirt between them. "See how his right hand hangs different?" He pointed through the chain-link fence to the boy across the yard. "Lost feeling in most of the fingers on that hand."

Lilly squinted to focus her gaze. Sure enough, one hand looked loose and limp. The boy's hair was shoulder-length, tucked behind his ears. Blond like wood shavings. She wasn't close enough to make out his expression.

"Then one day—this was after every last object in his room was taken away from him, all but one flat pillow—he kept damaging property; walls, floors, you name it— he started saying, *There's a blast coming that will change everything.* He said it to us, he said it to other boys, he said it to his caseworker. The caseworker before you started getting concerned, and come to find out, the boy had been communicating with some nutball latter-day white supremacists hell-bent on making trouble, thanks to some other kid who came through here who had connections with those idiots. So the caseworker alerted the Feds. It was around then that this one went silent. But his eyes . . . there's a world of shit in those eyes. All you're gonna get are the eyes. Whatever he knows, or doesn't know—these boys, after a certain age, they're just lost . . . When a kid like that starts to see that his own future has got nothing in it for him, he turns rageful. Fills up with whatever makes him feel like he exists." He spit.

"All the same, I need to meet with him." Lilly retrieved her own sunglasses and put them on. The guard just stood there, dull and thick and reluctant. "Now, please." She glanced back across the field; the boy was already watching her.

As she and the guard walked back to the main building, the boy seemed to track their movements. She thought about what she'd read so far in his file: Single immigrant foster father. Child maltreatment. Poor family-management practices. Low parent involvement. And yet he'd achieved high grades—very high—in elementary school. Until he didn't.

What put this boy in high-security detention was infanticide and patricide. Or so it was alleged.

The details were shadowed and layered, like some irrecoverable palimpsest. Some saw his case as prosecutable; others dismissed the boy as hopeless, a mental health casualty, with no known relatives, who'd slipped through the cracks. The evidence wasn't much, but the boy's fingerprints were everywhere—whatever that meant. (The alleged crime took place in his own apartment building.) If anyone had been around to give a shit about him, to take him in, he might have had an entirely different life. How the hell did he go from straight-A student, shy little misfit with glasses, possibly a savant, to this? There was no record of mental or physical illness in his files prior to the incident. No record of any trouble at all. Just a low-income immigrant foster father's oddball son.

And why had it taken years for him to land on her desk? Christ. The kid was fifteen now. When he was still ten, maybe she'd have had a chance. Kids you could work with. Boy teens, though, they were hard cases. Belligerent, pissed off, hormonal hard cases. Sometimes she wondered if boys carry all our sins for us so that the rest of us can feign innocence of the world we made—a world with less and less space for them to feel loved.

Mikael walked the yard, kicked dirt up with each step. He spit on his arm, rubbed the spit into his flesh until a sheen appeared. He studied the word he'd carved into his own arm with a sharpened-toothbrush shiv: INDIGO. He'd filled the letters with pen ink. Now he was no longer allowed to have pens or even a toothbrush.

He could see the woman across the yard. Yet another caseworker assigned to him. A thought crossed briefly through his mind: breaking her arms himself. Why not? His story had no beginning anymore, so his story had no ending. His story was lost to meaning.

A horn blared: return inside.

Back inside, he walked down the hall to his room, scraping his knuckles against the concrete wall as he went. He passed a boy of about nine, his pants too high, clutching his own forearms. Glasses, like he used to have. Mikael couldn't remember the last time he'd seen things properly. He'd stopped wearing them after that day in the yard when he stabbed a boy in the throat with one of the temples. No one tried to fuck him after that, or hold him down, or anything. He'd almost been sent to the adult system then, but the prisons were too crowded to take him. Now, as he walked past the nine-year-old, he knocked the boy's throat with his forearm, sending him like a slingshot to the floor. He couldn't remember ever being nine.

In the facility, when the other boys had held him down—one of them even put a boot to the back of his neck there on the concrete floor—he remembered smelling the knees of the boy forcing himself into him. The other boy's knees dragging bloody on the hard concrete surface of the facility floor. *Just be flat*, he thought. *Just wait. Later you can kill anyone. You're a killer now. It's official.*

He always remembered that smell, during the violence—the smell of pennies.

In Lilly's first visits to the library, on her off hours, she studied the system her father had occupied: the posts, the assignments, the ranks. She learned what position her father had occupied in the order of things. She learned what power he'd had, the kinds of commands he'd issued. It was easy; he was not an obscure figure. What did you think, that the information would be hidden? She learned that her father had no superiors. She learned that he'd had one of his own right-hand men killed for refusing an order. She learned about another order he'd issued, to sever the arm of a photographer who had taken his photo.

Butcher's Daughter.

Perhaps because she'd grown tired from trying to reinvent a life too many times; perhaps because she'd jettisoned what she'd known her entire life—that her father had recruited her brother first into abuse and then into barbarism, that he'd ordered her brother to execute a woman and child to prove that his loyalty could not be swayed by women and children—perhaps because she wished she were anyone else's daughter, a child beater's, a sodomizer's, whatever; perhaps because of all this, she directed her life toward the purpose of saving boys from becoming monsters.

She devoted the rest of her life to these floating boys—those who drifted away from a story that might have nurtured them into security and health, whose lives were lived on the sharp edge between violence and beauty, who took the place of the word *brother*.

What she could not decide from her own track record—a tiny three percent liberated from the juvenile detention system and recirculated back into supposed regular lives, some of them former immigrants, or refugees, or just strays—was whether she was helping or hurting. Who takes the side of boys or men who behave brutally, anyway? Who should?

In the library, going over documents, peering at screens, launching searches, she opened a notebook and wrote down a single phrase.

DAUGHTER OF A WAR CRIMINAL.

Then she tore the piece of paper from the notebook and ate it to stop herself from crying.

———

Those early days had been the hardest, when he'd taken a beating every single day, sometimes more than once a day, when he'd been made to eat dirt, or drink urine, or when they'd smeared shit on his face. He'd still been a boy then. A scared small weak soft boy. Repulsive.

There was no revelation, no equation, no scientific experiment that could change that. His boyhood obsessions? Nothing to open your mouth about here. Ever. So he hid his unstoppable brain deep down, at the bottom of some ocean inside his gut.

The hardest backhanded blow he'd taken as a boy happened when he'd collected every object in the false father's apartment—every fork and spoon, every salt and pepper shaker, every toothbrush and squeezed-to-death toothpaste tube, every cracked china cup and plate, every ashtray, cigarette pack, chipped cheap cologne bottle, straight razor, soap nub, discarded toilet paper tube, coffee mug and thick shot glass, ring of keys, handful of rags, stray matchbook, and can after can of beans, peas, peaches, soup—and lined them all up in an elaborate maze on the moldy orange-brown carpet of the main room. The artifacts of the opposite of family.

When his father returned from work, the big heavy backhand came, knocking his jaw hard to the left, throwing his glasses off his face, blotching the side of his cheek red, his ears ringing for days. *You have exactly ten minutes to clean this shit up. Exactly ten minutes to put every single thing back exactly where you found it or I'll take you to the woods and leave you there forever. What a goddamn mess. You goddamn idiot.*

But it hadn't been a goddamn mess. It had been a habitat.

To preserve himself, he started to draw on the floor of his room with pencils, his hand pushing graphite into concrete until the pencils

were ground to nubs. In his head, an entirely new world revealed itself, like a waking dream. The images were always the same: elaborate habitats of air, land, and sea strung together by bridges like webs
between worlds. In the air, individual dwellings were shaped like
giant hovering birds with large bellies and broad wings. On water, he
drew modules that fanned out in the shapes of starfish or curled like
conch shells in great spirals. Underwater, the structures he drew resembled the broad backs of turtles or the bellies of great whales. And
every habitat was connected by bridges and elevators, extending up
and down, side to side, in spiraling helixes.

Of course, no one who looked down at Mikael's elaborate habitat
dreams saw them as such. Of course, he was punished for his work
every single day, made to clean the floors he had covered with his
dreams. And every single night, he would reconstruct the drawings,
their intricate architecture becoming more and more vivid each time.
Finally, at the suggestion of a case worker, they took the pencils away
and gave him pastel chalk. Chalk was much easier to clean up was the
thinking. So he ate the chalk to spite them, and started breaking off
pieces of his environment—chairs, bed springs, bathroom fixtures—
so that he could scrape the drawings into the floor. This led to a
change in rooms, to a room with a dark-blue industrial-grade carpet.
The carpet smelled like petroleum. At night, the floor looked like the
bottom of the ocean.

After that, by necessity, he continued his drawings in a more co-
vert fashion, using his fingernails to create a perfect map of his world
on the wall behind the tattered chest of drawers, drawing images
from his mind's eye with blood from his fingertips.

Years passed.

Caseworkers came and went.

The drawings grew more detailed, more intimate; it was as though
the boy were engraving his DNA into the wall. Every night, he pulled

up one corner of the carpet to expose the floor, made his drawings there, and then replaced it before sunup. He even considered scratching and inking them onto his chest.

With time, in his drawings, he seemed to be growing the bones and muscles of some other land. Maybe even his land of origin, he thought. He thought about Vera's stories. He knew, from the occasional media access he had in the facility, that if he'd lived in the places she described as long as he'd lived here, he'd have earned the tattoos that indicate rank among young men who came of age in such violent, often war-torn wastelands. Which don't exist like the stories anyone cared about, of course, in the same way the abuse or neglect of boys doesn't exist.

One year, another boy his exact age came through the facility. The boy was almost old enough to be placed in adult detention, but he had landed here instead as a kind of last chance, since he'd never seriously injured any people, just property and himself. This boy liked to set off small improvised explosive devices. Mikael did not like him, though he did feel a kind of solidarity after hearing the boy's stories of being bullied and hated as a child. The two of them were not alike. But when they walked across a field or down a hallway side by side, their shoulders looked similar, squared off with about-to-be-men rage, the cover story for brokenhearted boys. The other young man's name was William. His hair was red. His great-grandfather had emigrated from Ireland. His parents divorced when he was ten, and he then had lived with his father, who was endlessly drunk and beat him severely.

William was only at the facility for a year, but in that year, two things happened: Mikael showed William his new habitat, drawing its outline in the dirt with a stick one day out in the yard. And William showed Mikael his prized possession, a letter he kept stuffed down the back of his pants. It was a kind of intimacy, to share one's private objects that way.

"I have plans when I get out of here," William said one day as they were hiding behind the dumpster. "I've been recruited by someone very important. No one should ever have to live like this, Mikael." And he pulled out the letter and showed him. It read:

"A man with nothing left to lose is a very dangerous man and his energy/anger can be focused toward a common/righteous goal. What I'm asking you to do, then, is sit back and be honest with yourself. Is this the life you want? Would you back out at the last minute to care for family or friends? Would you be willing to use your skills for something bigger than yourself? I'm not looking for talkers, I'm looking for fighters . . . And if you are a Fed, think twice. Think twice about the Constitution you are supposedly enforcing (isn't 'enforcing freedom' an oxymoron?) and think twice about catching us with our guard down—you will. Your family will lose. Make the righteous choice."

Mikael received a couple of letters from William after the boy was released, but they said nothing of any substance, leaving him to believe that what he'd bragged about before he left was true: that a major building had become a target, that William's ideas would become actions, and that people were going to die. It was that simple. There were boys like William everywhere, their hearts hollowed out by the world around them, willing to join or do anything to disrupt the landscape they'd been handed.

When Mikael thought of dead people, he thought about Vera. He thought about Indigo. He wondered if the targeted building might be full of women and children. If anyone had threatened Vera or Indigo, he knew, he would have killed them.

Inside his room now, inside his teen body barely existing in time and space, nothing: no pencils or pens, no shoestrings or sheets. Even the sink fixtures had been dismantled since he'd tried—or so they thought—to use the faucet parts to make a weapon. In truth, he'd been trying again to fashion something he could draw with. Now, instead of providing running water, they brought him a plastic jug with his meals, and he had to return the jug each night. Recently, after being tormented by another boy, he'd taken the blue plastic lid of his jug and jammed it into the boy's forehead, so hard that doctors had to be brought in to remove it and suture the wound.

Lying down on the cool of the concrete floor, Mikael stretched one hand out in front of his face and studied the lines of his own veins that crisscrossed the back of his hands. He thought about how veins carried blood to the heart, the motherload.

He closed his eyes and waited for this woman, who—like every caseworker before her—would mean nothing. No woman was coming to save him.

He dreamed the same dream as always: the sound of an infant, just out of reach. Only this time, in the dream, there was a blast as big as a building.

The Floating Boy and
the Butcher's Daughter

I n the detention center meeting room, Lilly stared at the feckless, rattling dark-green fan, moving less air toward her than a person would standing there blowing. The fan, the table in front of her, even the walls reminded her of high school—like a teen institution that had thrown up on itself.

The door opened. A pair of guards stepped into the room, holding Mikael by the elbows, and shoved him into the chair across from her.

The boy stared at her. Or not at her exactly, but at her cheek. His jaw looked like it could crack a wrist. His forearms were covered with marks—not the feathery traces of a serial cutter, but the gouged valleys of someone far beyond giving a shit. The guards chain-harnessed him to his chair, locked his handcuffs to a metal ring on the table, and stepped away.

Several seconds of quiet.

Then the sound of metal screaming and he lunged at her from across the table.

She flinched but didn't yelp, thank Christ.

He laughed, a kind of fuck-you growl.

She had the impression that they could sit like that for hours unless she did something to surprise him, catch him off his stride. She had exactly one move.

She reached into her bag, pulled out the object, and placed it on the table between them.

His laugh caved in.

The object sat between them, as silent as anything had ever been.

Lilly watched Mikael stare at the strange twist of flesh, dried into a husk, wound into a shape something between a letter *S* and a spiral staircase. She had expected the silence; she'd been reminded over and over again that the boy had long since stopped speaking. What she didn't expect was that, when she drew a breath to speak, she would be interrupted.

"Where did you get that?"

She recalibrated. "It was in with the artifacts and evidence left after the fire," she lied. "They said it was found inside—"

"A lockbox."

"Yes." In her head, a clicking sound. How was she sounding: Neutral? Aggressive? Benevolent? She had no idea. She looked at this boy-going-to-man in front of her, coiled in a spring of heated rage and dislocated want. Without permission, she thought: *brother*. How do you get a boy like that to open? How long had it been since this boy had even seen a woman? She hadn't seen a single one since she'd arrived.

She knew she had next to no shot. All she had going for her was adulthood, and her own reckless instincts.

"I have a recurring dream about a box," she said. She opened her shirt collar wider, exposing her neck. "A bad dream." He didn't move. "Really fucking bad."

He didn't speak. His eyes were fixed on her chin. Was there some danger in telling her secrets to this kid, about to disappear into a prison system that didn't give a fuck who he'd been or what he might be? He had nowhere to go but down. And she lived in a liminal space where no one gets saved.

Now or never.

"Yeah. The dreams are about my father. He was . . . a war criminal." Her throat was thick. She'd never said that out loud. Even in group therapy she'd lied, said her father had gone to jail for murdering someone. But her father had tortured and murdered thousands. He had turned her brother into a killing machine. Even the phrase *war criminal* barely covered it.

She stood up and walked over to the triple-barred security window in the cinder-block box of a room. She wondered if he was watching her ass, but when she turned around to look, he was staring at the ceiling. She could see a scar at the side of his neck. A big one. His Adam's apple, ungainly like any boy's, made her heart hurt.

"What's your last name?" Mikael did not stop looking at the ceiling.

Her breath cut short against her ribs—*he is speaking he is speaking don't fuck this up.* She remained near the anti-window, holding as still as a statue. "Why?"

"I can hear your accent. You think it's gone, but it's not."

"Bullshit." She palmed the scar at her own neck. Her skin felt cold, like uncooked chicken. A year of failed group therapy spent covertly cutting the thinnest line imaginable over and over and over again, just the whisper of a line, just to feel something besides nothing. She had no accent. Her mother had successfully escaped and relocated her, thanks to her American uncle at the State Department, long before her father was global news. She. Had. No. Accent. God. Damn. It.

But now he looked her dead in the eye. Could he see her scar? Was he smiling?

"Tell me your dream," he said. In Serbo-Croatian.

Little prick, she thought. And yet she realized she had no other game but this. She wet her lips with her tongue. The air between them crackled a little. Fuck group therapy. Roll the dice. In her own half-assed Serbo-Croatian, she continued.

"In the dream, my father is inside an upright coffin in my living room. The coffin lid opens like a door and he walks out, though he's dead. His skin is rotten, falling off—it's gray, like ash, but all his internal organs are bright colors, red and pink and bluish. His jaw is barely hanging from his head. He's reaching for me." She put her hand at her own neck again. She sees the dream in present tense, like it's in the room with them. Her father. Her throat constricts and the line of sweat between her legs goes cold, as if it were ice trickling down her inner thigh. "He's trying to say something or do something. I want to kill him, but he's already dead. I don't know what . . . I had a brother. My brother was good. My father—"

"There's a blast coming," Mikael interrupted.

Shit. He could shut back up like a lockbox if I say anything. But he was baiting her now. She couldn't ignore it. "A . . . blast?"

"A bomb."

"When?"

"Soon," Mikael said. "A van. In front of a government building. But I won't say where."

"Right. How do I know you're not full of complete shit?"

Mikael studied Lilly. "You don't. Women don't seem to get what has happened. We're all holding so many stories in here"—and he pounded his chest. "All of us. I could tell you one of a hundred different stories. I'm trying to decide which one to tell you. For instance, one story is, there are men out there who think their lives have been

stolen from them. There are men who want to recruit boys like us"—
he gestured in the air around his own body—"to do terrible things.
All over the world. No one wants boys like us," he said. "So the world
eases us into the cracks, lights us up like dynamite."

Lilly tried to make her jaw as strong and square as possible. "Well,
I wouldn't be here if I didn't give a shit." Her words meant to hold
steady like a bridge. "Are you trying to tell me you know something
about a bomb?"

"When I was a boy, I had a baby," he said.

Her heart lurched.

Mikael closed his eyes. Silence sat thick and hot between them.
Without reopening his eyes, Mikael began to tell a story. "Once there
was a boy," he said into the air between them, like the words were
trying to make a great journey.

"This boy lost his place in the world." Mikael's eyes were closed,
as if closing his eyes could shut out the present tense, as if he could
step back in time all the way through to childhood with the eyes of
a keen observer. Or a loving parent who had suffered a great loss.
The story of his boyhood spilling out of him in waves, the opposite
of silence.

"Once there was a boy who slipped from his story, but he carried
secrets with him, whether or not there was a place for him in the
world.

"This boy was different from everyone and everything around him.
The world looked strange to him, through his glasses—which were
always smudged—and the way he reacted to things didn't make the
normal kind of sense. For instance, he trusted mycelia, the tiny
threads that give birth to fungus, more than he trusted people. The
thing about mycelia was, they stick together. They're like a colony, a

close-knit mass of branches. They live in ecosystems on the land and in the water; they absorb nutrients and break them down. They're as important to decomposition as they are to life, which is a carbon cycle.

"Whereas the thing about people was, they're mostly individual meat sacks that own and devour everything in their path, and you never know when their insides will come out.

"One time, in his neighborhood, the boy saw a large woman get shot in the face, by a seemingly kind-eyed boy, as she was boarding the bus. Her mind never made it onto the bus with her. Blood splashed on the windows. People screamed. The driver made everyone get off the bus. Police got hold of the gun-boy, and as they took him away, he saw in the gun-boy's eyes that he'd been holding something that boys sometimes lose: the people they should have belonged to. That gun-boy looked right at him. He must have been from someplace else, like him, who knows where. Later, he heard that the gun-boy got sent away to something called a juvenile correction facility. *Like a foster home*, he thought.

"Finally, after the gun-boy was led away, another bus came and the kids were all taken home. When the boy got to his stop, he pushed his glasses up tighter to his eyes, felt the security of the thick black plastic above his ears. He stood and made his way to the front of the bus, passing various people along the way, though he didn't dare make eye contact with any of them, because who knew what might happen.

"He was worried that he wouldn't be able to ride the bus after that, but that would mean he'd have to walk, and his knees and shins already hurt from how far he had to walk just to get to the bus every day. The bus—no matter what risks sat inside—was still his best option. And the streets were dangerous. That was just true. You can't help where foster fathers bring you. America, the gun.

"The bus always smelled like worn rubber floor liners and too many feet, and he couldn't wait to get off, but even just stepping off the bus felt like a test to him. He kept his hands jammed into his pockets as he waited to get off, feeling the seams and bits of lint and the beginning of a hole at the bottom. He pushed his fingers through it till they reached the flesh of his thigh. He could feel his skin, his leg hair, which was barely there yet. His backpack felt heavier than it should. He wondered if he looked like a human turtle. He stared straight down, doing this thing where he made himself go a little deaf until danger had passed. Up front, the bus smelled like under-arms and pee and tires. For a minute, he thought he might barf, but then the sound of the bus door opening and the rush of cold air woke him up again. The bus driver was a guy he was actually fond of, but if the man said anything as the boy went down the stairs, he didn't hear it.

"The boy's cheeks flushed the instant the cold air hit him. It made his teeth ache. His eyes dried up like a forgotten ice cube kicked into a dusty corner. The tips of his ears pinched. He wished he had a hat. Weren't boys supposed to be sent off to school with hats, with peanut butter and jelly sandwiches, with a kiss goodbye? That's what he saw on TV, anyway. He trudged along, watching the tops of his shoes, wondering why one was scuffed and the other wasn't. He wondered what that said about him. Was there something weird about the way he walked? Was he doing something with his feet all day at school that he didn't realize? Did he kick things and not remember? Did anyone else notice?

"Sometimes the boy wondered how long he'd have to drag through this boyhood before he got to something better. Sometimes he worried he wouldn't make it to the other side. Sometimes he worried there was no other side, just some trick of height and weight and the sag of man-gut and the way men grew pouches where their cheeks used to be. And their noses and ears. *Men's noses never stop growing,* he thought, or maybe he heard it at school, or saw it on a screen somewhere. He pictured a man with a nose like a moose's, tipping over, unable to stand, falling on his face.

"His walk home changed every day. He took the same path, which helped him recognize his way, but what happened was never the same, which confused him if he wasn't careful. If he took a left but it turned out to be a right, someone might run a red light and hit the side of an old Buick hard enough to push it up onto the curb. Crowds could form out of nowhere. Cops. Dogs. Pigeons. One little change could have epic effects. Once, a man came running out of the mini-mart with armfuls of beer, and two bottles slipped from the man's grasp and shattered, splashing onto the sidewalk. The owner came rushing out with an actual rifle, yelling and yelling in some language the boy didn't know, or a language he did know that sounded different when yelled, until the thief got down on the ground and started begging or something—it looked vaguely like praying, or what the boy imagined praying might be. (Beer he knew about. Rifles and praying were from TV and movies and the nightly news.) The thief went down on the ground under the rifle and yelling, his cheek against the concrete beer everywhere. The boy saw the thief lick the concrete and cry.

"That whole day, the world seemed tilted to the boy. When he was almost home, he nearly missed the turnoff to his apartment building. All the apartment buildings suddenly looked like upset, crooked faces.

"The boy loved the thief, but he couldn't understand why.

"Now, as he was walking home, on an average day, two months after the shooting, the mini-mart just looked like a mini-mart. A dog barked around the corner. The smell of pee came in whiffs from every alley.

"From the position of the stop signs and fire hydrants, he could tell he was about halfway home. He aimed at cracks with his scuffed-up shoe: *five, six, seven.* If he hadn't been looking down and concentrating so hard on the geography of the sidewalk, he probably would have missed it. The thing on the ground. Or stepped in it.

"Right there, against the hard gray of the sidewalk, was something wrong. Something that was red and purple and pink and veined and wet, with a glistening gray wormish thing trailing away from it. He tilted his head and squinted through his glasses at it, trying to figure out what was the top and what was the bottom. It looked like butcher's meat it looked like an alien head it looked like what guts might look like if they were on the outside.

"He heard a siren, somewhere far away. He glanced up and spotted a Chinese woman two blocks away, hunched over, pulling a grocery stroller. A few guys on a corner, too far away to tell how old. Street signs and garbage and two crows and parked cars.

"He inched his scuffed shoe toward the thing, watched to see what would happen.

"It didn't move.

"He nudged it.

"It jiggled some, but then oozed back into its splatter.

"A taxi drove by, going the other direction. A woman opened her window and emptied a dustpan into the air. He squatted down next to his find. Down here, below regular people's sight, he could feel things shift immediately. Now he was at eye level with tires, with stacks of paper at the newsstand, closer to gutters and drains and bird poop and cats and the curbside. From this angle, the thing looked bigger and wronger. The veins running through it were blue-gray and white, fanning out like little rivers.

"It smelled like the butcher's it smelled like dead washed-up jellyfish it smelled like car exhaust and donuts. He was less than a block from his favorite donut shop. His stomach growled. His knees and thighs ached from squatting. He wished he had a stick or a fork or even a pencil, but all he had in his backpack were books. Then he thought of the parts of his glasses that go over his ears. He took his glasses off and stared at them. The black plastic was sturdy and thick. In truth, his glasses felt vaguely magical to him. He'd already survived gunfire, hadn't he?

"He took them off his face and used the temple to point at the glob. Then he poked at it. Deeply. When he pulled his glasses back, a thread of gooey ooze clung to them for a moment.

"That's when he heard the air say his name. *Mikael*, he heard it whisper. Then again, louder, till he snapped his head to the right and spotted the edge of a brick alleyway corner.

"It wasn't the air after all.

"Between the glob and the voice, he was hearing his name. If he followed the ick of the glistening wormlike thing, it seemed to point around the corner. Like a map.

"Was that singing he heard? He couldn't tell. His hands itched; his ears felt hot.

"He didn't want to follow the sound, or the trail that led from the mess on the sidewalk to around the corner of the brick wall, but as always, his body betrayed him. He stood up, shoved his hands in his pockets, and walked toward the sound. His backpack weighed down his shoulders, and he could hear the blood rushing in his ears. His glasses felt heavy on his nose and cheeks, as if they were pulling his eye sockets down.

"Even before he was around the corner, he realized what he was hearing: Vera's voice. Vera, who read stories in foreign languages to him as a child; who smelled like year-old lavender perfume; who petted his hair and adjusted his glasses and gave him goat's milk when he visited her. Vera was a place where he'd hidden from bullies like

Victor Michelovsky; where he'd waited for hours after school for his father to come home or not; where he'd come when the pilot light went out in the stove and he was afraid to try to light it himself. Vera was a place in the night too, pretending to be dead or asleep as he came and went with his father, but that was something not to talk about if you didn't want to get smacked in the jaw.

"Vera sometimes sang to him, if no one else was around, her eyes glazed over like indigo marbles, little worlds, her vision cast out of the filthy apartment window toward he wished he knew what. *Little folk songs* was what she called them. *From home.* And she'd put her hand on her chest above her breasts and he'd stare there for as long as he could.

"So when he finally got his head and eyes around the corner and saw Vera splayed out on the trash-stinking concrete, her blood and urine staining her silky slip that was shoved up above her hips—faintly blue, oh, blue like the springtime sky—the word *Vera* was already on his lips. The hidden world of her, as open and bloody and horrible as a tiger's mouth. He bent down to her, reaching out, toward what, he had no idea.

"He let himself look. In her arms, a squirming and grunting. Gray and red and white matter, like a cocoon covering skin. A terrible too-small mouth opened and sucked. The pink eye pockets closed as tightly as fists. A mewing mammal.

"*Not for a boy your age.* That's what Vera always told him, sliding a bottle of vodka behind her back, then putting it on top of the refrigerator. Or closing her blue satin robe over her chest, then smiling and petting his hair.

"To keep himself from having to see the things he looked at, he'd long since trained himself to think about a specific word: *indigo.* The word, and everything he knew of it, came from Vera. *You are an indigo child,* she told him, fluffing the hair on his head then petting it smooth. From her mouth, and the broad gestures she made as she spoke, he learned that indigo is one of the seven colors of the rainbow—the color between blue and violet, named for a plant called *Indigofera tinctoria*.

"She also told him that indigo represented the sixth chakra, the third eye. Indigo children would grow up with the ability to master complex systems. And they would know how to care for both animals and humans.

"When Vera said it, the word *indigo* took on a power, as if it were some kind of spirit, as if it were a myth. Like *indigo* meant something close to *life*. The boy pictured himself as an adult, in an indigo jumpsuit, working with elephants and bats and sad people in some kind of room filled with computer servers. It would be a large room, with lines of monitors and black lights and knowledge banks and straw on the floor for the animals. As he thought back on all of this now, he briefly forgot what was surging and moaning on the ground before him.

"A scent he knew the word for—*lavender*—mixed with the smell of gutter water.

"Then, a sound—the bawl of an infant.

"He looked at Vera's face. Her skin was so pale, he could see through it. It was full of veins and he could see the bruised color of bones and cartilage holding up her facial features. The holes in her face—her eyes, her nostrils, her mouth—suddenly looked wrong to him. Too big or too deep or too pleading. The fact of what he was looking at—her body—suddenly overcame him. He tried to focus on some small thing that might bring him back to human: A cigarette butt a few inches from Vera's head. An Anheuser-Busch bottle cap near a graying dandelion poking through the concrete. Water dripping off the corner of the gutter. He looked up to the top of the five-story brick building, past the dung-splattered wall toward a fragment of cloud. Then a sound he knew, Vera's voice, a voice he felt in his gut. He looked back down, right into her mouth. Her teeth were so small.

"*Listen to me, Mikael.* She pulled at him with a whisper. *You have to take her.*

"He shook his head back and forth in a panic, so hard that his glasses flew from his face and landed near Vera. With her free hand, the one not holding the infant, she handed them back. Vera pulled her stained slip back down over her hips.

"*I know,* Vera said. *Too much. You are just a boy.* She petted her own chest as if she were reaching to comfort him.

Not wanting to look directly at it, he closed his eyes. He heard differently this way, with his eyes closed. He could hear a fractured rasp nearby, like an animal clawing at garbage. No—not that. Something was wrong with Vera's breathing.

"*Shhhh,* Vera said, soothing him.

"His body slackened a little. His aching knees and thighs finally gave in and he shifted his weight to one hip, propping himself on one elbow, stretching his numb legs out sideways, so that he was almost reclining on his side next to Vera. The thing between them stilled and quieted. He almost forgot it was there, except that he couldn't look away from its mouth as it closed on Vera's nipple.

"Then Vera started to sing.

"When her voice trailed off, he realized he was smiling—a half smile, his eyes closed, his mind off where boys' heads go when women sing to them. As if now were like always. But when he opened his eyes, Vera was staring at the sky, her mouth too open, her skin wrong-colored. And the thing, the squirming pinkness of it . . .

"He stood up. Which took longer than it should have. He stared at it. For a moment, he considered simply turning around and walking away. Instead, he squatted back down and took his glasses off, holding them in the air between himself and Vera.

"Vera?

"He brought a temple close to Vera's face. Gently, gently, he poked her cheek. Her eyes did not blink the way eyes should blink. Her mouth retained its shape. He put his glasses back on.

"Wherever it was that he'd been born, in that other country with the other language that his mouth was fast forgetting, there were stories. Vera used to tell him the stories. The place he was from was cold, he knew, and they said it was *war-torn*, like some kind of ripped-up blanket. And he had the impression that death moved easily there, between people and things. It was a place cold enough that dogs were left to freeze in the street. Daughters were dragged off to sheds by soldiers in the night, laughing, vodka-drenched soldiers, the air full of sweat. Sometimes the daughters returned later, with their sight taken from their eyes; sometimes they were sold away forever.

"The sons were turned into dogs—or daughters—too, treated as whatever the soldiers needed the meat of them to be. Some of them were turned into guns, killers of anything for anyone, if they wanted to stay alive.

"He always wondered, the boys they used to be—where did they go? Did they recede into the folds of their brains like a well-tucked secret, something to be retrieved later in life? Was that kind of brutality a universal initiation into the world of men? Or did those inner boys just shrivel and disappear? What happened to them? Not the ones who died; they went to dirt. But the others? Did they go to facilities to be corrected?

"He used to hear his foster father's voice:

"*You should always remember how lucky you are to be here.*

"And he remembered Vera's voice, back in her kitchen:

"*Never whine for your fortune. No one likes a boy who cries.*

"Now he knelt by her body, his knees grinding on concrete.

"He stared down at the little pig of a thing. It grunted.

"He could see Vera was dead, but he couldn't think it. He placed his hands over each of her eyelids and shut them, the way people do on TV.

"Then the thing began to wail.

"*Shut up*, he whispered, looking around, adjusting his glasses. But it continued.

"*Shut up*, he said louder, and grabbed at the blanket around it, which came loose, and that's when he finally learned that the difference between a boy and a girl lived between the legs: a soft and tiny patch of skin slit where a penis should be. He stared at it. He looked around again—where were the humans? Nothing. No one. A dog barking far away. He leaned in closer. Closer still, until his face was nearly touching the wriggling infant. He smelled the place where its skin and slit were. Its legs jerking. He winced, shivered, pulled away.

"*Piss*, he said.

"But then it looked right at him. Silently. Half cradled but half falling from Vera's limp arm. It looked directly into his eyes, not crying but gasping for air or something. Then, wriggling its little fingers, it reached up to him.

"It could only have been him. Nothing else around them left alive.

"His chest felt inside out. He held his breath. His palms were wet. He felt dizzy, blurry. He closed his eyes and opened them and closed and opened them again.

"*Hey!*"

A voice he did not know swiveled his head around.

"*You there!*"

Ethnography 3

The moose here are hairless. The children blush and bloom
with rashes when they eat fruit or jam. Calves are born
with two heads, and there is a two-headed eagle. In the city,
the permafrost is melting; in the forests, the ice is taking
strange shapes. The fish in the lake are dead or mutated.
Underground nuclear tests. Industrial waste from mining.
Heavy metals dumped in the river. For years.

I was a factory cleaning woman for two decades. I did
my work standing at the lip of the Lena River, washing
out clothes. Where else would I go? I was born here. My
mother and her mother and her mother. We were a house
of women whose men left the moment they could. Women
labor into a void—our work to raise children and husbands and animals, our work keeping home and hearth
are not considered employment. My whole life's labor lives
in my hands. I stopped going to work when my hands
turned red, my wrists developed lumps, and they never
got better.

One day, I was washing the clothes—I remember what
was in my hands at that moment, a blue flowered dress—

and I looked up, and on the other side of the river, half of the shore just fell away to water. I stopped moving. I held as still as a statue, my washing suspended. Then I saw an entire house get swallowed up by the swollen river, as if the land had just given up or lost its meaning. A dog had been barking in the yard of that house. A babe had been sitting on the ground near the porch. A woman at the door was wiping her hands on her apron when the great rush came and then everything was going to water. I wept so hard.

I stepped back from the washing, from the river, and I walked back to our house. The chickens were squawking. I kept thinking about the dog. The babe. The woman. I wondered how long I would have before the river came for me too. The water comes for all of us, I think, like an answer.

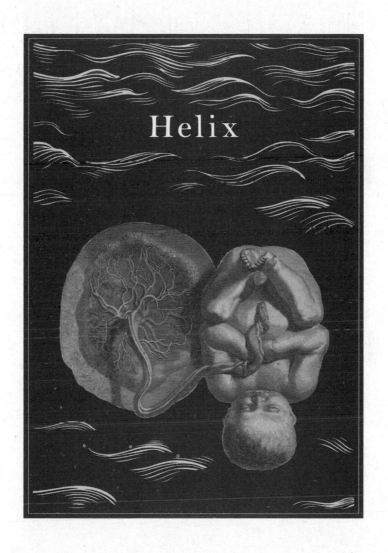

Helix

Cruces 4

One night, after a week of hard work, there was a kind of bonfire, with drinking and dancing, along the river next to the boardinghouse. All different kinds of workers were there—those of us working on the statue and every other kind of worker in the city, carpenters and shoemakers, ditchdiggers burying gas pipes and digging tunnels, stonecutters, meatcutters, and barkeeps, those who labored laying cable for streetlights, child factory workers and women pieceworkers and women of the night, butchers and bakers and opium den owners, trash collection workers and street cleaners and those who kept care of horses—all the workers underneath the gleam and glow and noise of the city.

I think we were all coming to an understanding that this project was moving toward an ending, and no one wanted to talk about the ending. No one wanted to think about whatever would happen next.

I wanted to dance with David Chen, but the firelight was too bright and too many eyes surrounded us, so I danced with Endora. I

don't know, maybe everyone thought I was dancing with a man anyway, as by now Endora had taken to wearing men's pants all the time.
But no one said a thing; no one looked at us. And anyway, it's not that
anyone couldn't dance with anyone else. It was my desire, and I knew
to keep it close.

What I remember most was her face, how it opened up in the firelight and night. When I spun her on her toes, so fast, she laughed so
hard that I saw something I never had before: Endora had joy. Until
that night, I had thought she knew only hardship and the strength it
took to carry it; even her face was hard and strong. But that night, as
she danced and threw her head back and flung her arms out to the
side, with me holding her waist, I think she felt free. A laugh came
from her mouth that seemed like it carried generations.

The four of us—David and John Joseph and Endora and I—stayed
after most of the others had gone, which was our habit. We all liked
to be there for the after-calm, to listen as the river water collected its
secrets.

On that night, a well-dressed man who was not the same as us
approached our little group near the last glowing embers of the fire.
His suit was of fine quality, but he was drunk—not belligerent, not
loud and boisterous, as most of our coworkers usually became before
passing out or turning in, just drunk enough to make him clumsy.
His eyes were big and glassy. His hair had been ruffled too often in
too many directions. His tie hung crumpled and undone.

"May I join you?" he said.

Before we could answer, he rested his frame on a box near Endora.

"I am Fred," he announced to no question, taking a large quaff from
a flask. "And you?"

"Danny," Endora said with no affect at all, without even looking
at him.

"A pleasure, Danny," he continued. "And your companions?"

Endora's shoulders stiffened. I took it as a sign to carry the story from there. "Sir, might we help you find someone? Something?" I offered. His eyes fell down toward his cheeks.

"Oh, come now," the man said. "I mean you no harm. I'm just on a nightwalk. I was just reminded of a project I worked on—different waters."

"Where is this . . . project?" John Joseph asked, looking around as if the stranger might have brought it with him.

"In another city, as it happens," he replied. "A fountain. But not just any fountain." He leaned into the fading glow of the embers, his enthusiasm igniting. He passed his flask to Endora without looking at her, and Endora being Endora, she took a sip without question and passed it on to David, who, being David, passed it without partaking to John Joseph. The man continued as if we'd invited him for this very purpose. His speech softening into slurry fragments.

"Cast iron. For the great exposition. I gave it to them for free! Can you imagine?" He laughed at his own narration. "Three basins . . ." He waved his hands in the air as he spoke, as if resculpting it there in front of us. "The basins held by three Nereids—"

"Nereids?" I asked.

"You would say . . . sea nymphs," he continued. "The base is covered in seashells. And Testudines spouting water!" He seemed pleased with himself.

"Testudines?" Endora said, the tone in her voice prickling.

"*Tortues!*" he said in French.

Everyone looked my way. "Turtles," I said.

"Yes! Yes, turtles!" He crouched toward us, using his hands to speak now. "The crown at the top spouts water. Water spilling from basin to basin illuminated by gas lamps. Do you see? It will be lit at night! Like our dear old girl." He farted and laughed, the belly laugh of a happy drunk, or any person without inhibition.

He finished his story with a flourish: "It's called *The Fountain of Light and Water*!"

I must admit I found that to be a fine name for a fountain. I think we all did.

"It's meant as an allegory, do you see? An allegory of . . ." He seemed to drift back into his own thoughts. He leaned back, then righted himself, crouching as if he were confiding a secret. "*Everything* is an allegory," he almost whispered. "Water. Light. Gas. All of this, in the city *moderne*," he said, waving his hand around.

"A toast, then?" I offered, and the flask made another circle. "To *The Fountain of Light and Water*," I said. And then: "My name is Kem." It seemed the least I could share, given what we had between us.

We toasted, and then his face fell to sorrow again. "Thank you, friends," he said, "for the pleasure of your company. Someone I love has gone from me." With that, he stood and walked unevenly away into the night.

In the firelight, Endora's cheeks looked like apples. She raised her flask and toasted us all. "Look at you lot. What a cast of characters we make! To the next chapter in our story!" she proclaimed, and passed the flask. "May we make something as mighty of ourselves here as our lady!" Her smile wide.

David took the flask, gave it a tender look, then paused before passing it to John Joseph. "Why did we come here?" He turned to Endora. "Why did you come here?"

Endora looked at the dirt in the strobe of the firelight. Her smile flickered, then faded. "For work," she finally said, then added, "For a better life." She hugged herself. The two answers were a story that had formed like a cradle in which immigrants sang themselves to sleep.

David looked at me next. The eye contact made my chest pound. "Do you think we were right? To come here? To this place, not some other? Any of us?" His eyes never left me.

I took a long time answering, partly because David so rarely spoke—his way of getting his meanings across did not depend on words like the rest of us did—and partly because I didn't know the answer, or I didn't want to know the answer.

Finally I spoke. "They say my name means 'the sun,' but that's only one story," I said. "In German, it means something like 'the combmaker.' Can you picture me as the combmaker?" I smiled and my smile drew laughter from everyone. "Or it might be short for *kemet*. In ancient Egypt, the word *kemet* meant "the black land"; ancient Egyptians were Black Africans called the Kemet People. *Kemet* is the root of words like *kam* or *ham*, a reference to Black people in Hebrew translations."

"What the hell are you going on about?" Endora asked.

"What I mean is, not even our names hold still," I said. "Who knows what our stories will turn out to mean. I mean, beyond right now. With this fire and one another. Maybe we came here just for this."

David smiled. It was as good an answer as I had in me, even though it was no kind of answer.

Later, in the newspaper, I came across a dispatch from the Centennial Exposition. Our visitor's fountain, his vision of light and water, has another name: the Bartholdi Fountain. We had shared our evening with our own sculptor. We had seen him before, we felt sure, but in such a rare time and space that he had seemed to be a different person.

When we saw the girl who came to us from the water, we told her about the fountain. The things he said reminded us of her, of how she emerged from water and how she would return to it.

Aurora, my eternal dawn,

How could I forget? Of course I remember the first night I came when we were young, my body shivering with know-nothingness, your perfect animal mouth filled with blood and laughter, just as I remember the first night I came into your Rooms after we reconnected as adults. You once told me that your devotion to me began where the flesh of your leg ended, because the leg that I made you had brought you to an ecstatic state. My devotion to you may have begun in childhood, but it evolved in your Rooms. Were it not for your Rooms, my visions would never have found form. They would merely torment me as phantasms. The three visions replayed themselves in my mind's eye for years before my colossus found her becoming.

The first vision happened to me in the Room of Kneelings.

Hog-tied and kneeling, so that a man's cock and balls rested on my face for hours—the cock sometimes engorged and ejaculating all over my face, other times as soft and velvet as a child's stuffed rabbit—I had the vision of an erotic struggle. A man, swollen with youth, strides into the frame. His body is the color between wheat and white. His torso is between muscle and the fluidity of pouring milk. With each step, the shapes of his body pulse and bend, so that in his watching, in the dream, his own eyes close, so that his mouth fills with spit, so that an unnamable pain rises in his throat. His teeth seem to float. His mouth becomes an entire digestive system. Soon, his whole head becomes a devouring.

The young man conjured in my dream is not turned in my direction, so in my mind's eye, the wood-curl tendrils of his hair stand in for a face. His unfinished body appears at times to glisten; at other times, it carries a kind of matte texture, light. It is excruciating to watch him, and yet, in the dream, it is not possible to look away.

Now there is a kind of riverside, a full-headed tree, water moving, rocks within the water, grass. The figure of the young man slides down upon the grass, his back—like every animal ever named, like the proof of physicality itself, like celestial excess—still facing me. In the dream, my strongest thought is that I do not want the figure to turn around. I want to build a world from never seeing this man's face. Seeing him might kill me. In fact, I am almost sure of it, since the pain of staring at the young man's back, his body—my god—is nearly doing the job itself.

I pray.

I pray for the young man to remain like that. Turned away from me. In the dream, turned away from me that way, as white as marble and smooth and muscled, he is the abstract idea of freedom itself. A young man's body leaning into man, there in the grass, next to an unending river. Yes, in the vision I pray—as I have never prayed before in life—that this man, still at the peak of youth, will not turn to face me. So that freedom might be immortalized, forever suspended.

The last time the stranger comes, he comes into my mouth, and I am glad. My hunger is endless. I am released and I curl on the floor for another hour like a spent cock.

The second vision came in the Room of Vibrations.

To this day, I do not know how you procured so many body-size furniture-like items, all equipped with vibrating stimuli designed and positioned to enter or stimulate or shiver the genitalia, but that Room is still ringing in my bones.

In the second vision, I want my mother. Had I been awake, this thought would shame me, even repulse me: my mother stone-cold, her hands as white as bones, her eyes gleaming black holes, twisting my guts. I am captured by her stern countenance trapping vision, heart, body. Come to me for a beating; you need to learn to be a man. Her hands a permanent grip. Her skin the hue of blue-white marble, as if the flesh itself has gone to granite—or is it a trick of the eye as I move closer, unable to pull away from the force of her magnetism?—my mother stone-cold, her hands as white as bones, her eyes gleaming black holes. I feel I might vomit. I double over, small as a boy.

Still, in the dream, she moves me—her own unmovable soul creating a vacuum toward her body, her torso and sexless lap. I am at once terrified and electrified, as if standing at the edge of death in the presence of the figure of my own creation. Mother, stone-cold, your hands as white as bones, your eyes gleaming black holes. The opposite of . . . of what I cannot feel, even as I am pulled and pulled. You will never be apart from me, I will always be with you, a love unto death. Come here, son, I will make you a man; I will bring you to your knees and raise you from your toes upward to the heavens; bring me your vulnerability for transformation, glory; you are not like other boys; you are not meant to be like other men.

I quiver, in the vision. I wish I could pluck out my eyes so that my sight might be liberated. My desire is to die so that I can outlive her gaze, her gaze making me, creating me against my very will; mother, a pull toward destruction, mother of cold stone, her hands as white as bones, her eyes gleaming black holes; there is no savior for a boy such

as this. There is no god. I haven't the strength to resist the black hole
of her. I lose myself in her abyss. Falling. Oblivion.

The third vision happened in the Room of Textures.

The marble corner of that room is a place where I would happily
die, preferably after my cock has been bound so long that you could
kill me by blowing air on it from an inch away. (I know that if you
answered you would select instead the fur corner. I can picture your
rapture.)

Miraculously, Delacroix's painted androgyne from Liberty
Leading the People *visits me in your Room of Textures. Like a*
muscled angel she comes, resisting the world, a corporeal revolution,
not man, not woman, but some body in between. And then it comes
into focus, in the dream, her womanhood, but not of any kind I have
known. This woman is beyond a woman, so far that she is out of
reach, her reach taking a nation through revolution to salvation. Oh,
if she could only save me from these torments, these night terrors
bringing me to the brink of death—if by death we might mean the
failure to create my colossus. This woman pure power—but neither
male nor female power. What was the artist dreaming? The opposite
of Venus. The musculature of her arm breaking heaven and earth,
her reach beyond law or order of any kind, her breasts and torso like
an unimagined armor against all wrong. Her passion larger than
mankind, so large as to be on fire, her clothes half torn from her
broad body, her momentum leaping a barricade over the bodies of
men, comrades, soldiers, dead matter. She needs nothing about anyone
even as she leads. Is she leading? Charging? Surrendering to death
because it is worth it?

Her body breaking language.

I am still haunted by the concept of freedom. I wonder, who on
earth has ever known freedom? Oh, we claim it for ourselves often;
as peoples and nations and individuals, we've inflicted countless

barbarisms and tortures upon our fellow man to prove that some of us have it by god, and others do not, will not, but that's not really freedom, is it? That is power. Ugly. Degenerate. Reprobate unless it has a corresponding release. Otherwise it gets cocked up in a body.

    My vision, my love, to you I owe quite simply everything.

Frédéric

Frédéric, my beautiful man-dove,

What a wonderful story! Verging so beautifully on homoerotic sentimentality. Are you, in secret, a novelist? Or merely as fluid as a woman in your erotic torments?

You want to give form to freedom, you say—the abstract idea of freedom? Let me tell you about freedom. Freedom is the body of a woman. The devouring, generating paradox of her body. Every law every aspiration every journey a man takes fails in the face of her body.

The women I know who sell their bodies for cash in this gleaming city are separated from the bourgeois married women by a membrane thinner than a scrotal sack. To wit: by law, any woman who has premarital sex is a prostitute. Our bodies—and by bodies, I mean our sex, our cunts, the sources of our reproductive worth—are held by our legislators at a level just above livestock, a fact I know you tire of me restating. Yes, it's true, women have and will always provide sex to men for any number of reasons: for food, for clothing, for entertainment, for housing, for a fiction of respectability or a fiction of whore-gasm. The commercial direction of the act, the production of the sex worker as part of the workforce, unveils the tensions and falsehoods embedded inside your precious word and fiction of "freedom."

Freedom? We need a new fiction that begins with the poor. The hungry. The filthy and the obscene. Not the exhausted bodies that bear the weight of a society's growth—women who bear children— but women who carry the surplus, the spent seed that adds no number to the population. Women who emerge from crossdressing men. Hermaphrodites and lesbians, nádleehi, lhamana, katoeys, mukhannathun. Look them up, dearest, if I've confused you. Bring me Kalonymus ben Kalonymus, Eleanor Rykener, Thomasine Hall. Bring me Joan of Arc. Bring me Albert Cashier and James Barry, Joseph Lobdell and Frances Thompson.

We need a new story of freedom that begins with the body of a woman with neither children nor the cyclops desire of the male penis entering or leaving the hole of her. We need a regendering of colossal scale. A manwoman.

Design that, my love, and you have yourself a kind of freedom.

But let me not leave without giving you a story. The story begins with the image of a naked dead woman whose commerce was sexuality. I have included a postcard—a POSTCARD! Produced from the event, borrowed from my considerable collection.

What event? That season, there was no other in the city, perhaps in the nation. The esteemed editor of the Herald, *upon encountering the body of murdered sex worker Helen Jewett, replied that he could scarcely look at it. At it! According to his later report, he slowly began to discover the lineaments of her corpse, "as one would the beauties of a statue of marble." A statue! Do you see, my dove? If you were here, I would read it to you aloud: "My God," he exclaimed. "How like a statue!" For not a vein was to be seen. According to him, the body looked as "full-polished as the pure Parian marble." He is speaking your language! "The perfect figure—the exquisite limbs—the fine face—the full arms—the*

beautiful bust—all—all surpassing in every respect the Venus de Medicis."

I give you exhibit A, wherein a dead woman is made eternally beautiful:

Do you know, beloved cousin, how the penny press we know was born on the night of her murder? There is no hotter fuel for consumption than cheap crimes against women and children. And blood.

Did she scream when the hatchet landed, or before? Of all the new accounts, none mentions a scream, or any sound at all. Nor was there any sign of struggle. This tells me that she knew her assailant, likely well, likely intimately. A young man of nineteen, so the story goes. But the details of the actual woman, her body, her life, were subordinated to the drool-worthy matter of the sexual violence, the voluptuousness of her body, half naked and expired.

I wonder what we have set forth into the world. Not the violence, which has always been there, men in love with killing women, but the story of it obliterating all other stories. A sexually unapologetic woman murdered and burned is the fact of it. That she was murdered again, by our consumption of her story, is the unacknowledged truth.

For your statue, cousin, remember those: the fact and the truth. Please keep in mind that woman's bludgeoned body, and what we did with her. It will keep my rage alive.

I have kept a collection of representations of her. Among them, I do believe Alfred Hoffy's lithograph is my favorite. You know the way I have designed my bedroom, my clothes, even my bookshelf—all of these were patterned after hers. Did you know that she created her own library inside her room? Books by Lord Byron. She even had a picture of the poet on her wall, and—oh, how you'll love this— a copy of Leaves of Grass *on her bedside table. With passages underlined. This dead woman, who paid so lavishly for the journeys of her cunt, was a literary adventurer. Brilliant. Likely more intelligent and creative than every cocksure narcissistic moron who brought his business her way.*

My dearest, I will answer your question. The reason I will not remove the images of this girl and her murder above my bed, the reason I cannot let go of this dead girl or, for that matter, any dead girl, is that she was a writer. In a trunk found in her room, she kept more than one hundred letters, and books, and other papers. Her worktable was littered with pens and ink and excellent writing paper. She wanted—was determined—to say something.

What became of her instead is the creation of an uncontainable story, now merchandised for erotic consumption. The beauty of her green velvet dress was reproduced as if it were an allegory for everything secreted behind velvet curtains throughout this city.

The beauty of her corpse created a hunger. Exquisite. Naked. Dead.

The other reason I cannot let go of this dead girl—this beautiful, sharp, creative girl—is that she knew exactly what to do with her cunt. She employed it as a means of resistance: resistance to reproduction in favor of capital. This was an inspiration, my cousin—this was deserving of worship. Where other people place a cross with an androgyne hanging from it that they pretend is a man—a hilarious icon if you ask me, with its double entendre, its sexualized, baffled, naked body up against some fiction of sin and redemption; could there be a more sadomasochistic image?—I prefer another image: The bare-breasted prostitute. In the long moment before the hatchet hits her skull.

It's more honest.

Love eternal,
Aurora

My cousin, my Eros, my confidante,

Your postcard has arrested my sleep, given me a kind of fever. But you knew it would. You are indeed a profound seductress—I am reading the Mary Shelley book and now I have opened the mail and the postcard too. Do you mean to kill me with this strange, erotic, morbid excess? Or just to haunt me? Dead women and monsters brought to life at the hands of a girl . . . you call images like Medusa to my mind's eye. You make me want to go back and look to see if we've got the story all wrong. You make me want to fashion a colossus that shoots flames from between her legs.

And, my god, how could I have missed the opportunity in front of me: a child of the city! A prostitute! What an incredible turn in my imagination you have engendered. This statue must carry something of the heat and thrust of cities.

Have you read any of the Darwin? A deal's a deal, my love.
Did you know Darwin married his cousin?

Yours and only yours,
Frédéric

My accidental idiot cousin,

Do me a favor, will you? Slap your own face as hard as you can. Hard enough to leave a mark.

No, I am not trying to conjure some metaphysical vixen in your head. I had no intention of planting a prostitute in your visions. Where in god's realm did you get the idea?

I feel nothing but rage with regard to your colossal misinterpretation. I feel I could break a man into pieces just to think of it—to rearrange him so that his head is up his own ass.

How comic. You hear my vision, and it takes for you the shape of some voluptuous whore? For male consumption?

You go from mother to virgin to whore? Could you be more dull-witted?

I must calm myself. I shall return to this letter when I can.

My lamb,

Let me tell you my new idea to rid us of this idiocy.

I want to arrange a theft from the British Library. A thief is an artist of extraordinary merit. Do you laugh? I will remind you that I have access to a wide array of clientele with undreamed-of talents and even more capital. What I mean to have stolen, my love, is the perfect object. Better than a painting or work of so-called art. Rather, a keepsake of profound meaning. Even to be near it, I feel sure, would make me tremble.

A book—but not just any book. A book with a kind of frame nested within its leather cover. Framed within one of two ovals on the volume's front doublure, or decorative lining, rests a lock of Percy Shelley's hair and a bit of his ashes; in the other is held a lock of Mary Shelley's hair. The volume itself is a collection of manuscript letters. Devised as a keepsake, it is so much more—a relic! More important to me than pieces of a saint. I want to touch them, these pieces of those extraordinary bodies. I want to kiss them. Even if I must return the object eventually, it would be worth it to have a moment within their aura, no matter how brief.

Your perfect thief,
Aurora

My love Aurora, I am kneeling. I am begging forgiveness, and I love it.

How could I have made such a mistake twice? Tell me how long to kneel and I'll do it. You know I will.

And a warning: Please do not become a thief. Please do not commit a crime.

Perpetually,
Frédéric

Oh, cousin,

You are, as always, my perfection. Forget not that you are a man of means and merit!

All is always forgiven, as I don't believe in sin and redemption. Forgiveness is dull. As there is no godhead that can hold me, I call and raise. In place of sin and redemption, I offer my Rooms.

Did I understand you correctly? Darwin married his cousin? Do you see the hilarity of that? He crafts a theory of evolution, with clear implications concerning bloodline and mutation, and he marries his own kin?

I've changed my mind! I want to meet him! I want to create a Room for him!

Aurora

Aurora's Thrust

There was to be a Raid on my house. On the day of the factory
fire, a client approaching from the back alley had seen our
faces pressed against the window; to him, we must have looked like
fugitives, all those faces of children like question marks. The client
alerted the authorities. When we learned of the plan—you'll not be
surprised that my sources extend to the city's official bureaus—we
needed an escape, and though I did consider other options, in the end
it was that otherworldly girl who won me over, by reciting to me with
precision exactly everything that had happened to me and to the
children in the last few weeks despite the fact that we had never met.

It was this all-knowing girl who offered the most promising plan:
to escape by water.

She sealed the case in an unusual way: by showing me a coin
she said she carried with her at all times, a one-cent piece from the
nation's earliest days, its central figure a woman with the hair of a
lion. "When this penny first emerged," she said, "people thought the

image was a horror. They thought she was monstrous, that she looked insane. *Her unruly hair*, is what they said." She turned the coin over and over in her hand. "Like mine," she said. Her own long black hair, wrestling its way down her back, was unruly—beautifully so. I reached out to touch it, but she pulled back. My hand hung suspended just above her head. Something about the coin, the girl, something about women and children and monsters, set into my abdomen.

There exists a city within this city, made by women and children.

Cagey, sly, and ingenious girls with barely-there breasts furrowing paths beneath the ebb and flow of city life. Bellicose wives with tongues as formidable as whips and torsos the size of battleships. Hopeless-to-the-point-of-reckless house cleaners and cooks and ladies' maids. Bands of little-girl thieves, their faces of hunger merging with their oncoming sexuality and drive to survive. Tiny ambitions in collision, or collusion, with desire. The city they inhabit inverts its own alleged social structure. *Women and children first* may be its cover story, but women and children creating their own society—their underground economy, below where its very sex sits—that is a deeper story.

This girl, she had an unimaginable plan for our escape. I remember feeling a little dizzy from the sheer will of her. But the story she told, in trade for my trust, won me over.

"This is a story from my father," she said. "But it is actually the story of my mother. Aster has carried it long enough, though. I think perhaps he is dying from carrying this story," she said, and the sorrow on her face seemed larger than a body.

"This is the Tale of the Fur Spinner," she told me. "Sit down in that green chair and I will perform it for you." And then she began.

"The moment my father first saw my mother, Svajonė, he had a seizure. Sometimes I think he wishes he'd died right then, inside the image of her following his fall to the ground, kneeling to put his head in her lap."

"What kind of seizure was this?" I asked. I had not yet been enveloped into her storytelling.

"Epileptic. People with epilepsy have suffered greatly, you know. They are thrown into places with criminals and mentally ill people, just like prostitutes and poor people and orphans are. If we ever meet again, I'll tell you the story of the Salpêtrière—which started out as a gunpowder factory and later became an infamous hospital. In your time, it will become a teaching center for those who study the brain."

I was restless for her to continue. "But what became of your father?"

"There is nothing wrong with my father. Sometimes he just slips time because he can't hold the weight of his life. That is the story I came here for. But you need to listen. Can you hold still while I tell it, as still as a statue?"

From that moment, I understood. My task was to listen.

"My mother was studying the Yakut indigenous language. My father's mother had been Yakut. When my father met my mother, he knew only a few phrases, words really. The village he grew up in within Yakutia rested inside a tension next to a former Siberian gulag. Former gulag prisoners taught the villagers how to grow potatoes, how to fight for a life—so many things about the space between living and dying. After the collapse, most of the villagers became hunters and fishers. The villagers simply never found someplace else to go. A woman who lived alone in the woods where my father grew up gave him a bone necklace that she claimed belonged to his mother. The woman had no idea if the shards of bone were from a human or a reindeer or what.

"Maybe it was from his mother, maybe from some other woman. Stories multiply and disperse in a village like that.

"His father was an exile—or so the story goes. They said his father murdered a soldier. No one knew what kind of soldier, only that he had a uniform and a rifle. A guard? Or was he military? His father— my grandfather—was maybe a Yakut, but maybe not; everyone my father spoke to was hazy on this. Some villagers described his father's hair as black like night; others thought it was blond; some said he was a Jew, or Ukrainian; still others shook their heads no and said, *Turk!* or something else. He could have been anyone's son from any-where, and yet he knew, whoever he was, that there had been ice and water and earth and blood all around him.

"Both his mother and his father were dead and gone before my father reached the age of three. Both shot dead in some kind of Raid, the story goes. Both buried in ground near the village, near enough sometimes that he could still hear their bones singing in the wind. Or he thought he could.

"The village raised him. People who'd been exiled or forgotten, indigenous Yakut people mixed with Siberians, Ukrainians, Lithua-nians, Albanians, Turks, Russian Jews—even an American or two whose wits had atrophied. He still knew some people in the village who knew more Yakut words than he ever would, so when this woman arrived to study the languages, he offered to help her.

"That woman was my mother.

"Svajonė came from Lithuania. In her case, there was no question of who she was or where she came from. She came with a real story— an important lineage. Her grandfather had been a famous book smuggler, a *knygnešys* during the Lithuanian language and press ban instigated by the empire. Her father had continued the tradition later by opening a bookstore in Panėvežys. It is thought to this day that, had the *knygnešiai* never existed, the Lithuanian language itself would have slipped away forever.

"Language slips away sometimes, like objects, like peoples.

"Svajonė became a linguist in order to study what happens to languages under siege. She understood profoundly how power could drive individuals underground and reshape them into a new species capable of a kind of resistance and resilience no one had dreamed of. When her grandfather was caught delivering books to a secret transport on its way to America, he was shot on the spot. Her grandmother swallowed a wail larger than a country as she stood unmoving next to his body on the ground. All she had were her eyes locking eyes with the murderer as he spit on the ground, laughed, and walked away. My mother's grandmother and mother raised money to send her away from her country of origin to receive an education, away from the violence of a family narrative. But the violence never left her body.

"Stories have a way of burying themselves underneath skin.

"Svajonė was the most beautiful woman Aster had ever seen. According to my father, she looked nothing like him or anyone. She looked like she'd been spun from moon and water—her skin alabaster, her eyes a clear blue, her auburn hair falling down her shoulders in unkempt tendrils. She had tiny lyrical lines around her eyes and mouth—lines that looked like writing, he said, like a poem trying to write itself on her face when she smiled. The first time she spoke to him, my father wanted to touch her face. This continued for the rest of his life. He wanted to leave everything he'd ever known to enter the world of this woman, who knew more words in his so-called ancestral language than he did. Did he even have an ancestral language? From whose mouth?

"I don't know if this was love or not, but if what he felt about her was love, it was love-unto-death from the very beginning.

"Everyone and everything there loved her. In a desolate place, she was life—a woman giving meaning to what seemed like a dead environment, dead animals, dead vegetables, dead people, dead hearts. It was the power of her desire to learn that brought them all back to life.

"He loved to listen to her mind race. *The fascinating thing is, 'rain' in Mohawk is* ayokeanore. *In Turkish, the word is* yaghmur. *Can you hear it? The Turkish word for 'five,'* besh, *is also the Cayuga word* wish *and the Mohawk* wisk. *The Mohawk negative* yagh *is the Turkish* yok. Waktare, *an Iroquois word—well, I shouldn't say Iroquois, because that's an idiotic French colonizers' word for the Haudenosaunee people, I should say People of the Longhouse—anyway*, waktare *means 'to speak,' and the Yakut word is* ittare. *'To hide' in Haudenosaunee is* kasethai *and* kistya *in Yakut. The word 'three' is* ahsen *in Mohawk,* ahse *in Tuscarora,* uch *in Turkish,* ush *in Yakut . . . Do you see how exciting?*

"My father would stare at her and smile, as contented as a child listening to a fairy tale. But he did not see. He just wanted her to keep narrating sounds and languages to him for the rest of his life.

"I believe that this itself was a kind of love . . ."

The girl stopped for a moment, staring into space or maybe time. I considered offering some comment or question, but then she looked at me and her eyes seemed to hold me silent. *Do not enter this story. Do not reroute its meaning.* She continued.

"What did she think of him, my mother who fell into love with him, who agreed to take the most dangerous journey with him across water so much bigger than the hubris of a man? Why did she agree to go to North America with him? For what? Because he could not stop the rush of fever dreams telling him to go? To leave forever this forsaken place? To *protect his family*? Or for some dreamstory about America? Or for some even smaller reason? Because a man needs work to have worth, or a violence grows inside him?

"When the permafrost began to thaw in their area, the tusks of ancient mammoths began to rise from the mud like giant bony fingers. The past was not so dead, as it turns out, though the smell of death was everywhere. Of course, as always happens, some people made themselves rich by recovering the ivory.

"Yakutia had once been rich in farmland. But the melting of the permafrost turned the farmland into swamps or lakes; whole fields just caved in until they pulled down the ground and whole villages sank. Rivers around villages ran so fast that they swept neighborhoods away.

"My father worked for a while as a reindeer herder, but the pasturelands gave way to the rotten stench of plant and animal life that had been frozen for thousands of years, their decomposition coming back to life, an invisible stream of carbon dioxide and gas pluming into the atmosphere.

"They'd heard of massive craters popping open on the Yamal Peninsula, created during the eruptions of methane gas that happened as the permafrost thawed. They were all waiting for the ground under their feet to explode.

"One of the last times my father herded reindeer, he found a she-calf stuck in a mud lake. One of its eyes had been gouged somehow. My father pulled the calf free and took it home. He thought about slaughtering and eating it, but Svajonė wouldn't let him. Instead, she sewed its eye shut, nursed it with a bottle, and brought it back to health. When I was a baby, my father told me, I sometimes took naps curled up on a blanket next to the reindeer's stomach. The reindeer protected me, or so Svajonė believed.

"When my father was just a person living on the edges of wanting to be alive at all, nothing really mattered to him. Who he was—if he lived or died—didn't matter in this place no one knew existed. After Svajonė, everything mattered so acutely that he almost couldn't breathe. One night, he broke down and told her he was afraid. Afraid for her. Afraid for me and my unborn brother. He knew she was happy, but he begged her to leave. He told her he knew someone who could find him work in America, or what was left of it.

"She stared at him a long time. Then—as if her mind had already arrived at the place he meant to take us—she said, *The Haudenosaunee languages include Mohawk, Oneida, Onondaga, Cayuga, Seneca, Tuscarora, and Huron-Wyandot. Among others. When we leave, those are the languages I want to study next. The death of languages is what precedes the death of the world.*

"They married in the woods, my mother and father, a ritual of their own making.

"My brother was born shortly before they tried to leave to cross the waters.

"In that moment of time, we were a family. Now, all of that is lost forever. Like a lost language. Like a forgotten word."

She fell silent.

I felt the room soften when she stopped speaking. She'd been using her hands a great deal while she spoke; now they dropped to her sides like objects without use. A lamp flickered and then went out, giving the moment an eerie punctuation.

Her story held me caught, like some great epoch brought to stillness after a seizure. The story of a mother's death, maybe also the story of all mothers, the dead and the living. "I don't know what to say," I said in a kind of breathless gasp. "Your story, your song of your mother, is beautiful." After that, I would have done anything for this girl.

Before I die, I want to give everything back.

To mothers. Everything our mothers took from us when they couldn't understand how to exist inside the impossible contradictions;

everything that was taken from our mothers as a means of keeping
the house, the country, the world in order. I would give them back
their arms, their legs. Return to them their heads, their hair, their
lips and eyes. Mothers, here are your bound and heavy hearts, stricken
by the beatings they tricked you into. Mothers, I give your body back
to land, your original intimacy. Most of all, I give mothers back their
breasts, their wombs, their cunts, their desire.

I would set us free from the word *mother*. May your body be yours
again; may your blood belong to you again. Even to the dead mothers: may your body belong to whatever you might have become, had
you not been strapped to the service of breeding.

And to the blossom of every girl ever born: May that violent rush
of cosmic possibility in your body, between your legs, be let loose from
reproduction. May you open yourself to the cosmos, creating new constellations. May it wreck the wrong world back to life.

The Lament of
the Butcher's Daughter

Mikael's story—of the boy, and the woman on the sidewalk, and the life she held as hers escaped—made Lilly's gut feel numb. The more he moved toward its inevitable conclusion, the heavier and hollower her own body seemed. She could almost feel what his next words would be, but she didn't want them to be real.

As he narrated this story of a boy—as if some other boy were the matter—the fact of him sitting there in front of her receded. He was not a young man on the constant cusp of violence. He was not her lost brother. He was . . . possible again. His voice a storyteller's. She needed the bathroom, but no way was she going now. She crossed one leg tightly over the other and kegeled and told herself, *You will hold this in, no matter how much it hurts. You will hold this in if your eyes water an ocean.*

Mikael looked different now as he spoke. He sat up and he used his hands. Lilly noticed how long his fingers were, how delicate his gestures. His hands were beautiful. His story began to make shapes in front of her. His voice traveling through time, or so it seemed.

"He picked the thing up and held it hard against his chest, like a ball. The baby girl. He'd caught a football exactly once in his life, almost by accident; the ball was meant for another boy, but he'd seen the physics in the air and reached up to snag it because he knew he could. Most of the time he'd spent around boys and balls involved getting hit in the skull, in the face, hit so hard in the chest that it knocked the wind out of him. He'd spent most of his physical education classes sitting on a stupid wooden bench alone, just him and his glasses, but now the coach yelled, *Bring it to your chest, hard!*

"And he did. With both arms, hard to his chest, he ran.

"In the furnace room, in the basement of his apartment building, the boy knew every hidden space: a million shadowy corners, tucked behind piles of things in storage. The room was as warm as a tub for hatching chickens, a device he'd seen in his science class. That was the thing: the warmth, and all the old things stored there, made the basement feel like a giant nest. And the sounds down there were *cacophonous*, one of his very favorite words. The furnace roared, and whatever it was connected to growled, and the pipes moaned and screeched, and just being at the bottom of things—all those floors above them, the cooking and cleaning and families and husbands yelling at wives and mothers yelling at children and women like Vera making their body songs all day and night—it felt like all that sound might hide them.

"He'd learned how to use an eyedropper to feed baby chicks or baby birds fallen from trees. He knew how to feed abandoned kittens or puppies, even a baby ferret once, with food he'd chewed in his mouth first. Mother eagles did this. It was called *regurgitation*, another favorite word—not for its meaning but for the syllables.

"And the best thing of all was: he knew how to read better than anyone in the entire school, possibly including his teachers, which meant he could find whatever he needed to know about the idea of *mother.* In fact, the more he thought about it—about resting the baby girl inside his coat and an old blanket he found, and then carefully laying her down in an old wooden box—the more he believed he had a purpose. For the first time in his stupid boy life.

"He stared at the girl as she lay there, in the box, cooing like a pigeon. Then his heart seized: How to make the box rock? He scanned the room, spotted an old bike leaning against the wall. If he brought his father's hacksaw down, he might be able to cut a rim in half. He ran upstairs to retrieve some water and saltines, which he chewed up while walking back down to the basement. After letting her suck on a washcloth doused in water, he made a kind of mush of the water and saltines, and put a little at a time on the end of his finger for her to suck. He had so much to learn.

"For the first time in his life, he'd found a reason to survive school. He set about constructing a kind of fort in a dark corner of the basement, away from sight and sound, where the box would be safe and protected. A place he could visit every moment he had: every morning before school, every afternoon as soon as he got home, and every night after dinner, before he went to bed.

"On the second day, he began to feed the tiny girl with a bottle. He warmed the milk patiently next to the furnace.

"On the third day, he stopped going to school. He pretended to go, he rode the bus, he got off the bus, he walked around the buildings, he walked home.

"On the fourth day, someone heard crying in the middle of the night.

"On the fifth day, his father found out he'd been skipping school and hit him so hard across the face that his glasses ended up in the next room, but he said nothing.

"On the sixth day, the baby smiled up at Mikael, and his entire world shifted on some imagined axis.

"On the seventh day, unbeknownst to Mikael, his father followed him down to the basement. He tried to take that beautiful baby girl. All that was left of Vera.

"On that day, the boy from nowhere had a choice to make."

He looked at Lilly dead-on. "Didn't he."

Lilly was not sure she had taken a breath in more than an hour listening to Mikael narrate his story. Narrate a past that was forever gone to him. A self that simply slipped, like those of so many foster kids who go violent or dormant with trauma, or those who stray when it becomes clear that no one and no place will have them. An image of her own brother, lost to unimaginable violence—Was he alive? Dead?—crept up her throat and lodged in her temples. A sea of lost children surged in her psyche; most of the minors she worked with were lost to the system or worse.

"You see?" Mikael said, his voice now hard again, as his teen eyes sank back into the cinder-block room. "He was going to take her." The fact of it seemed to punctuate his sentences. "When he bent over, I hit him. In the head. I had a bicycle-tire pump, so I used that. Did it hard, four times, so he couldn't come back and attack me. I hit him harder than he'd ever hit me, I think. The second time, I heard a cracking sound. There was blood everywhere. His eyes were open, but he wasn't alive.

"Then I went and got her box, her little box on rockers, and I put it over by the door where I knew I could grab her quickly. I had an old plastic lighter, and I started touching it to everything in the room that would burn. Then I grabbed the girl out of the box and I ran, with her tucked against my body. Up the stairs, out of the basement, out of the door, into the night. She did not cry. I ran and ran.

"I made it to the railyards, and I climbed onto a train before it left. We rode that way all night till we were in another city. Where they found me. After the building burned and all those people died."

Now he looked at Lilly again, as if somehow what he knew, the story he told, had restored to him some temporary grasp on his life.

"I left her there, in the new city. And I want you to look for her."

He reached up to pull back his collar, twisted his neck to show Lilly something that wasn't there. "She has a little tattoo, right here on the back of her neck. I gave it to her with a needle and ink and fire. It says INDIGO. She cried when I did it, but only a little. Like she knew. I would never burn her in that basement—but I burned a word into her, so she'd have it and no one else could take it."

Lilly knew something too. From the file. She couldn't say it, but Mikael could tell.

"I know about the skull they found. I don't know whose skull that was, what baby it was. But I heard about the police report. Maybe someone killed their baby there because they couldn't feed it. I don't know. People in the building were always doing things for money. One man sold his wife, his young wife, Albanian.

"They said someone saw me with a baby, but no one saw me. Except my father.

"I want you to find her. I left her on the doorstep of a blue-painted house in that city. The one where they found me. You must have it in the notes. I told them all, but no one here believes me. Go find her. He was going to take her. My father was an animal. But only to children. Do you understand? My father is not my father. He stole me. He took a baby. To sell for money. Only no one wanted me. He was a *fucking thief.*"

Mikael slammed his hands onto the table, loud enough for the guards to hear. He picked up the twisted gray rope of umbilical cord, nestled it under his shirt, and dared her with his eyes to tell.

She would not. But neither did she have any clue what to do with what he'd told her. Who would believe a story like that?

The air in the room disappeared, as if some vacuum had sucked it away.

Lilly felt marooned—in a time between her life and his, between foster fathers and war-criminal fathers, between lost sons and daughters untethered from families. Mothers emptied out of children and left for dead. Lost in a scatter that was both ancestral and geographic.

Brother.

Was there really a baby out there? Or was Mikael just a hard teenager making up a story about a lost girl just to save his ass, a boy lying on his way to becoming a violent man?

Dearest Aurora,

I've had to position the hand in Madison Square Park to raise money.

She is beautiful, the isolated limb. The wrist rises to the tops of the trees in the park and above the rooftops. The torch tips are visible for almost a mile around.

I wonder what the casual passerby thinks—someone on his way home from work, some exhausted mother demoralized by worry over how to feed her children. Do they see it as a monstrosity, or does it spark just a bit of imagination? Are they tempted to drop their fatigue and hopelessness for a moment and venture into the park to see what stands there, amid the trees, or do they tell their children to stay away from it, as if it were some ghostly extremity?

This woman must emerge in pieces.

The hand in the trees needs money. Damn this gift from one nation to another without the funding of either.

I know what the papers are saying. They seem confused and act superior. They all snipe that the supposed gift from one country to another has apparently failed to produce a whole entity—that perhaps this is all there is, this giant hand and torch performing without a platform in a city park. Like an amusement park feature. I hate what they've written.

I watch the well-to-do stride up to the hand in all their silk and velvet, their parasols and cigars and shined shoes. They carry the look of people who feel obliged to perform some understanding of the object before them. Wealthy people always perform knowingness, whether or not they possess any. Vapid bubbleheads in colorful clothes, they tête-à-tête together as if exchanging brilliant observations. I don't care. The object itself, even in part, creates mystery and suspense and interest; it is like a spider's web. It's not their understanding I want. It's their attention. I want their lust drawn out by the object. I learned this from you.

You understand this, Aurora: The colossus is not for them. It is for a world that doesn't exist yet. I want them to want. *I want their want to be overwhelming—for them to demand,* Give us this statue so that we may say that it is ours, that this vision is our vision. *I want their desire to travel like fierce electrical current to those whose money shapes the world.*

When Viollet decided upon the nature of the frame—wood-slatted, covered in plaster, that plaster sanded down to a texture that can approximate the curves and lines of a bodily form, carefully crafted wood ridges along the edges, sheets of copper hammered around the molds and structure—I felt giddy. I could see the body before the body even took shape. We have much to figure out still; chief among our questions remains how to get the body to stand. You will want me to say "her body" here, and so I will: we need her body to stand. Upright. Forever. In spite of construction, of its several distinct pieces; in spite of weather and time. In spite of the entire world.

To that end, we have created a system inside the studio involving ropes and metal. (I hope those two words conjure something in your body when you read them.) My beloved assistant Jean Marie and the artist Monduit realized that we must render her in slices. The base, feet, and dress hem: one slice. The dress, shins, knees, another slice. Her head and shoulders their own slice. To accommodate the engineering and construction, we have assessed the model with strings and measurements, and replicated the entire system using hefty ropes dangling from the ceiling. Can you see them? Will you perhaps come to see them? May I show you how to wrap a body like an animal's and swing it toward pleasure? Perhaps you have something to show me?

I've left the best for last, though. As to the problem of her interior, I had a gift of imagination from an old friend: Gustave Eiffel. Or perhaps his idea simply merged with the truth of you, my beloved, and everything I know about your body as a woman in this world. He told me, Build a giant metal corset—but one where the woman's lungs are fully and freely expanded rather than contracted. There is no more perfect answer.

A corset built not for beauty, but for freedom.

I always leave my encounters with you wanting more—but not from you, love, I did not need to ask you for more. When I say "more," what I mean is that I created the condition for more, based on everything that was between us, and then I filled the space between us. I created a space in my sculpture workshop where men might be free to be fully men with one another, in a world that makes men opt instead for war and violence and money and wives—those great masculine sublimations, those cultural underpinnings that keep men from exploring and creating their own desire for each other. It was during the construction of the giant woman's substructure that the idea first seized me. As I watched the metalsmith working so close to the metal—the flight of electric sparks, the delicious flex of his forearms—my imagination locked on two things at once. The first was a phrase you said to me in our youth, and which I've held in my body ever after: Hold as still as a statue.

The second was the word liberty. *I saw in an instant what I must draw, and I left instantly to draw it. I began first with the shape of winged victory—but I imagined her internally, the iron structure. I then reimagined the image as a metal full-body brace that could hold a man suspended, unable to escape or move, arms spread like wings, legs spread wide enough for entry, body held, neck held, head held in a suspended kind of flight. And what to do while inside the brace would be to hold still. Hold still while Viollet removed his velvet jacket. Hold still while he undressed, the fourteen-inch satin cuffs of his shirt covering his hands falling to the floor. Hold still while my dear assistant with his sinewy willow of a body began to caress me. Hold still while Viollet cupped Jean-Marie's ass enough to feel him push back, enough to make him reach for my cock. Hold still when Viollet moved to burn the hair around my nipples from my chest with a match, a little at a time, as carefully as an artist, until the hair itself filled with blood and lust.*

This construction is far superior to the threesome-facilitating chair I designed. This structure would bring a blush from Daedalus, that perfect sculptor who built the Labyrinth. These wings would not melt in the sun. Were you to be suspended in my winged metal sculpture, your breasts would hang like illuminated globes, your lips would suck open in their reddened splendor, your derrière would open like a mouth.

The leg and ass holsters can be adjusted.

During the day, when workers were working on the pieces of woman for the statue—long hours of arduous physical work—no one asked what was behind the thick velvet curtain I had fashioned exactly as yours in your Rooms, only larger, more monstrous. Just as I never even asked, except once, what was behind that door in your home and place of business—Room 8. I knew from your first stare when I inquired that the door was not for me.

Sometimes, I confess, it feels good just to hang there like that, alone, open to the world. Is that the space of woman? I can feel each limb one at a time. My limbs remembering something like wings or flight? Phantom?

Yours unto death,
Frédéric

My most clever, creative cousin,

Pay attention. I have a story.
A story about severed limbs.
In fact, this is a soldier's story.
I do not believe I ever sufficiently thanked you for building me my leg. To put this another way: I will spend the rest of my life devoted to you for doing so.

As I write this, I am sitting next to a pond watching swans. A single swan swam right up to the edge of the pond to stare at me— and such a stare! One thinks of swans as beautiful, demure, winged things. But this gaze! My god. As if she knows something of what we have done to the world. I would call it silent rage if not for the indulgent error of that anthropomorphism. It was the stare of that swan that gave me the mind to tell you, at last, exactly what happened the night I lost my leg.

Some history. In the summer of 1863, when I was twenty, a Union burial excavation in Pennsylvania made a discovery of sorts. In addition to the soldiers they expected to find, they unearthed something unexpected: the body of a woman soldier.

Not unexpected to us, of course—we women soldiers, I mean. We were all well aware that hundreds of us were fighting alongside the men, for the same reasons they did: for family, for country, for money, or for that reason no one likes to mention in good company, for freedom. No, not the freedom of a nation, but of an individual. To enter the war as a man was to feel free from the burden and binds of womanhood, freed into being and motion from marriage and sex and domesticity and reproduction. War was a form of useful work in a way breeding and caretaking and cooking and cleaning will never be. We used different names. We altered our marks. We bound our breasts and erased our figures easily without corsets or skirts. We trained with all the other citizen soldiers, away from our hometowns, with scowls and dirt on our faces.

I was not a soldier, rather a field nurse. But my first year as a field nurse was filled with soldiers and their injured bodies.

My dear friend and the bravest soul I ever met—Frances, who was wounded twice serving with the 1st Missouri Light Artillery—was with me when I was shot. The bullet struck me between breast and shoulder as I stood outside in the woods near a field hospital. The blood shot out in a splash—I could see it, and then I could not, and then I passed out. The rest of the story, there on the field, is Frances.

What I remember most about Frances was not her skill with a rifle, which was considerable—she took out the bastard who shot me down—but the curve of her cheekbone when she set her face near the rifle, the way she never flinched or even closed an eye when she took a shot, the way her shoulders—broader than a man's—barely moved from the kickback. I do believe I have a permanent shoulder bruise from bracing my own rifle butt against my shoulder and taking its pounding. I could shoot well enough, but shooting didn't like me.

She killed the man who wounded me. She brought me safely back to the field hospital. She made sure I was attended to.

I've never met anyone who kissed me more perfectly than she did, her tongue not jammed in bluntly but curious and sly. I've never met anyone who came harder than I did with Frances.

Frances returned to the field.

My leg happened later that night.

I had a fever dream. I woke up twisting in my own sweat, with no pants, with a man—a doctor, a soldier, some man wearing the bloodied and filthy white garb of a field doctor—pressing his hand to my mouth and his weight on my frame, trying to shove his cock into me. With my good hand and arm and shoulder, I did what any soldier under attack would do: I clocked him hard to the side of the head. He fell to the floor. It looked to me like I may have broken his jaw. A soft jaw, perhaps, the bone of a man who had turned his softness inward into hate. You'll regret this, he hissed at me. You'll regret this for the rest of your life. Then he pulled something from his pocket, which must have been a rag soaked in chloroform. Everything went dark.

When I came to, I was on the operating table, bound at the wrists, gagged at the mouth. Standing over me, a doctor and some young male assistant—a boy who looked to be among the walking wounded, who was probably threatened if he refused to assist. I struggled as much as I could, but I was drugged repeatedly. It must have sounded and looked like an emergency amputation, like a normal procedure in that place filled with moaning and bleeding, with the bodies of mostly men making all manner of noise, some begging for death. Where had the nurses gone? Men and women?

The next time I woke, days later, I had one leg ending in a foot and one ending in a knee.

I always wanted that leg back—the leg they took from me. I wanted to hold it, swaddle it, coo to it. I even asked after it, but most of the amputated limbs were burned quickly.

I lost my leg because I hit a man in the face for trying to fuck me after I'd helped to heal the wounded. No one in the war had ever threatened me, attacked me sexually, or even stared at me in any way that ever said anything but "brother in arms."

It's a myth what people say about those of us who are amputees: that we did not receive anesthetic during operations. That we just had to "bite the bullet" during surgery. Very few did. More than eighty thousand were injured. Most received chloroform or ether by means of medical technology. (You know where the phrase "bite the bullet" comes from? Bullets were found on battlefields with teeth marks in them. You know who bit them? Pigs, rooting around in the blood-soaked mud of a battlefield.)

I will visit your statue's limbs. Of anyone, I will love them the most.

When your Big Daughter is finally Erected, I will worship her at her feet.

Frédéric, if you should ever find me gone, look for a gift soon after. The gift is an important object between us. Take good care of this gift. Objects that can no longer be re-created retain power in a profound way that keeps us human. If you lose me, remember to stay human. Remember to invest your colossus with presence in time and space—a presence that someone will be drawn to as if it carried singular magic.

I am eager to try your contraption.

I am eager to receive you in my Rooms.

With a desire that obliterates lust,
Aurora

Aurora and the Water Girl

A nd so, in anticipation of the coming Raid, I decided: we would empty the very womb of my Rooms, leaving only the evidence of pleasure and pain. They would find my creations, but not these children.

In advance, I made three choices that I knew would create great consternation among my clients, my colleagues, and my friends: I chose not to tell my dear Frédéric, with confidence that the grief and loss would only contribute to his artistic practice. For grief and loss, when they do not kill you, engender creation. I would leave him a parting gift that he could not forget.

I chose to believe a girl I barely knew, a girl who claimed that the water is the only way; it seemed insane. I don't know what to think about the story Liza told me. But the pull she seeded within me was unstoppable. And so we struck a bold trade, one that will hold whether or not we succeed in saving these children. In all times, it is worth the attempt. Children are what was or is or will be the best of us. Stand at the gravesite of a child who died too young from this wrong world we've made, as I did too many times during the war, as I have too many times when a child's labor is exploited to death. Tell me what you feel in your body as you stand at their grave. What you feel? It has no linear time. It does not exist in linear time. The grief crosses all times.

This was the last night I would create a Room for my beloved Frédéric, but he did not know this. I had mapped out the plan on that odd night when I met Liza and made our secret trade, and I held the secret inside my body as if my body could still hold treasured secrets. The scene we played out reminded me of what was last best about both of us, that we had once been unafraid children who could imagine anything.

As for the children from Room 8, we invented a private ritual for our journey. Each child held an apple in a half bite in their mouth. They stood in a great circle, all apple-mouthed. Then, on my command, each child knocked the apple from another's mouth, so that the rest of the apple flew away, leaving only a small bite between their teeth. The force of knocking the apple from another's mouth a reminder that anything a woman or child wants in the world will be forcefully taken from them unless they bite down—an animal truth. One boy accidentally socked another boy in the jaw, missing the apple at first, because he still hadn't mastered coordination with his left hand, having lost his right. But the two boys simply tried again and got it right the second time, punching each other in the shoulder upon completion.

And the girls? One lost a front tooth, her mouth left bloody, the tooth lodged in the apple. She laughed. I felt something like love, I think. Or perhaps just kinship.

When we completed our ritual, Liza led us to the river's edge. The night and dark were kind to us. There was a fog. One by one, when

Liza said jump, we leapt into the river—with Liza herself directly
behind us.

Liza gathered all the children around her in the water, then reached
out and commandeered a rickety stray boat floating nearby, herding us
all over the side into the boat, placing one strong girl and one boy at
the oars. Once we were safely under way, she placed what looked like a
squirming bald baby rodent into my hand. I recoiled but managed to
hold on to the thing. "Oh my god," I said. "What is this creature?"

"A leucistic axolotl," she said, cupping my hand in hers as if to
guide me. "Now, you must swallow it."

I must . . . ?

I was less than thrilled.

She thrust the creature toward my face. "Do it now, please. While
we are on the water."

"Why on earth should I swallow this creature?" A reasonable question, you might think, but even as I uttered it, I realized how unlike
me it was. I felt immediately ashamed for my lack of courage—my
lack of *imagination*.

Liza looked down at my skirt. Reaching over, she lifted the fabric,
then knelt down, at knee level, and traced the roses on my prosthetic
with her hand.

"Your leg," she said, and then she did something unexpected: she
stood up again and gestured dramatically at the axolotl in my hand,
as if she were on stage. "The axolotl can regrow its limbs, you know,"
she said. "*Ambystoma mexicanum*, in Latin. The Nahuatl word *axolotl*
means 'walking fish.' But it is not a fish. The axolotl is an amphibian.
Scientists are obsessed with it, because its body can do things humans
cannot. It can regenerate its tail, its legs, its central nervous system.
The tissue of its most complex organs—the eye, the heart, even the
brain." Her eyes, I noticed, remained fixed on the prosthetic under
my skirt.

Liza must have the heart of a scientist herself, I thought, for as the boys pushed our boat through the water, she continued her monologue on the traits of this amphibian wonder. Amniotes, I learned, deposit their fertilized eggs on land—or inside the mother—whereas anamniotes, such as fish and amphibians, lay their eggs in water. "Amphibians are anamniotes. They are able to exchange oxygen, carbon dioxide, and waste with the water that surrounds them—so that their embryos can complete their own growth without being poisoned. And axolotls are unique among amphibians, because they don't develop lungs." Instead, she explained, they had four different ways of breathing—a fact that I'll admit did fascinate me.

Now my imagination was in thrall to two creatures before me— the resourceful little being squirming in my hand, and the black-haired girl regaling me with knowledge. How had she managed to seize my attention so thoroughly?

I looked again at the squirming being in my hand. It had a pinkish tint, little black lidless eyes, and a fan of feathery external gills on either side of its head. It did not look appetizing. But this girl had saved the only family I had ever known from a Raid. I owed her everything. So I picked the creature up by its tail, closed my eyes, said a tiny internal prayer that I would not throw up, whispered, "My apologies and my gratitude, tiny beast." Then I improvised a toast—"To the Mother of Oceans!"—and swallowed it whole.

Liza must have seen the look of misgiving on my face as I swallowed. "It will be okay," she told me. "I asked her first. The animals are coming back from everything we've done to them—but we have to be in our bodies differently. Swallow and breathe through your nose, so you can gain hold of the rest of your body and cross time. You can go get your leg, Lilly—and your son."

I thought about legs. I pictured lilies. *Your son,* she'd said again. Maybe I'd misunderstood; maybe she was talking about the sun. If

she could help me get these children to safety, I would be happy ending up anywhere under the sun.

I thought as hard as I could not to think about the taste of the
axolotl, but instead about the taste of eggs. As if the word itself had
gotten inside me.

Ethnography 4

Like so many others—maybe more than seventy-five thousand—my father was promised citizenship after the war. For years and years after he returned, he built and worked a ranch. Then, one day, his neighbors had a secret meeting and held a secret vote. In a group, they came to his door and knocked. My mother asked them in, and they came, though they looked uneasy. Eventually, it became clear why: the neighbors wanted my father out.

Before he had this land, my father had been a vaquero for a wealthy rancher in the next county. He had a good working relationship with a wealthy white rancher nearby, and he enlisted his advice and help. My father took the matter to court; the judge permitted the legal case to proceed—but the case dragged on for years. It was said that the Office of Surveyor of General Claims would sometimes take up to fifty years to process claims or finish the permissions for trials. My father lost all his money, and the ranch itself, in his effort to argue for his own rights. Rights that had been given to him by so-called law. Government promises. After that, my mother had a stroke—or she just stopped wanting to live, I've never been sure. She had to get a job as a maid; maybe she just worked herself to death. After he lost everything, my father started doing dangerous mining work. He lasted two small hungry exhausted years.

In our last days on my father's ranch, there is one day I will never forget. My father was on horseback, tracking down a stray calf. My mother was drying dishes at the kitchen window, smiling, humming some little tune. My brothers were in the barn, probably shoveling hay or shit. I was at the kitchen table, eating a hard-boiled egg. I was a kid, so what did I know, but for a moment, it felt like we were real. Do you know what I mean? Like we could be a father, a mother, a son, my brothers laughing and cutting up in the barn, all of us making a life, near animals and land. It seemed so simple. Like a dream anyone could walk into and just . . . rest.

For the rest of my life, I dreamed about that egg.

Portal

Cruces 5

We rode the waters to and from her like tides.

Back and forth and back and forth to the island, where she rose up and up. The pedestal was too wide for scaffolding, so after the iron frame was erected, some of us dangled from ropes and swung about inside, joining the pieces of her body. Endora was highly skilled at riveting. David was the most artful and efficient. I was quite delicately skilled with my hammer in hard-to-mold places—her nose, her eyes, her ears. We swarmed over steam-driven cranes and derricks like a swarm of human ants, conspiring and recombining, joining her body together.

Under our breath, we blessed the things we touched and made. From our different bodies and mouths and languages, blessings fell like flowers from our lips onto the ground and into the copper of her and into the water, every single day and night. Some of the blessings were for family members: *May my mother or grandmother live through the night. May my husband be safe. May my brothers and sister find enough to eat. May this boy or this girl survive while they are held in the hands of others.* Some were for the materials or the tools or the ropes and pulleys, or for the weather that surrounded and buffeted us: *May this wood and plaster hold and carry us and all of our labor ever upward. May this steam-driven crane move her mighty neck and shoulders in the rhythm of our labor. May this storm pass us by without injury.* And some of the blessings were malformed, half-thought, missing parts: *May no one discover my fears, my secrets; may my family members not be deported; may the desires growing inside my body never be taken from me. May swirls of opium smoke comfort our suffering; may the laugh of an ample woman help me to breathe full in the chest; may this ache under my belly where my very sex seethes meet an equal want; may my desire be whetted without punishment or shame.*

Because underneath our labor was our hunger.

We were men and women and humans and children of all different kinds. We were driven by our embodied existences: the need to eat, to shelter, to fuck, to work, to protect other bodies. We the body were driven to earn the money, since money was the only path to everything we needed: food and electricity and heat and blankets and medicine. Our bodies labored to the point of fatigue, so deep that we moved as if in a trance, like sleepwalkers.

It was our sweat that made her come. Our fucking burst open our fatigue and bred lust; our lust combusted into children. Some men loved women and the women loved the men back. Some men loved other men; some women, other women. There was a free flow of physical demand in the spaces we worked, in the workshops and warehouses and alleys and docks. Some of the children who worked among us had parents and others did not. Certain jobs were served best by small hands; others required a delicate touch. Some bodies did heavy work and some bodies bent and curled, tracing the shapes of the details we crafted. Some of us washed and cleaned and swept, carving an endless S in our backs. We worked together in waves and weaves, and when we went home at night, we were just ourselves again, apart from the work.

No one who worked to build her body died.

The girl slept on a blanket under Endora's bed for many nights in a row. One night, after everyone else was asleep, the girl came to me. "You love David Chen," she said, standing over my cot in the room I shared with John Joseph, Endora, and David. I could hear a symphony of soft snoring around me. But she was awake, and she meant for me to understand that she could see me. "You love him more than you've ever loved anything in your life. You desire him unto death."

Her voice made my body tremble.

I looked across the room to where David lay sleeping. I had chosen a bed as far away from his as possible, but also one that would give me a good view of his back, so that I could watch over him as whatever voices and bodies and suffering moved through him in his sleep.

I do desire David unto death, god help me. His body, a color between white and wheat. His hair, the color of night. His torso, between muscle and some otherworldly fluid, its heavy grace apparent every time he moved in his sleep. When the sheet fell away, and I could see the glistening marks on his back, I thought of hundreds of feathers or wings. As if David were turning into a great crane. I wanted to crawl onto his cot and cup his body with my body, like a double parenthesis, something held inside another, where no one anywhere could find us. I want to push my cock into him I want to tendril my arm around to his waist to the velvet pulse of his cock I want to hold him and work the desire out of him in a rush. I want to put my face at the back of his neck I want him to violently throw me off him and then push my legs up until it feels like they will snap from my hips I want him to shove into me, sweet suction sweet thrust.

I also want none of this. I want David Chen to stay turned away from me, so that all there is of him is his back, the hieroglyphics writing the unsaid story of whatever happened to him, his back the new world. If he stays turned away from me, if he stays asleep, nothing and no one can ever take my love for him away. There is another kind of freedom in that.

Bless this man's body. Bless his skin, his cock. Bless his sleep.

The girl pulled something from underneath her shirt and brought it over to me. A perfectly coiled white rope. "When do you feel most human?" she asked me.

I didn't say anything. I just looked at David's back: His hair. His shoulders. The rise of his hips. His feet. His sleep.

"This is *kinbaku*," she said. "*Kinbaku-bi* means 'the beauty of tight binding.' This rope is made from hemp." She placed the rope on my belly. "In the late Edo period in Japan, Seiu Ito studied the art of binding prisoners of war. *Hojojutsu* was used to capture and restrain prisoners, and sometimes to hold prisoners in place for execution or crucifixion or death by fire. Someone's limbs might be tied to decrease their mobility. Rope loops at the neck, or anywhere blood vessels and nerves are, so that numbness might be achieved during struggle." There must have been some look in my eye—a look of something unknown, unresolved—that made her pause, then continue. "Ask Aurora. She knows a different story from torture. David has met Aurora. He knows how to find her Rooms. Freedom isn't what they say."

I don't say anything to the girl. For the rest of the night, I hold the rope tightly to my chest. My mouth goes wet, then dry, then wet again.

The next morning, she was gone. I'm not sure what the four of us were thinking about her anyway—did we think we could make a family inside our shared labor? Make this girl one of us?

But her words stayed with me. I did find Aurora. And her Rooms. And so did David.

It is possible that desire needs to let loose, here and now, before it is snuffed out by laws meant to suffocate and kill it. It is possible that we need to find the doors of the Rooms where we feel most human, and open them out toward the sky, the water, the world, and back to one another's bodies.

I keep thinking about the broken shackle, the way it was supposed to be prominently held in the statue's hand for all to see—and how it ended up near her foot, like something hidden or disappeared.

I keep thinking about how her skin changed from copper to green, its own kind of vitiligo.

After our work was completed, after we had no more reasons to be bound together, we broke apart. The breaking apart of the body of us happened in the same streets and political forums where Reconstruction had crumbled even as we were working. It happened in the same courts that crushed the rights and protections that had made us feel part of something larger than ourselves, as if we were living in a country that could see us and count us as real. It happened in the tightening grip of laws mandating separations of peoples in public schools, public places, public transportation, pulling us apart in restrooms and restaurants, pulling our very lips away from fountains of water.

Every day that passed, we were told in more and more ways that we could not fully exist. Could not vote. Could not hold a job. Could not get an education. We faced arrest, jail, violence, death, each of us in our own way. And I began to emerge between us, purely for survival reasons. It felt like the we of us couldn't hold.

Endora found work at an orphanage. As a groundskeeper.

John Joseph returned to the nation north of here. He returned for many more ironworks projects in this city as it grew. So did his descendants.

For many years, Endora, John Joseph, David, and I would meet up in the fall and ride out together to see the statue. We'd make a toast together at her feet, smile and reminisce, then go back to our lives— the lives where we had to make a go of it, as Endora said, no matter what came next.

The statue did turn color over the years.

No other girl appeared.

Sometimes I found myself checking the level of the water.

David and I . . .

I can see the head of the statue over David's shoulder through the window of our loft. The room is not large, but the windows stretch out for an entire wall. She's something like a secular angel, crowned and stern, our labor inside her forever.

David stirs but does not wake. A light rain whispers morning.

Bless his exquisite form.

The story of workers is buried under the weight of every monument to progress or power. Our labor never reaches the height of the sacred. No one ever tells the story of how beautiful we were. How the body of us moved. How we lifted entire epochs.

May our story survive the rise of this city.

The Apple

"Cunt."

The air in the room vibrates.

"Say it." Aurora looks down at me kneeling beneath her on the carpet. "Say, 'My cunt.'"

I do.

"Hold still," she says.

I do.

Between her thighs, between the folds of her labia majora, is an apple. Most of the apple is visible. The rest of the fruit is nested inside her.

A quivering apple.

Her legs are neither pressed together nor apart; the space that exists between her legs is the width of the small red world.

This room and every object and texture in it—the lushness of the indigo carpet, the cherrywood tables and chairs, the deep-green velvet curtains skirting the floor like a woman's dress, the mahogany bed layered in linens and satins of red and umber and black and blue, gold and orange and bone white—the hues of the body's internal truths—makes a pocket for my soul in a way that life does not.

On my knees, in the Room of Kneelings, my hands bound behind my back with an intricate weave of rope braided from human hair, head and neck and spine already aching from looking up and up at the colossus of her, my face less than an inch from her cleft, I can see her labia and the hot wet seeping sap of her already making a kind of halo around the apple.

Between her legs . . . oh, but I can never see her legs as legs.

One of her legs, yes, is a leg. It stands her upright from beneath red and black velvet waves of skirt, spliced up the middle and pinned back like open curtains.

The other leg—there is no other leg. Where the other leg should be, to my right, is the leg I built for her. Rosewood inlaid with gold-leaf roses from ankle to hip, its hinged knee patterned after the Salem Leg but modified to mirror the fullness of a woman's thigh, its slender foot painted with delicate red toenails.

The apple, deep red with a bit of yellow at the top curve—that yellow is somehow maddening; any painter would agree—is situated so close to Aurora's cleft that it seems to convulse as she pleasures herself. I try to look past the apple, up toward her head, her eyes. It hurts to try too hard to see up the length of her. My mouth is as open as I can make a mouth, as she requested. My jaw torques, the apple suspended between my lips and the gaping mouth-sex of my cousin.

From this angle, she looks larger than life.

"Hold still, Frédéric," she admonishes in a whisper, "or else." Her fingers making tiny furious circles around her bulging and rouge-red clitoris. Her hips move in waves almost imperceptibly, making the motion all the more painfully ecstatic. My hands, bound behind my back, writhe like fat little hungry snakes.

An apple, the world.

I can smell the sweet inside the apple. I can smell her sweat and sex, a tang, a madness.

I don't know how much longer my cock can take the waiting. I grind myself against air, careful not to make contact with Aurora lest she arrest her motion, wishing for some other body weight to meet the ache of mine, something, *anything in the world,* to push back against my anguished hips and purpled cock even if it kills me. It would be an acceptable way to die. But no weight comes.

As much as I can make myself a statue, I do not move. I see the heave of her breasts bound up in a slate-gray satin corset above me as her breathing cocks like the moment before a gunshot.

"Don't breathe," she commands. Our eyes lock.

It makes me feel a little insane to hold my mouth open while simultaneously holding my breath and staring hard enough at Aurora's eyes—not the apple, not her sex—that my skull feels ready to break open. My bound thoughts my bound hands my stretched neck and spine now shrieking.

I want to bite more than I want to be alive.

Then sound.

Aurora's moans animate the entire room. Her head rocks back. Her breasts spill from her corset. Two dangerous eyes.

She tightens her cleft around the apple, and for a moment, it looks as if the apple will be swallowed by the other mouth of her.

Then and only then does she come, hard enough to flood the apple, to send it into the waiting mouth of me. I catch it in a perfect bite. I come now too, in a full body spasm. I don't recognize the sound I make.

Something feels final about this.

I surrender my body to her thrust.

The Water Girl Carrying

Repeating things helped make order. To make a good trade, a carrier needs not to care about transgressing time. A carrier needs to slip her way into the barter. Sometimes you had to use objects and signs differently from the way other people did.

Penny.

Cord.

Apple.

Rope.

Laisvė pulled the umbilical cord out from her shirt, its purpled winding shape wet with river water. She smelled it, touched it with her tongue, then tucked it back beneath her shirt, next to her skin.

Thanks to the turtle's mapping advice, she had traveled from one bay through ocean through another bay, finally to a river called the Patawomeck, an Algonquian name. The name the fish in the river used on her journey. The Natives in the Chesapeake region included the Piscataway, the Mattaponi, the Nanticoke, and the Pamunkey—the people of Powhatan. In 1613, the English colonists had abducted Powhatan's daughter, Pocahontas, who was living with her husband, Kocoum, in a Patawomeck village. Now, on the edge of the river where Laisvė had climbed onto the shore, a tourist plaque stared back at her, confronting her with the story.

Laisvė closed her eyes and took her mind back to the volumes of history she'd read in The Brook, still likely stacked against the wall of her father's apartment. (In her chest, an ache hole around the word *father.* But it wasn't time to go get her father, not yet. He had not reached the surface.) Laisvė remembered the drawings of Indians accompanying the stories in history books. Those books were filled with lies about people and objects and animals and land. Stories they called history that were really stories of conquest. Of seizing and holding something too tightly, of ending something not yours.

Somewhere amidst the loose fabric of the lie that Pocahontas saved the English captain's life after his capture by Opechancanough, behind the romantic notion that she often brought provisions to save the colonists from starvation, beneath the myth that she continued to serve as a sort of English emissary ever after—underneath all this, a different story seethed. The story of the baby born as Amonute, who also went by the private name Matoaka before she was abducted by English colonists and accepted Christianity as a means of survival. The possibility of any other story in the world. A hundred other possible stories of a girl. What was her suffering? Her bravery? Her desires? Her delights? Who among us can go back to recover the story of girls made into false fictions?

The umbilical cord underneath Laisvė's shirt seemed to wriggle a bit.

She reopened her eyes and read the plaque confronting her.

INDIANS POISONED AT PEACE MEETING

According to the plaque, in May 1623, another English captain had led his soldiers from Jamestown to meet with the Indian leaders here in Pamunkey territory. The Indians were returning English prisoners taken the previous year during war leader Opechancanough's orchestrated attacks on encroaching English settlements along the rivers that joined here. At the meeting, the English called for a toast to seal the agreement, gave the Indians poisoned wine, and then fired upon them, injuring as many as one hundred and fifty, including Opechancanough and the chief of the Kiskiack. The English had hoped to assassinate Opechancanough, who was erroneously reported as having been slain during the incident. (They would not succeed at this until 1646.)

Laisvė spit on the tourist plaque; she wasn't quite sure why, except that it was a static marker of story, which made her angry. The river made her the opposite of angry. "Thank you, river, for bringing me here," she whispered to the water. "Thank you, trees, for witnessing the stupidity of humans." Unlike people, rivers and trees and animals did not misunderstand her.

There were exactly three people in Laisvė's life who could almost understand her way of being in the world: Joseph, whom she'd met in her close future when he was younger and she was older than now, as well as in her present when she was younger and he was the older one. Aurora, whom she'd met in the deep past, and who had said, *Well, there's nothing about your story that's harder to believe than some idiotic old man living in the heavens spewing commandments and invading the bodies of women.* And her mother, who had gone to water. None of the slippages in time or lives or ages made any difference to her. None of these people ever rejected her or doubted her; all understood that time moves, or they were people for whom life no longer had edges.

They did not perceive living as more important than not living; they were not afraid to die.

None of them was her father, though, and that was a fact that hurt her heart. Her father could only live and die inside the space of their present tense, and for that reason, their love for each other had a corresponding mortality to it. Her watermother's words: *Listen, my love. You cannot save your father or your brother or me or anyone or the world even though you want to. But being multiplies and moves. That is the beauty of life. Not death, but energy in a state of constant change.*

Something like a gap existed inside her father, perhaps evident in that place he went to during his seizures. Laisvé believed the place was real, just like the places where dreams live, or grief or pain or ecstasy. She believed that these places all carried a kind of vibrating pulse that only some people understood, although animals and trees and water and dirt and the sky and space all seemed to be woven through with it. Just as she believed in what her watermother had told her: *Listen, my love . . . you can do something quite useful. You can turn time. You can move forward and backward. You can become a free-flowing form in motion, a bridge between being and beyond-being. You are no one's hero. You are a living moment between time and water.*

But what did beyond-being mean, exactly? Was the living moment between time and water a real place? When? How?

Tomorrow she would deliver the umbilical cord to the person who needed it. Tonight she nestled herself at the foot of a sycamore across from several box maples. She covered herself in leaves: tulip poplar, northern spicebush.

She thought about animals—about the short bursts of intense variation within species that occur after geologic catastrophe or upheavals in the environment. Like a meteor striking the earth, or the rapid diminishment of the ozone layer that led to glacial melt, the great Water Rise, and the social collapse of nations. A species could split and its evolution could take different paths. Any speciation event you could explain by anagenesis could also be explained by cladogenesis.

Hyracotherium *evolved into*

Mesohippus *evolved into*

Merychippus *evolved into*

Pliohippus *evolved into*

Equus: *Horse, a direct ancestor of* Hyracotherium, *small changes over time gradually, for example, from three-pronged foot into hoof.*

Or:

Hyracotherium *goes extinct.*

Ancestor X gives rise to Mesohippus.

Mesohippus *goes extinct.*

Ancestor Y gives rise to Merychippus.

Merychippus *goes extinct.*

Ancestor Z lineage gives rise to Pliohippus.

Pliohippus *goes extinct.*

Equus: *Horse carries seven extant species traces that branched and braided.*

When Pangaea split into Laurasia to the north, and Gondwana-land to the south, and then into continents, species living on the land masses split with them.

Polar bears and brown bears shared a common ancestor with the extinct Eurasian brown bear. Glaciation made movement southward difficult, isolating them. When the glaciers melted, inside the speed and power of climate change, hybridization between brown bears and polar bears quickly followed.

Laisvė pictured the Hawaiian archipelago. In her mind's eye they looked like pieces of land breaking away from each other, each land mass forming its own ecology. She thought of the earless Hawaiian monk seal, an endangered species. The hoary bat, also endangered. The vesper bat . . . extinct.

Could stories break free of stasis and equilibrium, give way to bursts of radical change? Could stories themselves become extinct? Could history? Could stories carry us differently? Could children branch off, away from their ancestors, like a body disassembled and reassembled in an otherwhere across time and space?

Laisvė pictured her baby brother breaking off from the ferry ride like a puzzle piece, traveling to another formation, or family, or species.

The woman she meant to meet next did not know yet that Laisvė carried an object that could help deliver something profoundly lost to a different boy.

She fingered the cord against her chest until sleep came for her.

Umbilical

Morning. The scent of river water, dirt, tree bark, and tiger lilies and a tiny grunting sound. Being awake meant moving toward a fountain, as the turtle had said: "Go to the fountain with the turtles spitting water." Laisvė opened her eyes to orange and yellow: the smell of orange and yellow, the image of orange and yellow, and that curious tiny crunch or grunting sound that came with the colors. She pushed herself to sit still, with her hands in the dirt.

The dirt moved.

A tiny voice emerged. "It's not a problem that you're here, girl," the dirt said. "Just don't get in the way of our labor."

Laisvė focused her attention closer to the ground. Terrestrial invertebrates. Class: Clitellata, order: Opisthopora, phylum: Annelida. Earthworms. Hundreds of them. Crawling and grunting and eating their way through the roots of a patch of tiger lilies hard by the river. Now that she was paying attention, she could hear a kind of low hum, the chatter of the worms as they worked.

"I'm sorry," she said. "I didn't see you."

"Typical human. Just mind the ground," the worm said. "We've got all this organic material to get through—protozoa, rotifers, nematodes, fungi, bacteria . . . and the project at hand, these invasive fuckers. Look at them. With their showy arrogant orange heads. Makes me sick."

Laisvė didn't need encouragement to admire the earthworms: their fluid-filled, hermaphroditic coelom chambers, their hydrostatic skeletons. Their central nervous systems, with their subpharyngeal ganglia, their ventral nerve cords, their bilobed brains made from a pair of perfect pear-shaped ganglia. The profound, all-consuming power of their guts. Even their commonplace names were beautiful to her: *rainworm, dew worm, night crawler.*

But mostly she loved their burrowing and their mating. How, as they drove down into the wet earth, they ate soil, extracting nutrients, decomposing leaves and roots and organic matter, their little tunnels aerating the soil, making way for air and water. How, after copulation, each worm would delightfully be the genetic father of some spawn and the genetic mother of the rest, the mating pair overlapping each other, exchanging sperm with each other, injecting eggs and sperm into each other inside a kind of ring formation, the fertilization happening outside of their bodies in little cocoons after mating, their families untethered from gender or the stupid false suction of the nuclear family in humans. Parthenogenetic.

"The tiger lilies," Laisvė said gently, aiming her voice down at the worms. "They are so very beautiful, though."

"Beautiful my *ass,*" the worm groused.

Laisvė heard a kind of raised murmur of agreement from the dirt.

"That's how things go, isn't it? The flashy beautiful thing gets all the goddamn attention. The so-called ugly thing close to the dirt gets the contempt. *We* move the goddamn earth around this entire planet. No credit. Not from humans."

Laisvė considered this carefully. Aristotle had called earthworms the intestines of the soil. A few years ago, she had liberated a book of Darwin's, *The Formation of Vegetable Mould Through the Action of Worms*, from the library to give it a loving home with her and her father. She held worms in high regard. "I am sorry if I offended you. Anything I can do to help?"

"Your lot doesn't *help*. You destroy. We were just talking about this with the mycelium. Hey, mycelium, what were you saying before? About the Amazon?"

A tender fan of white threads surfaced up through the dirt, speaking in a hundred tiny whispers. "It's true. My god, your ignorance about the flora and fauna of the Amazon—staggering. Do you know there are around *four thousand* species of trees alone that none of your scientists have even named, much less analyzed? You have any idea how many fungi? I heard you finally 'found' a few new species of electric eels, that cobalt-blue tarantula, a couple of new river dolphins. I think also a tree that's a hundred feet taller than the tallest tree you thought you knew of. At what point do you rethink your whole idea that these are 'discoveries?' How does that word even have any meaning for you? Something exists just because you finally 'found' it? You 'discovered' it?"

Laisvė looked away. Her eye lit restlessly on the bark of a nearby tree, then back to her own skin. She felt something like shame except deeper.

Another worm picked up the point. "You ever seen a waxy monkey tree frog? That's a more spectacular species than you. You know all the problems you're having with bacteria resistance? What a man-made, idiotic problem. That frog's skin could form the basis of a whole new arsenal of antibiotics. Did you know their skin has a protein that contains dermorphin, an opioid fifty times more potent than morphine?

You know what you knuckleheads use dermorphin for? Doping thor-
oughbred horses. So your racehorses can ignore the pain you're putting
them through and *run faster.*"

The mycelium joined in: "There are seventy-five species of poison-
dart frogs, in more colors than you have names for, with more than
four hundred novel alkaloids *in their skin.*"

The first worm raised up some off the ground for emphasis. "You
spend so much time mythologizing monsters! The vampire bat? Sure,
it bites its prey, sucks the wound—but it also carries a unique anti-
coagulant in its spit. The vampire bat produces this substance you
call draculin. Someday you'll 'discover' that draculin is an effective
agent for retarding clotting. But you're too busy making up cutesy
names and blaming the damn bats for *your own idiotic diseases.*"

Laisvé knelt down into the dirt.

The mycelium curled around her knees. "There are literally thousands of Amazonian fungi you haven't even noticed yet. And all of you
who don't live here, who live in cities full of corporations and pollut-
ants and death-driven, war-centered behavior, far away from the mil-
lions of people and billions of species of plants and animals who live
outside those cities—what do you do? You let it burn."

"Can I please help?" Laisvé felt infinitesimal. Not in size. In soul.

"Well," the worm said, its tip leaning toward the tips of other worms
as if conferring with them. "You could just pull up the tiger lilies
around here. That way at least our work will be a little easier. But listen, word on the street has it that you're after a lily of your own."

Laisvé had already started pulling up flowers, strewing their
carcasses in limp heaps, but now she paused. "What do you mean,
worm? After a lily?"

The worm raised itself up from the dirt like a question mark.
"Turtles sent word ahead of you. You're after a girl, aren't you? That's

your lily. She works about two miles from here, on foot, I think. But she's not there right now. She eats her lunch nearly always at the foot of the fountain in the botanical gardens. Even when it rains! Stupid human. We don't measure distances the way you do, but one or two miles on foot—that's my best guess. We measure in eating and shitting and aerating soil, so our metrics won't mean much to someone like you. Your kind should try it sometime."

"Try what?"

"Eating dirt," the worm said. A tiny chorus of worm laughter.

"Oh, that. I *have* tried it. When I was young, I used to eat handfuls of dirt, straight out of the ground. And apple cores. Seeds. Balls of paper. And pennies," Laisvė said. "My father said it was pica. I never understood why it needed a name."

"I see. Then we have some things in common. You should also try getting it on with the earth instead of destroying it with your own endless reproduction. You humans are all so full of yourselves! What a waste of being. Anyway. Go that way. Or just meditate on the word *lily* . . . I don't know what kind of girl you are, but sometimes human-child spawn can travel differently, I've noticed. Once your species hits adulthood, it's all over. Dead matter. Stasis. Stuck inside their own dramas."

"I travel by water. Backward and forward in time," Laisvė said.

"Well, there's always the sewer system if you don't want to walk. Unless swimming through shit is a problem for you. Humans are so . . . *averse*, to—what? Their own damn organic matter."

A tiny group chuckle.

"All righty, then. Back to work." The worm joined its worm brother-sistermotherfather bodies in their labor. The sounds of their labor receding, Laisvė began to walk in the direction her imagination pulled her. In her mind's eye, she could see a fountain with mermaids and seashells and turtles spitting water. She held it there as if it were a beacon.

On the streets, in this city and inside this time, garbage blew around on the ground. The closer she got to the buildings, to the city blocks in which they were arranged, the more the colors around her faded and a kind of monochrome took over; she felt surrounded by the smell of concrete and steel and hot dog stands and car exhaust. The more she walked, the more the cars multiplied. Streetlights and the clack of heels on pavement. Oddly curated lines of trees and shrubbery and lawns. A tidiness that made her tummy hurt. This time looked familiar—a history not so distant from her own, except that the buildings were intact and the electrical grid seemed functional and people looked to be engaged in things like jobs and driving to and from places and eating and business transactions—their labor hidden behind suits and high-rises and blocklike institutional buildings. The wind moved differently here, diverted by man-made things. By city being. The sound of the airspeak drowned out by engines, tires on pavement, horns, whistles, the occasional whine of a siren.

Laisvé heard the voices of people moving around her.

Then water.

Then she saw it: a fountain, as she had already seen inside her mind. Perched on the surrounding marble bench, a woman in a suit, her legs tucked under her like a doe's. The fountain, more than the woman, drew Laisvé's attention—the glory of it. Three Nereids, sea nymphs, served as corporeal support for basins above and below them. Atop the fountain was a crown, from which water spilled gracefully, falling from basin to basin below. The figures stood on a pedestal decorated with seashells. At the base, jets of water sprayed from the mouths of—yes, it was true, just as Bertrand said: "Look for a fountain with water-spitting turtles."

A plaque on the fountain read THE FOUNTAIN OF LIGHT AND WATER, but in the sculpture, Laisvė saw only her mother. Not really her mother, but a kind of symbol, a reimagined archetype that set her mind and heart at ease. This was the place. She felt sure.

The woman seated there, eating a sandwich, looked rumpled— not her clothes, but her face. Something less than wrinkles but more than concern.

Laisvė walked up to the woman. She had a lanyard dangling from her neck, with a tiny image of her on a name tag—she looked crumpled there too—and a name: LILLY JUKNEVICIUS. Laisvė stared at her.

"Can I help you?" Agitation pricked the edges of the woman's voice.

"No, but I have something important to trade," Laisvė said.

"Oh," she said, distracted, opening her bag as if looking for a scrap of food. "Listen, I—"

Laisvė persisted. "Do you have something for me?" She was certain what she needed was near. "Lilly, right?" Laisvė pointed to the name tag.

Laisvė watched as the woman rummaged around in her purse. At last, she sighed heavily, a *nope, nothing here* sigh, part performance, part relief.

Laisvė sat down next to Lilly. Lilly scooted over a bit, alarmed by the proximity.

"Try your sack," Laisvė offered.

Lilly stared at Laisvė, who could read what she was trying to hide in her expression: *Can't a woman eat a fucking sandwich in peace?* But something was happening within the stare this girl held her inside. Without looking away from the girl's eyes, Lilly reached for an apple she knew was in her brown sack. She handed the apple over to the girl, who slowly, without speaking, reached into her clothing and pulled out a strange-looking purplish twist of unknown nature, as if some kind of trade was actually going down. *Jesus. What is that, rotting meat? Some kind of dead snake? Just accept it and walk away, Lilly. At least you've given her something to eat.*

Laisvė took the apple and released the twirl of purpled rope to Lilly. "This will help you help him," she said.

Before Lilly could say a word, a speeding black van swerved up over the curb, skidding to a halt nearly right on top of them. A side door slid open and two men piled out, both dressed in dark clothes and glasses, both armed. Vests and helmets. No identifying details. Lilly gasped and curled backward, clutching the purplish object toward her breast as if it had great value.

"Your name!" she yelled.

Lilly's chest constricted; her breathing locked in her throat. She could see the apple in the girl's hand and hear her voice—then the two men snatched the girl's small body up, all in one motion, and swallowed her into the belly of the van. Before the doors slammed shut, the girl said, "Liza! My name is Liza! It's okay, it's okay, I know where the story is going." Then the van screeched back into gear and disappeared into the river of traffic alongside them.

Lilly felt a full-body *oh my god* overcome her. She began to shake.

Inside the belly of the black-windowed van, Laisvė makes a compass of her body. She needs to know what's what.

The men in the van drive fast.

She is strapped in by a network of belts. Her mouth is covered in duct tape.

A black bag on her head smells like dirt.

The black van makes a lot of stops and starts and turns for a while; then not.

Open road to somewhere.

The belly of the van is dark, like the insides of whales or deep water.

The inside of the bag is dark.

Inside the dark is fear. Inside the fear is a memory, one she has carried too heavy, a piece at a time, in all the chambers of her heart. Of the Hiding. The way memory can spring you back in the space of a moment.

In this memory, she is cradled in the warmth of her father's pickup. At a certain point in the workday, after taking a bite or two of a peanut butter sandwich and drinking some water, Laisvė had crawled up into the driver's side of the truck to look at things. Her baby brother was nearby, nestled in blankets on the floor behind the cab, sucking on a bottle, spit bubbles forming on his lips, eyes droopy with sleep.

She could see the workers quite clearly. The pickup truck was parked very close to their worksite, probably dangerously close, but Aster and Joseph needed to make sure they could see the truck, the rusted red beast holding the children inside. Most of the laborers were on the ground, working to complete a base about the height of six men stacked vertically. But it wasn't these laborers who had Laisvė's attention. Joseph was so high in the sky, he looked non-human, except that he walked across his rusted-orange iron beam one human foot at a time. Just below him, Aster was walking a different iron beam in the opposite direction. Each man had a rope tied around his body—secured to something, she imagined—but before she could puzzle out how the harnesses worked, she felt a spike of fever. Her vision doubled, then tripled, then blurred into a hot haze. But she did not close her eyes. Something was emerging, coming into focus, just as it might underwater. Her breath fogged the window of the truck.

Laisvė took her fist and rubbed a small portal through the fog on the window. Where first she had seen only her father and Joseph, now she saw Kem and David Chen, John Joseph, and Endora too, all swinging around the iron, the body of them in motion like an organism, sort of coming apart but also holding together, like bees in a honeycomb. David Chen the most graceful of all, swinging between beams, almost in flight, the people in and out of time, in and out of vision—and then she was with them or in them or something; she was so close, she could see the sweat on Joseph's biceps and forearms, the bite of Endora's jaw and her unruly hair and eyes, the blue cross on Endora's neck, and a hint of the white feathers crawling a bit up the neck of David Chen. She could see her father's eyes—only now they looked unusually deep, like pools or moon pods, not dead as they often were with the weight of loss and grief. The nexus of past and present and their bodies and their work—all these together, she realized somehow, *were* the fever in her. And a kind of calm came with it.

In the van, Laisvė smells the sweat of the uniformed men. Power smells like the sweat of men mixed with the scent of gunmetal. Laisvė thinks of how people often see danger where change is happening, and then her fear floats away.

In the van, she closes herself up.

The sweat of the men becomes the smell of salt.

The smell of salt becomes the possibility of an ocean.

She thinks, *I am in the belly of a whale.*

Since I am in the belly of a whale, I can go anywhere.

Imagine the bottom of the ocean, motherwaters.

No, don't imagine it. See it. *In this dark underneath this hood.*

Let loose your imagination.

The floor of this van is the belly of the whale.

There are no wheels or walls.

There are no men; the men in the van washed up on a shore somewhere,
thrown onto land from a wave.

Just baleen plates, sifting foreign matter out and nutrients in.

In the belly of the whale, she rests and rolls in wet.

The Water Girl and the Whale

L aisvė puts her hands on the inside wall of the whale and closes her eyes. A great humming emerges, threaded through the sounds of their travel. The humming vibrates through Laisvė's entire body.

"Have you ever swallowed a man?" Laisvė asks the whale.

"What on earth?" the whale responds. "No, I've never *swallowed a man*. That's absurd. Do you have a name, dear?"

"Liza. Do you?"

"Well, *Balaenoptera musculus*, but that's in your language. If you like, you can call me Bal. I think humans are comforted by names, isn't that right?"

Laisvė gives thought to the question. "Yes, I think names and naming do matter a lot. For good or bad. Also, I think names can slip their meanings."

The whale continues. "I see. You may be right about that. I'm not familiar with meaning-making gestures in your species—you seem so lost and angry all the time. Like you have no songs in you. Anyway, the mythology that we *swallow men*—that didn't come from us. That story emerged because the moment your kind catches sight of us a fear emerges in them from our so-called monstrous size, or maybe from a fear of drowning; and that fear needs someplace to go. Or that seems to be true of most humans, at least. The more interesting of you seem to be more inclined to see us as an instance of the sublime. Anyway, I've long understood that our size is the key. That's the whole idea of monsters, how you got from *monster* to *monstrosity*. You've turned my gaping mouth into an icon of danger even as I go on eating krill, not men, as I always have."

Laisvė looked around the belly of the whale: luminescent pinks and blues and grays, surfaces slick with digestive goo.

"Think about that," Bal said. "Krill! My teeth are not like daggers. They're more like enormous unruly hair. They're not even teeth, really—they're plates."

Laisvė stared at the roof of the whale, then out toward the baleen plates. "Yes," she said. "I know. They're filter-feeding systems. You take in water filled with krill, then push it back out in a great heave, so that the krill gets filtered by the baleen. I read that it's made from keratin. My fingernails and hair have keratin too."

"Girl, are you considered different from others on land?"

Again she gave the question silence and thought. "Yes. I think I am. That's one reason I need to be hidden. I think maybe I'm not quite right. I talk too much about too many things and sometimes I make mistakes. I read books from the library." She paused, caught by a memory. "I did read a story, once, about a whale swallowing a man. But I didn't . . . *believe* it, exactly."

"I see," said Bal. "Well, the evolution of my mouth began before you can imagine. Maybe in the Oligocene epoch, when Antarctica became more isolated from Gondwanaland and the West Wind Drift was formed. It's possible we had teeth then. Some stories say so. Some ancestors believe the stories. If so, our teeth must have evolved over many years into baleen. I don't know where teeth go across epochs. Have you read about the Antarctic Convergence, where the warm waters of the sub-Antarctic meet the cold water of the Antarctic? That stirs up nutrients and food chains for many species. Including the upwelling of krill. You see?"

Laisvė nodded.

"I'm thinking that all those stories about leviathans may have been connected to the evolution of teeth in my kind. So many stories. Always *swallowing men*."

Laisvė stood up. "In the Christian New Testament, Jonah appears at least twice. In the Gospels of Matthew and Luke. The 'sign of Jonah' is invoked by Jesus—it's a miracle, since he comes back to life after living for three days inside a whale."

"Can you picture that? Living inside a whale?" said Bal.

"Not until just now," Laisvė said.

"What's it like for you?" Bal asked.

"Amniotic," Laisvė said. "I am a very good swimmer. In Judaism, the Book of Jonah concerns a minor prophet included in the Tanakh. Jonah, in Judaism, was also swallowed by a giant fish and brought back to life. The Book of Jonah is read every year in Hebrew on Yom Kippur. In this story, the fish is said to have been of a primordial era. The inside of the fish was a synagogue, and the eyes were windows."

"That's not a bad metaphor," Bal said.

"In the Quran, Jonah appears as a prophet faithful to Allah. Dhul-Nun, or 'the one of the fish,' is swallowed by a big fish," Laisvė continued. "He stayed for a few days in the belly. A Persian historian named Al-Tabari wrote in the ninth century that Allah made the body of the fish transparent so that Jonah could see 'wonders of the deep.' He also reported that Jonah could hear the fish singing." She walked toward the front of Bal's cavernous gut. "I've always loved that image. A transparent whale."

Bal sighed hugely. Her gut shook and Laisvė fell onto her back. "So many stories. Heaped upon one another. I've never eaten a man. No whale that I know of, in any lineage, ever has. But the stories seem important to your species. Doesn't it seem strange, in all these years, that no one tries to learn the truth from the whales? I could tell you stories . . . the ones we tell about your lot, for instance. You wouldn't like them, though."

"I might," Laisvė said. "I am unusually fond of storytelling. Try me."

"Here's one. In 1830, in the waters off the island of Mocha near Chile, an albino sperm whale was killed. The whale was said to have more than twenty harpoons in his back. Sailors at the time described the whale as a ferocious monster. No one asked the whale. Or any whales around. At the time, your people called him Mocha Dick, after the island. You probably know him by another name, from a story about a monstrous whale. But we have a different story.

"Our story is about those twenty harpoons in his back, about the glow of his magnificent skin at night under the moon, about his son and his daughter and those kindred souls he swam with. How he led the great journeys through the Antarctic Convergence, where the roil of the waters stirs up nutrients for many species. Those twenty harpoons? To us, they were points in the night sky."

"You mean like an undiscovered constellation?" Laisvė asked.

"No, no. The constellations you people imagine are nothing to do with us. For us, the points in the night sky are like story maps."

"That white whale who carried the harpoons in his back . . . the stars in the sky are a map to where?" Laisvė asked.

"To our dying grounds. Where our bodies, as they decay, become the life source for other ocean species. And the white of the whale is understood as dying light, like stars, and the black of night, like the black of many whales, is seen as lighting the way for the living."

Laisvė's eyes stung with tears. "You mean like beacons or guides? Black light in the water?"

"Yes," Bal said. "Black is the cosmos. Creation. Life itself."

They moved in silence for some time.

"I've heard recordings of whale songs," Laisvė said. "They're not ferocious. They are beautiful."

Bal's voice inside the belly vibrated her whole body now. "Here is a story for you—about your species. We will all die, we whales. But your species will not care about the history we are carrying. You won't care how much older we are than you, how we care for and carry our dead, how we emerged from the time before time, how much older water and mountains and trees are than you. Your species will likely continue to obsess on things like whales being sea monsters, or black being dark or without light—or on idiotic economic things, like the fact that the Antarctic current helps preserve shipwrecks from wood-boring shipworms. You'll keep searching for buried treasure, at the bottom of the ocean, in the melting ice of Siberia, under the ground. You'll keep destroying yourselves.

"You will all die too, is the thing. But you haven't figured out how to make death-stories, and death-places, that have generative power."

Laisvė took the story into her body without flinching.

"Tell them I've never swallowed a man, will you, dear?" Bal said. "Tell them that, when whales die and sink to the ocean floor, our decaying bodies create life, just like your shipwrecks create a new habitat."

The whale paused a moment, then smiled. "I did once swallow a *girl*. But that story takes a hundred different forms, a hundred different songs. You can tell 'em that."

Aster's Wail

The holding tanks, made of metal, are underwater. Aster can see the soldering, can imagine the process as a metalworker. *So this is where they take us.*

Aster's anxiety about being underwater lives near his sternum. He thinks perhaps his *oh god* got stuck there—the *oh god* when his wife was shot and fell, the *oh god* of Laisvė's plunge from the ferry, the *oh god* of never again seeing his infant son.

And not only those: the *oh god* of Joseph's disappearance one night, the *oh god* of the air around Aster's life shifting forever.

Right now, though, what he knows is that he can't feel his feet. He wishes he could tell Joseph that the opposite of walking the iron is being at the bottom of the ocean, in an enormous puke-green steel tank with no windows and nothing to see except terrified people waiting to be taken away.

Taken where? There were rumors, but no one knew for sure, and no one ever came back. In place of all that nothingness, stories emerged.

Maybe the detained people scooped up in the Raids were executed, their bodies dumped as fish food out in the ocean. Who would know? Maybe people were taken to some other island or country or piece of the world, to be deposited like trash and set loose to evolutionary entropy. Wasn't Australia once a penal colony? Hadn't Laisvė recited all that to him once, listing it all off the way she did? And what happened to Joseph? Did he sit in a tank exactly like this one?

He looked at his own arm, hooked up to an IV next to his shitty rickety cot. He did not feel particularly drugged, so perhaps the IV was simply a saline solution to make him look briefly cared for. He studied the faces of the others around him—their faces all like gray deflated balloons in the halting artificial light, as if all trace of race, class, or meaning could be erased simply by draining a detainee of blood and agency. Every once in a while, a low and strange vibration shook the entire tank, shook the floor, shook their cots, shook their shoulders and hearts. It was the sound of more detainees arriving, or perhaps someone coming to take them out and away through a kind of side orifice in the holding tank. The uniforms on the men who handled the people made no sense to Aster. They weren't even uniforms, really, more like ad hoc military hand-me-downs, with boots. (Name your historical moment: there were always boots.)

Whatever happened next, he knew it would happen without his daughter unless he could get free of this place, and as his gaze traveled the walls of the holding tank, its ceiling as tall as a skyscraper, he thought of the story of James Bartley. Laisvė had been obsessed with the man, who was supposedly swallowed by a whale and survived. Aster knew well that the veracity of the story had faded with time, but Laisvė never lost interest in the story, the man, or whales. She had a kind of strange faith in their existence. She often drew pictures of the man inside the whale's belly, cooking dinner, caring for his daughter, as if the whale's belly were a room or a house.

"They say he was found bleached of skin from the whale's gastric juices," she said.

"That story isn't true, Laisvė."

"It is physically possible for a sperm whale to swallow a person whole. It is."

"But not for the body to survive inside," he said.

"How do you know? How would anyone know?"

And the question would hang suspended in the air between them—like most of her questions, which probably had answers but left him feeling lesser when he offered them.

Laisvė loved to tell Aster about whales. "When a whale dies in the ocean, it falls to the bottom and becomes a giant mound of food for fish, sharks, underwater animals. Some breach on the shore, or the half-eaten ocean carcasses wash up, which means more food for birds and other land creatures. Mammologists at the Royal Ontario Museum found a blue whale washed up in Newfoundland. They salvaged the heart by plastinating it."

"Is *plastinate* even a word?" Aster knew the answer; he was just trying to keep his daughter talking, keep her telling these stories that so delighted her. He knows that *plastinate* is a word thanks to Laisvė, who has already recited this story to him, explained the word and the process, showed him a photo of a whale heart in a book. In his head, he can hear her.

First, extract.

Then dilate.

Ship.

Plastinate.

Cure.

During the plastinate phase, the heart is submerged in acetone. Over time, all the water molecules leave the tissue. Then the heart is soaked in a silicone polymer solution and left in a giant vacuum chamber, which drops the atmosphere around the heart to conditions resembling those in space. The polymer fills the organ.

"When the heart finally emerges after it is cured, even the grimy little hands of children in museums couldn't penetrate the plastic-encased organ. Look! A blue whale heart is bigger than a person. You could actually climb inside one of the chambers."

How do you search for a daughter when the world wishes you were both swallowed up and gone?

Laisvė had always wanted to know who she was, where she came from, and he could not answer her. He put his face in his hands. He felt the concave of his eye sockets, the mound of his nose, the hair on his face, the slit of his mouth. *Where is my girl?* And then a fact he knew well, as well as his own face, maybe better: *She won't go to the safe house. She will go to water.*

Aster pulls the IV out of his arm, lets the line twirl and dangle like an umbilical cord. Blood, but not much; he holds a hand over it. He has no idea how long he has been in the holding tank, so he turns to the nearest person and asks. That person starts to cry. Aster leaves things alone.

When the Raid came, Aster was standing in the kitchen, cooking stew. He saw the cusp of winter through their window that day; soon they would be reinventing how to heat themselves, again calling on the best thing they had, their imaginations, to conjure survival. Heat bricks over fire in an alley. Wrap them in towels and put underneath bedcovers at night. Wear layers of newspaper or cardboard or plastic bags between your clothes and your coat.

Try not to have a seizure.

He saw snow, he remembers—the first flakes of snow, not yet fall-ing, blowing directionless in the air. Laisvė's red coat was hanging on a nail on the kitchen wall. When they came, she didn't even have time to grab the coat.

How will my daughter survive without her coat?

Did they track her and find her? Did they enter the throat of the crawl tube under the kitchen sink and climb down after her? He feels as if his own heart might stop, might plasticize in his chest like a petrified apple. Did they find strands of her hair in the tunnel, perhaps where it took a sharp turn? Was there the faintest trace of blood? Did she hit her head in her rush to crawl as fast as her hands and knees could carry her? Did she scrape her skull against the wall looking back over her shoulder for me? Did they find any pieces of her at all? A shoe?

Or one of her beloved objects?

A few cots away, another detainee—this one a small child—starts to cry. A boy, barely more than an infant, yet already beginning to take shape, the way children evolve. The tank holds the hearts of too many submerged children. Aster walks over to the boy, sits next to him, puts his arm around the smaller body, then cradles him.

Everything Aster knows about tenderness he learned from his friend Joseph Tekanatoken.

"You're the same age as my grandson," Joseph had told him over and over. Joseph who took him under his wing, Joseph with more lines in his face than a map, Joseph whose father and grandfather were neither Canadian nor American but who traversed nations for work, Joseph from the Haudenosaunee Six Nations ironworkers, generations who built most of the city's most famous buildings and bridges. Joseph from seven generations of Mohawks who walked the iron.

Joseph who disappeared in a Raid.

If Aster only knew who his ancestors were, he would have given that story to Laisvė. The men he worked with on the Sea Wall had taken him in because of a story he *made up* about his ancestors; Aster has no idea who his ancestors actually were. Maybe he was just a random man from nowhere, laboring on a massive ironwork, living illegally in this place, trying to feed his daughter.

She wanted to know who she was. He had no idea what story to tell.

He rubs the small back of the boy. The boy's crying gets swallowed up by other ambient sounds.

Aster's feet tingle. At the bottom of the holding tank, his body feels pressurized. His ears ache and his limbs are as heavy as lead. It isn't true that men who walk the iron are not afraid of heights. He can vouch for it. They just want work and are willing to do what others aren't to get it.

"In history and in the now," Joseph always reminded him. Aster's chest still convulsed every time he walked the iron. His hands still felt like a hundred butterflies alive in his fingertips. His legs still went numb. But his feet found the iron.

"Aster," Joseph often told him. "You could close your eyes and your feet would still find the iron." Then he'd add, "But goddamn, don't ever close your eyes, okay? Don't be a fucking idiot."

Who are men when they're untethered from fathers? From mothers? From daughters?

Is his son weightless inside, a floating boy somewhere out there in the world?

The boy beneath his hands—someone's, anyone's son—stops crying.

The Water Girl
and the Wail of Father

I know my father is nearing the surface of the water. I can feel him in my belly. Bal showed me how to feel the map between a belly and the stars.

I know what current to take to get there.

I know he's probably wondering what happened to me. But he's wondered that for a long time, ever since I first dove in after my mother.

The last thing I heard that day, before I dove into the water, was the wail of his voice. That's how I know how to find him now, by the vibration he carries in his body.

I don't know how old I am in this moment. It doesn't matter. Though I feel like I might be midlife inside my body. And anyway, in the belly of a whale, there is no time.

I don't know if my memory of the stories my mother told me is real, or if those memories are mixed-up fragments from my time carrying objects and turning time. I know that my mother was studying

Yakut, and the people of the ice forests of Siberia, when she met my father. My father had no idea if he was related to those people or not, but they acted like he might be. They were kind. They didn't treat him or any of us like outsiders. They helped my father to heal my mother when she was spit out of the prison.

So maybe the stories in my head are from her, or from the people we met there, or maybe they're mixed up with stories my father told me. Or maybe the stories just keep multiplying, accumulating from my own witness of animals and trees and objects and water, repeating and repeating in waves.

So know this: When I say I remember my mother, I could mean anything. When I say once I had an infant brother, I could mean anything.

The currents are fastest near Antarctica if you are traveling through the time portals west to east, the same as if you were on a ship.

Highways between buildings and cities are not like riverways or oceanic currents. Man-made highways don't lead to anything larger than themselves.

I do remember my mother telling me about Olonkho. The stories known as Olonkho are a collection of folktales from the Yakut. The Olonkho are like poem songs. Or like the singing I heard inside the whale belly. Or maybe like the sound I hear when I go to water, which has waves and repetitions I can't explain properly to anyone. Or maybe like at night, when I look up at the Pleiades and see a girl with a sieve measuring out star showers where other people see other things.

My mother told me that anyone who performed Olonkho had to be a truly great singer or actor or poet. Many Olonkho have more than twenty thousand verses. I've never even heard of anything that long recited from memory. Then again, memory is just making stories, like I said. I once asked my mother if she could sing one to me. She said no. To sing a true Olonkho, she said, could last up to eight hours. Some Olonkho could take more than a month to perform. She said they're not written down; that's when she explained to me what oral traditions were, and how they are handed down by mouth from generation to generation.

She said, *Just studying a thing isn't the same thing as being part of a thing.*

She said, *Don't take things that are not yours.*

She also said, *Step into stories at the places where they cross each other, at the cruces. Bring gifts. Let go of them.*

I asked her if we could make one up. Our own pretend epic story. She laughed. When she laughed, her eyes made little wrinkles and I always wanted to climb into her lap then. To be inside her laughing. Inside her voice. Inside her body. All I remember about the story we started making together is the beginning.

The girl fish loved her water life, swimming with currents and against currents and rolling around onto her back and flipping her tail and breaching briefly midair with a sky twirl, suspended like an idea before plunging back into the deep-water world. There was nothing better than being a girl fish and there never would be. She lived in a building made from amber, with other girl fish, with turtles and whales and dolphins and seahorses and starfish.

We even made sure to sing it, and so we changed it a little every time we sang it, which didn't matter, because that was part of the performance.

But that was as far as we got. Before my mother went to water.

My father's wail is louder now. I think we must be close.

Traveling in a dark van and traveling in the belly of a whale and slipping across time and space are all very similar. To be a girl inside the gut of something bigger than you is a form of adaptation. Your body moving from one form to another.

Think of an object of great value sinking, slipping, moving through water. Sunken treasures have a way of rearranging the story. A ship at the bottom of the sea folds gently over into sand and barnacle and sea-creature ecosystems, losing its former worth and moorings, for a ship is built to float. Its sinking is a kind of failure—and yet, when someone finds the sunken thing, new value emerges. The ship changes forms when it goes from sailing the surface to wrecked at the bottom. The wreck changes forms after the dead people disintegrate and the cargo settles to sand.

For a time, unless the wreck is discovered, no one owns anything. The fish find homes and hiding places. Radar sweeps can take years to detect the great masses driven off course. Whole histories, life stories, and meanings fall away from existence, only to be rediscovered and attached to the new stories we make up because we need things to mean something besides nothing. We need human history to mean something. We need the things we do with our hands to mean something, not nothing. We need the sunken treasure to mean that something of human value, once lost, is found again; that something of ourselves has been salvaged and brought back in pieces to the surface; that something we thought dead and gone yet holds life. Delicate truths, delicate artifacts.

Fish need nothing from ships.

Whale bodies become a life source for fish and other ocean life when they decay.

I don't know what happens, over time, to dead mothers at the bottom of the ocean. Or to brothers who float away.

We never finished making the story. Our mother-daughter story.

I can feel my father nearby now, inside the belly of a holding tank. Like a heartbeat inside a giant metal container.

When we arrive, I ask Bal to rest on the ocean floor.

She does.

We hold as still as a sunken statue.

"Memory is proof that imagination is a real place," Bal says.

The whale's body begins to dissolve, the walls of her gut begin to shimmer and soften and liquefy, until I am surrounded by the cage of her rib bones. Then the rib bones rise, slowly, with me embedded inside them, up and up from the ocean floor toward the surface. Colors go from black blue to deep blue to green blue and then a kind of indigo before what was the rib cage turns into the hull of a boat on the surface of the water.

The boat has a hull sturdy enough for passengers, blankets, and food and water. It is a kind of ferry between epochs. This carrier, like the whale, is and is not a boat. It is an allegory and it is real. I understand that now—what my mother taught me, what Bal said. How a story can be anything at any moment if we need it badly enough.

"May the boat travel well across time and space," I say up into the night sky. I think I can see the white whale's star map.

A small distance away from me, I see a great plume of aquamarine bubbling up on the surface. The gush of water is also a gush of bodies. Some of the bodies are alive; they thrash and squirm and yell. Some are dead; they float facedown with a melancholic serenity. Some of the bodies begin to sink; others are drubbing around to save themselves. I see a man trying to hold a young boy up so that the boy does not drown. I see the man's gasping and struggling, I see the boy's fear in his eyes.

Then I see that the man is my father.

As I row toward him, I sing the song my mother and I made up, inventing new words with each stroke. When I reach him, my father is crying amid the salt water, amid the sinking bodies around us. "*Svajonė, Svajonė*," he wails. In his drowning, he must see me as my mother.

And then, "Laisvė!"

I can tell his strength is leaving. I can see he is on the verge of drowning. I climb down a rope ladder on the side of the boat. "Kick your legs! Hard," I yell. My father looks like he is beaten by the water, but he is beating it back with his legs. Once my father is close enough to me, he lifts the baby boy above the water with both arms. With his last breath, he finds the strength to hand me the floating boy. He is right, the boy is heavy.

For a moment, my father and I lock eyes. The water between us calms. I reach out to him. He just stares at me, barely treading water. I say, "Father?"

"Laisvė, my love. My life." He gurgles barely above the water's swell, "This is the end of my story. The beginning of yours. I love you. Let me go to her. Svajonė. Let go."

I remember my mother's words: *You cannot save your father. You cannot save your brother.*

I remember the strength of dreams and water and stories, how they move differently: repetitions and associations, images and accumulations, fragmentations and displacements.

I feel Aster surrender to the gentle fall of the water. When I can no longer see him, when the image of Aster's hands and arms and face are lost to dark water, I look up.

So many stars. Constellations that seem to come apart for a moment, then reunite, then part again. I close my eyes and reopen them. Suddenly, the stars seem to stitch new stories across the sky.

I put the toddler in the hull of a boat. I wrap a blanket around this child and ask the boat to hold it in its belly. I speak a prayer for protection up to the white whale stars in the sky.

Then I dive down after my father.

Motherwaters

F ear is not with me on this journey. For to enter the depths has become a part of living a life. The baby I left on the boat is a floating boy. The descent I make now is toward father. At the bottom of the ocean, mother. Between them, my life, like a language you can endlessly rearrange.

In the ocean, bubbles rise like a second skin around my body. The water goes from dark green, to indigo blue, to midnight. The deeper I go, the more I enter a realm between light and dark. When I reach the floor of sand, tiny flickers of color blink and glide around me. Silver and blue fish make their undulations in huge schools. Underwater hills and valleys rise and fall. A glorious aquamarine and green octopus with hot-pink suckers on her tentacles slithers around coral and disappears into a rock cave. Neon-green anemones and red-stained starfish clutch geoformations, looking like decorations. Purple urchins and tube coral the color of rose blush dot rocks. The bell shapes of orange and blue giant jellyfish dangle their tentacles and oral arms like fluid lace as they pass by me.

What if home is this?

Why wasn't I born to it? Why was I made to leave the lifewaters? Couldn't I have been left like a creature from a fairy tale to inhabit a story?

My own hair sways before my face, black seaweed. Something is coming. A shape as big as a man. I part my own hair like a curtain. "Hello, Aster."

"Hello, my beloved," my father responds.

Aster does not look drowned. He looks as he did in life, weighted with grief, handsome but lost. The water between us brings him in and out of focus.

"May I bring you back to life?" I ask my father, although I can tell he is already in an afterdrowned place. I don't know if I can revive him on any surface.

"I want to show you something," Aster says, and he holds out his hand.

I take his hand underwater, there on the sea floor. We walk slowly. It is not possible for humans to do anything underwater quickly. We've lost our tails and skill. Our bipedalism keeps putting us upright. We walk some distance. Two seals tease a playful visit in my periphery, circling each other. Something looms ahead of us. At first, I think it's a whale, but it is not.

As we approach, I make out the shape: some enormous sunken shipwreck.

"This is the SS Oregon," Aster says, his voice reverberating. "In March of 1886, just fifteen miles from landing, the ship crashed into a schooner. There were only enough lifeboats for half of its 852 passengers. Another ship arrived shortly after the crash, so the passengers were saved, but the ship sank here. Until that moment, she was the fastest liner on the Atlantic."

I can see what's left of the hull and the iron frame of the decks. I can see the engine standing about twelve meters above the ocean floor, I can see several of the ship's boilers, the propeller, the masts. The iron is covered with ghostly purple, green, and gray anemones. Small striped fish swerve in and around the carcass of her. Sea bass and blue cunners navigate the maze of sea fans and coral. Mussels line the shipwreck's bones, strange thumb ridges. Limpets and barnacles adorn the spokes of the helm.

"Beautiful." I sigh, not knowing what else to say. Aster is smiling. I try *to remember other times I saw him smiling. With peace. I cannot. I start to ask him a question, but my mother appears, standing next to him, and I think maybe my heart swallows everything about me. Standing there together, they look wed.*

Wet, I mean. Beautifully wet.

"There are more than three million shipwrecks spread across the planet," I add. "They carry history."

"Hello, Laisvè," my mother says.

Whatever happens next, I know that I will be leaving the water alone again. This time, truly alone. But I also know that there is a floating boy in a boat above us, and I will not abandon him, even though my heart feels like it is rising up my throat into my mouth.

"Is there a story?" *It's all I know to ask.*

"Yes," my mother says. "My love, listen carefully. A tsunami is coming that will raise the waters even higher—"

"Tsunami—it means 'harbor wave' in Japanese," I say, reaching back into my memory library. "But that's not entirely accurate. A tsunami has nothing to do with harbors. Some people call them tidal waves, but that's wrong too. Tsunamis have nothing to do with the tides, or the moon or the sun . . ." *It's hard to breathe. A world of words and images scrolls through my head: migration histories. The face of Bertrand. The voice of Bal. My brother as a baby. The laughs of worms.*

"Do not be afraid, Laisvè. You're right, my dearest. About the waves. These waves will destroy the rest of The Brook. They'll destroy the Sea Wall too. But anything de-storied can be re-storied. These waves will reshape the order of things. But you are not part of the ending."

"When will it happen?"

"It's happening now, my soul. Do not be afraid."

The sea floor lurches and vibrates. "I left a baby boy in the boat; I have to go—"

"It's okay, Laisvè, love, the boat is also a whale. The floating boy is safe.

The whale is descending. You'll want to take the beautiful baby boy to the place where lilies meet the dawn. There you need to collect a different boy, a young man who is on the verge of creating new life—you have done so well, my love. You are so brave."

"Who is this different boy? Is he a boy or a young man?"

"Everything about him is in his hands. He is not like other people. He doesn't think like other people; he doesn't speak or act like other people. He is misunderstood. He's trapped in a time and place that cannot understand him. In that liminal space between boy and man. Like you are, between girl and woman."

The sea floor undulates. Not violently. Gently.

"Is he like me?" My chest tightens. There's never been a girl like you—*that's what my mother told me when she was alive. I don't think she understood how heavy that would be to carry alone.*

My mother stares at me. Her eyes glow very blue. Is it love, her eyes?

"A little," she says. "Yes. The two of you both understand how water moves, how water will change the story. Sometimes you have to believe that people can yet be moved, even when it seems that they cannot. You both understand things differently, not the way other people do."

Aster comes close to me now. He is still smiling. His smile is like a new word that has never been said. As if he's entered a dream he never has to leave. A good dream. His smile is the answer.

I put my hand up to his face, his cheek. "Aster, is this your seizure place?"

"Laisvè, my perfect daughter," he says, and I hear in his voice for the first time the absence of grief. I hear a giving way. "Do not be afraid. We are with you into the everything. We are in the air and the water and the earth, the plants and the animals. We are even in the night sky; we are made from everything in the cosmos. We arrive, we leave, we emerge, we dissolve. We are in the meteor, in this tsunami, in all the bones of whales on the floors of the world's oceans. All the fish and creatures, all the roots and branches of trees, everything reaching into everything else."

Is it love, what Aster says? I think this may be love. A great swelling of the sea that overtakes every story we have been told. The chance for a different story to emerge. Godless, and filled with animals and rearranged history pieces and the motion of elements.

"I love you. I think—" I say to them. Beautiful Aster and Svajonė.

The story of a star and a dream.

When I leave them, I enter the great waterways as a carrier, untethered from time and space. Perhaps I was meant to be a sea creature after all, but some slippage, some cosmic rupture, sent me through my mother's body and spat me out on land like a wave throwing rocks onto the shore. Leaving me something like a marine mammal, or a terrestrial fish, or some creature from a folktale.

I think some people slip time and enter a life wrongly—or, if not wrongly, at least formed differently, mismatched with the material conditions around them. I do not think any god with some odd intention put them where they are. I think that beings emerge and decompose endlessly, like cosmic or oceanic particles, so whoever we are and wherever we were emerges and dissolves endlessly, like all matter and energy.

The innocence of children is the most complex system on the planet. We've simply gotten the story wrong, and thus raised legions of wrongly dispatched beings. We pretended that "innocent" meant "without sin." But that's not what innocent children born into this world think. No one asks us what we think.

Once I killed a boy to save another. The killing was easy, compared to blind cruelty.

Once, in the river water as it moved toward the sea, I asked Bertrand if he believed in god. He said, "What do you mean by 'god,' girl?" I said, "Some divine creator or creators, not wanting to give special privilege to any religious cosmology."

Bertrand said, "What if I told you there's a magical teapot between Earth and Mars, a teapot revolving around the sun, and that all life on this planet emerged one day from that teapot, poured out like tea? And what if a whole group of kooks got together and decided to formalize the story of this invisible teapot and, worse, to develop their own set of rules and laws of behavior based on their theories of teapot logic?"

"That just sounds stupid," I said. "There's no magical teapot in the sky."

"Exactly," Bertrand said. "This god business is absurd. It's a fiction untethered from matter and energy. It's got you all mucked up out there. I fear for your species. I always have. You keep looking up or down and inventing all manner of nonsense when everything about existence is neither up nor down, but always in motion and rhythm, all existence connected in waves and cycles and circles. I don't mean to be rude, but your species is . . . well, not the smartest shrimp in the sea.

"By the way, I told the worms you were coming. Don't be surprised if they're grumpy. Worms aren't too happy with the state of things lately."

The whale returns. Her body brings a beautiful black glow to everything. A black shimmer everywhere. She gently opens her mouth and swallows me away from Aster and Svajonė, from their beautiful story. Through her baleen plates, before they close, I can see them; they hold each other close—a father, a mother—then dissolve. The baby boy is safe and sound inside the belly of the whale. After a few days of travel, the whale becomes a boat again, carrying us in her hull, ignoring human ideas of time and space, bringing us back to the surface of the world, where the sun is coming up and the lilies are blooming inside a different story.

Joseph and the Whale

The first time I met Laisvė, she was twenty years old. I was twenty years old. I know, you'll say that's not possible. Just let me tell the story, okay? Stories are quantum.

She was the most beautiful anything I'd ever seen, with the possible exception of a corn snake. Corn snakes, man, they have it bad. They often get mistaken for copperheads even though corn snakes are harmless to humans. They kill their prey by hugging them to death—ha! I mean constriction, of course. But I digress.

Laisvė's skin the color of desert sand and her eyes a clear blue and her crazy black hair falling down her shoulders in unkempt waves.

At the time, I was living with my father, Flint, near a grain store. My father and I worked together on the early iron frame of the Sea Wall. We walked the iron up top. I don't know if anyone understood fully how bad things were about to get; maybe we did, maybe not. The last great collapse was on the horizon. The great Water Rise. We heard about Raids here and there, to sweep refugees away, but not on any mass scale. Still, the signs were there—even about my father. One morning, one of the carabiners on his ropes failed and he dropped about eighty feet from the top beam we were working on. Right next to me. I mean, he fell like a stone, then jerked to a stop as the harness caught his fall, then dangled and swung. I saw the whole thing. There wasn't time to be shocked, it happened so fast. But the image of him falling stuck with me. Like a felled bird, his arms outstretched, his back wide and strong.

The rats and mice were plentiful in our cabin next to the grain store; the corn snake was fat and so orange that I swear it glowed in the dark. Corn snakes are docile. They don't like to bite unless they have to. The oldest corn snake in captivity lived to be more than thirty years old.

That corn snake was gorgeous. But no, not as gorgeous as this young woman walking into our cabin. She said, "Are you Joseph?"

My father named me after my ancestor John Joseph. Our families all originate with a female ancestor, but I never knew any of mine. My mother left my father when I was five, so I don't think of her as an ancestor; I don't think of her sisters, her sister's daughters, or any of their daughters as ancestors either. I don't know where any of those women are. Maybe the women leaving is why there are so many of us Josephs. I don't know.

Living with men made a bitterness in me, but it was a bitterness I could trust. No one brought us into a longhouse to live. My father and I lived in a shack he built near the grain store. My father told me about my ancestor, John Joseph. He said that John Joseph was the best sky walker anyone ever knew. My father and I both walked the iron; our skill probably came from John Joseph, I don't know.

Anyway. That night I was taking off my muddy boots to leave in the mudroom at the front of the cabin. First, I caught a glimpse of the snake. "Hey, snake," I said, and I swear she smiled. But then I saw something moving that wasn't the snake. It was a young woman walking into the mudroom. So I said, "Hey," again, still taking off my shoes, trying to act cool.

She asked if I was Joseph, and I nodded. Then she said, "Throw water on me."

I just minded my shoes. Didn't look up or anything. Finished my business. When I finally looked up, I tried not to look too interested. I mean, maybe this girl was crazy. Maybe she had a weapon. She had something in her hand for sure, clenched in a tight fist. Finally, I replied: "Why the fuck would I want to throw water on you?"

"Well, it's a fast way to figure out if I can trust you or not," she said.

I sat there and stared at her for a bit. She didn't look crazy. She looked beautiful. I could see her better now, half in moonlight, half in shadow. Jesus, man, I was tired. We'd worked our asses off that day. I knocked off before Flint, walked home on legs so tired they felt like someone else's. I probably stank too. "You don't think you can trust me? Ask the snake," I said, gesturing to the corn snake. Then I pulled my shirt off. I had the intention of going to the outdoor shower. I stood up and began to walk toward the back of the cabin.

"I need to tell you something," she said, following me.

"Is that so," I said, not looking back.

"Yes. I need to make a trade with you. My mother told me to find you. She told me you're a member of the Haudenosaunee Confederacy. People of the Longhouse."

"Uh-huh," I said.

"My mother was a linguist. I love histories that live underneath history."

"History. Okay. Right."

I reached the shower stall and opened the chest-high wooden door. Once inside, I took off my pants and draped them over the door. I eyeballed the knife in the shower, just to remind myself where it was. She just kept talking. Almost like she couldn't stop.

"I've read all the names, if you don't believe me. Mohawks, People of the Flint; Oneidas, People of the Upright Stone; Onondagas, People of the Hills; Cayugas, People of the Great Swamp; Senecas, People of the Great Hill; Tuscaroras, the Shirt-Wearing People. I know about the clan mother structure. Oldest participatory democracy on earth." She stopped talking and stared at the snake.

It was weird listening to her recite all that at me. I have no idea who her ancestors were, though she was definitely in the ballpark with mine. But me and my father were laborers—urban workers, city people, more than we were anything else anymore. We didn't talk about ancestors much. Besides, how is anyone supposed to know who they are anymore? As I listened to her, the words seemed like they might belong to me and my body, even though they were coming out of her mouth and her body. Ordinarily, I would have just ignored her, because typical white person ignorant gibberish. But I couldn't tell if this girl was white or what; she looked like she was from someplace else.

Then she came over to the wooden shower door and peeped over the top. "Are you the first people?" she asked.

Whoever the fuck this girl was, she had strong-ass orenda.

I finished washing off and put my pants back on. (Ordinarily, I would have walked naked back to the cabin but, well, this woman with all the words was here.) When I opened the door to the shower, I noticed her squatting down to talk to the corn snake.

"Snake, you are neither of the sky world nor of the underwater world below," she said. "You are of the earth, floating on the back of a turtle. Bertrand told me."

The snake didn't say anything. Or, if she did, I didn't hear it. (I did bring the knife in with me, though.)

I let her follow me into the cabin. I wondered where my father was; it was past time for him to be home from work. In the kitchen, I took an apple from a bowl on top of the refrigerator, then pulled the knife out of my pants pocket and cut it in half. When I handed her half, she pulled out a smaller knife of her own, cut her half into smaller pieces, and fed one to the snake.

Even if this woman was crazy, I'd decided, she was okay.

We ate our apple pieces looking at the floor. My hair hung wet on my back, cooling my body from the heat of the day's work.

"I have a trade to make you," she said.

I didn't say anything. The snake uncurled and recurled herself in a corner.

Finally, she opened up that clenched fist of hers. She was holding some kind of coin—not shiny but dark; maybe dirty, maybe old.

"What kind of trade?" I said.

She started whispering, some kind of list, her words aimed at no one.

"The Flowing Hair cent. The Liberty Cap cent. The Draped Bust cent. The Classic Head cent. The Coronet cent. The Braided Hair cent. The Flying Eagle cent. The Indian Head cent. The first Lincoln penny."

Then she turned back to me. "Some stories say that the figure on this penny is meant to be a woman in an Indian headdress," she said, handing me the coin.

"Indian Head penny," I said. "Yeah, that's some bigoted shit, isn't it?" Then I rubbed it and looked more closely at it. The year read 1877. "Hey, is this worth anything?"

"Not as much as the Flowing Hair cent," she said. "At the time it was born, everyone says the cent woman looked insane." She walked over to me till she was standing a little too close. Her hair smelled like night. Her eyes were the color of water. Her shoulders underneath my height made me want to touch them. I could feel her beauty in my jaw. No, not beauty like you're thinking of it in other women. It was more a beauty from the inside. A beauty screaming.

"I'll give it to you," she said. "I'll give you the whole collection—if you lie down with me. Now. Tonight."

I took a step back. "Collection? What collection?"

"Your father isn't coming home," she said.

My heart started pounding.

She started to take off her dress, a dress I could now see was covered in indigo flowers. The flowers seemed to quiver, or maybe that was just my eyes playing tricks on me. I was about to try to stop her, but . . . my god. Her body. Her collarbones. The barely-there dip between her breasts. The skin of her belly, so soft that it looked like sand-colored velvet. Her hips. And down to the dark hair covering her sex or leading me down and in. And that goddamn coin. Which she put on the kitchen table. And then another—the crazy-hair-lady coin. She started pulling coins from her hair, one and then another and another, until coins were falling to the floor all around us. Where were they all coming from?

Then she got on top of the kitchen table. I eased my pants off my hips and down my thighs and over my knees, which, goddamn, were shaking some. Pulled my feet free. Climbed onto her. Coins everywhere.

On top of her, I could see the snake in the corner birthing her eggs. The piles of coins at our feet were growing all around us. The air smelled like copper and our sweat.

She was right; my father never came home. Not that night, not the next day, not for the weeks she stayed with me. He had fallen. He had died.

The grief and loss were as heavy as iron. He was all I had. He was a son of a bitch most of the time, but he was my son of a bitch. And

he was the best iron walker there was. Ask anyone. The only one
greater might have been my grandfather, John Joseph, but I never
met him. He was just a story.

She said, "I will enter desire with you inside your loss. I will carry
it with you inside our lovemaking until you can breathe again. Grief
is an object you have to carry over time, like a body. Someday, you
will be able to take care of me and my father in return."

One night, as we lay coiled around each other, I asked her how she'd
known what had happened to my father. This is the story she told.

"There was a whale." She drew small objects on my chest with her
finger. I could feel her speech and breath on my skin.

"I was in the current, on my way to an otherwhere, and the whale
swallowed me. After I scraped my way beyond the baleen, and crawled
across the tongue, and made my way down the tunnel of the whale's
throat, I could hear the whale's voice vibrating the whale gut as well
as my whole body. The whale was singing. Inside the whale's belly,
she carried me through the Antarctic current. I could hear the speed
of things in the walls of her. The vibrations shook my whole body.
We made our way through water. After a while, she stopped and
vomited me out.

"I made the rest of my way through water to children. Then the
whale became a boat. Then we came to my father, Aster."

"The whale became your father?" I asked, her head against my
skin and shoulder. I wanted her to become my body—I wanted to
forge her to me, to solder our bodies together.

"No," she said. "I mean, my father's people . . ." But then she fell
silent and licked my nipple instead of finishing her sentence. She
straddled me.

"What about your father's people?"

"I was going to tell you something about the Yakut, about Yakutia, but that's just a story I could tell. Truth is, my father doesn't have

any people—as far as he knows, as far as I know. There are a hundred stories I could tell. One of them is about how the prisoners were rounded up in Yakutia, and about the long Road of Bones, where tens of thousands of prisoners were sent to gold mines and work camps and gulags in Siberia. More than a million laborers and prisoners traveled the Road of Bones. Geologists looking for gold deposits are still finding piles of soggy coffins and decaying bones. Everything there is resting on bones."

I put my hands on her hips, then her breasts.

"Isn't everything everywhere resting on bones?" I said.

"Yes, the past gets buried like that, and then comes back when people least expect it. Like ice melting away. Or water rising. The Indigenous death toll in this land, where we are, was probably more than thirteen million, but that's not the story that got told."

She leaned over me. Mouthed shapes on my neck. Her hair keeping the rest of the world out of sight.

"You are going to meet my father. When you're an older man, I mean. My mother told me. You're going to meet me again too, only I'll be younger, just a girl. I know, I know. Don't be afraid or confused. My father and my baby brother and I—when you're older, you're going to take care of us for a little while, like I'm taking care of you now. I am carrying you through this grief so that you don't die or become terrible. Your father is gone. My father will die too. Everyone goes back to the motherwaters eventually. Then becomes something else."

Laisvė stayed for a month. When she told me she'd be leaving, I gave her my knife. An object to carry, to prove we were real.

The next time I saw Laisvė—the second time—she was a child, just like she'd told me. Her father was frantically looking for work and somewhere to stay. And I was an older man. There was a baby boy too, but that story took a very sad turn.

When I met Aster, I wasn't entirely sure it was her. But I knew Aster was a man who needed help, like a boy who'd lost his parents. I could feel it radiating out of him. Turns out, he'd lost his whole heart. He was gutted, living a kind of ghost-life. From what I understood, his wife had drowned, and his boy would float away, and there is just no way for a body to bear that weight. I understood I should love him. I mean, for fuck's sake, whatever *love* means.

Love isn't what we've been told it is.

Time isn't either.

What it amounts to is, I met that young woman, I met that girl, out of order. Stories don't care how we tell them. Stories take any shape they want. Not all stories happen with a beginning, a middle, and an end. I've come to understand maybe they never do. End, that is.

I remembered something about my own mother when Laisvė left that first time. I remembered her saying to me, *This is not the end of your story. It is the beginning.*

Over the years, I always thought that Laisvė must have wanted a baby—that that's why she came to me when I was twenty and she was a young woman. I even wondered if maybe she got pregnant when she was with me. But when I met her again as a child, I saw the error in that story. She didn't want to have a baby.

I know because of something that happened when I met her again, when she was a girl. One morning, I was drinking coffee and Aster was showering and Laisvė was standing near the front window looking out at I don't know what. I started wondering aloud about what she wanted to do, or be, when she grew up. "Someday you'll fall in love," I said. "Maybe start a family." I don't know why I said that. Maybe because of the piece of her future that I'd seen, or maybe just how her mess of black hair fell down her back and the way her shoulders squared off against the light from the window. She didn't know what a beautiful young woman she would turn out to be.

She turned around and looked at me. "That right belongs to the planet, to plants and animals," she said.

"What right?" I asked.

"The right to make a family. Species, genome, family . . ."

I'll admit, I worried for her after that. I wasn't sure of how she was in the head, of how she could possibly deal with it all. But when she came into my life with Aster, and I was an older man, I could not have loved them more. What else was there to do but love them? It was my turn to take care of something besides myself.

Ethnography 5

I started working at *The Crisis* in 1918. I worked under Jessie Redmon Fauset. What a time that was. The novels she would write changed my life. Her characters were Black working men and women—professionals. She was more than a mentor to me. So much more. She was a mirror I could use to see myself; she was a portal I could step through to something more. She wanted literature to split open so that more voices and stories and bodies could get through—forging a second passage as proud and profound artists. She birthed and nourished so many important voices: Langston Hughes. Countee Cullen. Claude McKay. Jean Toomer. Zora Neale Hurston. Arna Bontemps. Charles Chesnutt. Her younger half brother Arthur Fauset, the folklorist and activist.

I worked hard for Jessie. I proofread and typed up notes and just swam inside the ocean of her creative and editorial waters. As she started writing for *The Brownies' Book*, the children's magazine, I worked with her on that too. Nothing is more important than giving children stories they can grab on to and live by. Stories about gender, race, class, pride; stories that inspire children, that show them where they came from. For years, Jessie created the large majority of the content in *The Brownies' Book*. Its pages were filled with African folktales. Before I had that job, most of the stories I read about Black girls were about slavery, or rape, or violence against Black women and girls. But even the advertising in *The Brownies' Book* was devoted to education, schools, training classes, colleges, and universities.

Sometimes it seemed to me that Jessie did the work underneath everything that was gleaming on the surface of our lives. You know, like how mothers do. Like she was a creativity mother, but she was also an intellect—an intellectual mother. Sometimes, when I think about what work is, I think of that—how there is no place that recognizes "mother" as a form of employment, recognizes how many women mother us back to life.

Epistle

Cruces 6

S ometimes photographers came to document our labor, to capture our motion in a stilled image.

At first, we might have felt seen. Once, when her hand was still plaster but not yet covered with copper skin, we gathered around it, posing like children. We looked so small there, next to her enormous hand, but without our labor, she would never have been born, so standing together there made us become, in that moment, a single body. The photos were made into postcards, which were sold—another means of financing the project. Our names were not attached to our bodies, but when we looked at the postcards, we could see how tall we were standing next to our work. The organism of us. My name—Kem—never appeared in any story. Nor did the names Endora or David or John Joseph.

But the photographs were not about who we really were, or our labor, or our lives; they were about the story she was becoming, the spectacle. Sometimes newspaper stories would make their way to us.

We read and heard many insults against her, even as we were still building her. One in particular stood out to me, from the *Cleveland Gazette*: "Shove the Bartholdi statue, torch and all, into the ocean until the 'liberty' of this country is such as to make it possible for an inoffensive and industrious colored man in the South to earn a respectable living for himself and his family, without being ku-kluxed, perhaps murdered, his daughter and wife outraged, and his property destroyed."

None of us said anything out loud when the insults and challenges came, but those words went into our bodies alongside our labor, and we ground them into us, maybe the way the bodies of the people who built the pyramids were ground up into the stone and grain and blood of the structures.

I told Endora and John Joseph and David about the *Cleveland Gazette* story one day, after it lodged itself in my dreams. I started to have nightmares about Black bodies in boats. I didn't want the images to take over my life. My father and his father and his father had moved through slavery stories, had carried them forward like the bodies of sons.

I thought about the revolution in my country that no one here ever told stories about. How self-liberated Haitians had fought successfully to overturn French colonial rule. I thought about John Joseph and his stories of genocide perpetrated under the brutal cover story of discovery. How his ancestors' stories got buried like bones. I thought about Endora being haunted by a dead infant buried in the ground next to her church in Ireland—how many babies were likely buried in that ground, how at night the wind and dark were their only solace. I thought about the scars on David's back, how I wished I could tongue them away.

Could we ever become part of the story of this place? Or was something always slipping away?

I thought about the girl who had come from the water, and the

woman we were building between the water and god. Then it occurred to me that I had never met grace in any god like the grace in
David, Endora, and John Joseph. God was just a story.

The day her body became a freestanding statue, a joy got into all
of us. But so did a sadness. Looking up at this body we'd built with
our hands and arms and legs and sweat and hearts—it opened up our
throats a bit, stretched and stiffened our spines. Seeing her gaze out
across the water made our chests open up, as if that were something
hearts could do, as if you could just open your arms to the universe
and sky and tilt your head up and open your mouth, and suddenly
your heart would be something more than a muscled-up fist pump-
ing in your chest. As if the beating of all our hearts might be something different than the life of one person.

The day before she was presented to the world, with pomp and
presidential speeches and tickets sold to well-dressed onlookers and
wealthy businesspeople, the body of us climbed off the last scaffold-
ings back to the ground. We spent the night before her birth cele-
brating beneath her shadow, with beer and wine and chocolate and
music and rabbit stew and potatoes and sausages cooked over open
fires, and puddings, breads, and cakes; we the body filled time and
space with dancing of a hundred different kinds, so much dancing, to
fiddles and guitars, pipes and harmonicas and concertinas and drums
of all sorts, a singing made from everywhere we came from in waves
of voices. Howling deep into the night. The sparks from the fire rose
up toward the sky; our voices made bridges between people and land
and water and animals and trees. Some of us slept right there on the
ground, drunk on one another's bodies, drunk on the end of things.

But it turned out that it wasn't the end of things.

Is there ever an end to things?

For us, the statue stood unfinished, in a way. Or maybe what I
mean is, she stood always on the verge of becoming.

My dearest cousin Frédéric,

I have nostalgia for apples. The story of our becoming! I have thus included in this letter reproductions on a theme: the Fall of Man.

My three favorite paintings of the Fall of Man are Jan Brueghel de Oude and Peter Paul Rubens, The Garden of Eden with the Fall of Man; *Hendrick Goltzius,* The Fall of Man; *and Michelangelo,* The Fall of Man. *In that order.*

My choices are due to the arms and bodies of the women, although my most beloved of all has a singular feature that distinguishes it from the rest: the animals. In the shared gaze of Brueghel and Rubens, the humans are no more visually important than the animals and trees. And the snake looks like a snake, the apple like an apple, the woman like a woman.

Second place goes to Goltzius, because the woman's back and arms are strong. As strong as a man's. Her sexuality is not foregrounded— and the little-girl face on the snake? I must admit it makes me laugh. I know I should be outraged, but it delights me. And the tiny apple! What idiot would condemn a species for eating such a diminutive . . . what is it, anyway? A crab apple? Be serious. The cat does look pleased though, as cats do.

Third place goes to Michelangelo. My god. Have there ever existed more masculine women than his? She could take Adam in a wrestling match. Even his snake exhibits feminine musculature. The split image, the not-quite-a-diptych composition, fascinates me to no end. Both the snake and the avenging angel appear as branches of the knowledge tree. But my obsession with this painting rests on a missing element.

There is no apple.

In Michelangelo's vision, the tree is a fig tree on its fruit-bearing side, and an oak on the punishment side.

In the fourth century AD, a scripture scholar named Jerome was tasked with translating the Hebrew Bible into Latin. This endeavor turned out to take fifteen years. The word for evil and apple, in Latin, was the same: malum.

However, in the Hebrew Bible, the fruit might be any fruit on the planet, because the word peri in Hebrew is a generic term. Peri is not an apple, not necessarily: It could just as easily be an apricot. A grape. A peach. A pomegranate. A fig. (Am I incorrect about the specifics? Perhaps. But you see what I am getting at.)

I don't know if I am correct about this, but I do believe that Albrecht Dürer was the first to paint the tree as an apple tree— which, to be clear, makes nearly no sense. And that moron Milton codified the apple as the sinful fruit of women in his Paradise Lost, *a book I have repeatedly thrown across the room. In many ways, the story is one of our teeming wriggling thriving city, our capitalist drive and thrust, complete with a snake-oil salesman.*

What is behind desire—behind the endless waves of pleasure and ecstatic pain—is one thing: the fact of a body. A body untethered from the stories we've been told in an effort to contain us. My dearest, the rest of the Darwin story—yes, I finished it; I admired his drawings of animals—is that the human body has been hog-tied, stunted, kept from its own evolutions. All in the name of power and progress. We've been assigned roles inside a predetermined myth, roles that keep us contained. Some of us more than others, but rest assured, we are all imprisoned by the great narrative of ourselves as masters of the universe.

What a sorry lot.

We could have been anything! We could still.

Did you know that under a microscope, pig and human embryonic material share many traits?

I'm rooting for the pigs.

Listen: I know why women such as I make a more sophisticated species of pervert than their male counterparts. Women, of all creatures, remain bound to their object status in this world we've made, whereas male artists—you, my love—are allowed to apprehend pleasure as a sublimity.

Between inert and pervert, I choose pervert.

If Eve showed up on my street, I'd buy her a drink and bed her in an instant. In lieu of that, I created the Room of Eve as an homage, as a reclamation, where an apple has a quite different significance. You are the only person I have ever allowed to enter that room.

I am leaving, my love.

Do not look for me.

Remember us.

Aurora

The Water Girl
and the Floating Boy

A lone in his detention room, Mikael stares at the withered umbilical cord on his pillow.

She was real, it tells him. The baby was real. And Vera who sang was real—and he had been real too, a long time ago, as a boy. This tiny lifeline to nowhere, the last evidence of them all. Why does no one listen to children?

He does a childlike thing. He puts the crinkled object underneath his pillow, climbs onto his bed, and puts his head on the pillow. He closes his eyes. He can't really remember what she looked like, but he does remember the tattoo on her neck, so he pictures that color.

Indigofera tinctoria. Indigo, Vera told him, represented the sixth chakra, the third eye. *When they grow up, indigo children will have the power to master complex systems. And to care for both animals and humans.*

As near as Mikael could tell, he was no master of anything: he could not care for a child, he could not master complex systems, he could not care for animals and humans. He felt as dead as the crinkled object underneath his pillow. No use left for him. Besides. The only part of "indigo children" he didn't think was full of shit was the word itself: *indigo*.

He can't sleep but he can't not sleep either.

His hands make fists. He wishes he could hit something. He considers getting up to hit the wall, which he's done many times before. If he cannot draw, he thinks that what is stuck in his body, in his hands, will kill him or someone else.

He knows they'll find the object; they always do. There is nothing he can keep, nothing that is his, not even a self.

He thinks of William and bombs.

He thinks maybe the world deserves to be bombed, given what the world has done to children.

He wonders if he will ever get out of this place, and if he will become like William, not for any real reason other than the deep aloneness.

He rolls onto his side and faces the wall of his room. He punches the wall hard and quick. His knuckles bleed. He sketches a nautilus shell on the wall with the blood.

Then he hears water running. The running water sounds like it comes from his bathroom shower, but that seems nonsensical unless someone else is in his room, which never happens, because they think he will harm other boys.

He slides off his bed onto the carpeted floor like he's slipping into water. His T-shirt rides up a bit; the carpet scratches his skin. He slides like a snake across the floor toward the bathroom, using his elbows like flippers. For a moment, he stops to put his cheek against the carpet. Heat and texture against his face. If death could just be this, as simple and animal as this.

The falling water recaptures his attention. It is his bathroom shower. A bit of steam like fog coming through the half-open door. Whoever is here, they shouldn't be here; no one should be here, even he shouldn't be here, especially right now when his ears are beginning to ring and his head feels hot and he is beginning to grind his teeth. Whoever is here, he will hurt them.

When he is very near the bathroom doorframe, before he can push himself up off the floor, a figure emerges. Standing there before him is something not possible: a girl. A naked girl, her hair wetted and making black S shapes against her body. She towers over his body, his belly still against the floor. He studies her a glance at a time: her feet, her shins and knees, her thighs, her sex glistening with water droplets, her hipbones, her belly, her ribs, her tits—mostly nipples— her shoulders, her neck, her face, her mouth. She looks to be about his age, maybe a little older. He wants to bite her. He has no idea why. The urge to bite her is so strong that he drools a little.

"Are you a scientist? Or an artist?" she asks, her words falling gently down at him.

Is he dreaming?

Is he dying?

"Yes," he says.

"When is the time in your life that you felt the most human?" she asks.

He doesn't want to talk to her, he doesn't want to acknowledge anything about her, but his body won't listen to him. "There was a baby. A long time ago." He slaps his own jaw to make himself shut up.

Something moves between them.

Her hand.

With her right hand, she parts the lips of her cleft and fingers her way to her own blooming; she makes small rhythmic circles with her middle finger above him.

Why shouldn't he kill her, this naked girl in his room? She is clearly not meant to be here. Is she a hallucination? Or some insane person who has somehow snuck in to murder him and steal his possessions? He thought of the shiv he'd been working on; it was lodged between the mattress and the bed frame, not quite done yet, but sharp enough.

A thief.

Probably a crazy thief.

"I have something to give you," she says, holding her left hand out to him.

He gets up off the floor in a quicksilver snap, the way teen boys are able to do. Now he can see it: he is taller than she is, but she's a little older than he is.

But that's not what matters in the moment. What matters is that her face is flushed.

What matters is that her right hand is furious with her own desire. He's never seen a girl's desire before, only held and ravaged his own in his hand, his ejaculations captured in his own sheets or wiped up with socks.

What matters is that his cock is so hard, and his rage is ramping up, and this girl is so naked that it feels like a crack in the world is about open up.

The impulse to bite is so strong.

"Kneel," she says.

What?

"Hold as still as a statue," she says, and without knowing why, he does it. There in front of her. His face close enough to her hand and sex that he can smell the salt of her. "It's not wrong to want to be loved," she says.

His mouth lolls open.

Something is emerging between her legs, behind her hand. He stares so hard that he shivers.

An apple.

An apple blooms from between her legs, and she pushes her hips toward his head until the apple touches his mouth, and finally, the bite of him can come.

Then the apple is blood, or his mouth is blood—blood gushes between her body and his head. He pulls back. If they find a dead girl in his room, a bloody scene, his life is over—if he even has a life left to be over.

"My god, are you okay?" he screams.

Blood covers the floor. A tide of it rises in the room. The blood comes in waves, impossible waves, until they are both near drowning. He is terrified, but when he looks up at her face, she is smiling. Then laughing.

"We have to leave this place," she says, cradling his head. "The waves are rising. Your drawings will come to life where we are going. You are not dangerous. You are not violent. Your drawings are not wrong. They are just in the wrong time and place."

She smiles again as she treads the bloodwater. Though he knew no such thing was possible, he watched as the blood bored a hole into the wall of his room, like a mouth opening, like a portal, and they slid out of the hole together.

The Butcher's Daughter at Dawn

Had she lost him forever? Another boy falling away? What happened?

Back in the heart of her city, Lilly walked the network of streets leading to her own apartment, but she kept turning away from home. *You had one job*, she chided herself, hating herself even more for the stupid fucking cliché.

Was she helping or hurting?

Who takes the side of boys who don't belong to anyone?

Who steps inside male violence in some small hope of rerouting the story?

Who should?

How many boys had she failed? How many had she lost?

Mikael was gone. There was a hole in the wall of his detention room, as if a bomb had gone off, but there was no record of any bomb, except the news about Oklahoma, the homegrown terrorist loner, too many dead people to fathom.

The only thing left of Mikael was found later, scrawled underneath the shitty-ass carpet of his former room. A complex layering of drawings and carvings and scratches and clawings, full of shapes and buildings and strange forms no one understood. Like a landscape of chaos inside his mind.

She turned it over in her head as she listened to the pattern of her heels on the pavement. She hated the rhythm of her own feet, wished something would drop out of the sky and land on her, get it over with. She stopped. She looked up at the sky, the high-rises on either side of her stretching upward, constructed, unshaken. A pigeon flew by. Nothing fell from the sky to touch her. Not even pigeon shit.

She looked down at the ground, because that's what a stupid woman whose guilt is eating her alive does after looking up at the sky, right? There on the ground near her foot was some kind of stain, dirty and brown and ugly. Or, maybe, a coin.

She squatted. Picked it up. Yeah, that's it, a coin.

Rubbed it between her thumb and forefinger. An old weird coin. Some kind of penny. A fucking *penny*. Probably worthless. It figures.

She dropped the coin back on the ground.

But there she was, alone on a city street, hunkered down on the sidewalk. She closed her eyes and took a breath, inhaling so deeply that her bra nearly cut off her circulation. When she opened her eyes and looked up, she realized she was in front of an old favorite bar: the Tabard Inn.

"Well, let's give the old girl a drink," Lilly muttered. She stood up and pushed her way through the door.

Nostalgia is a funny thing. At certain moments in life, it can hit you so hard that your whole body vibrates with it, almost like you're on the verge of time travel. Lilly's skin began to tingle—with the history of the place, and with her own memory of the last time she'd been there.

The story was that the Tabard Inn had been run by Marie Willoughby Rogers, who named the place after an inn from Chaucer's *Canterbury Tales*. Lilly went there originally because it was female friendly, not the usual misogyny cave. During the second big war, the inn had opened up as a boardinghouse for WAVES—the navy's Women Accepted for Volunteer Emergency Service. She liked that. She liked the dark wood and she liked the low lighting and she liked the tiny indigo flowers stitched into some of the upholstered seats.

The last time she'd been there, she'd gotten into a fight with a woman she'd slept with exactly once before deciding she was too clingy, too needy, just wanted too much. The last thing the woman said before she stormed out was, "I'm not *needy*, Lilly—you're just Antarctic." If only the woman could have seen what Lilly needed most, which was to be cut open, aggressively, like an ice-cutting ship parting a frozen bit of sea. But all the woman wanted to do was kiss—incessantly, like some kind of fruit fly you can't bat away—and cuddle and engage in a little sixty-nine. Absolutely meaningless.

In the bar today were four women and two men, and a girl bartender who looked to be about twelve years old. Youth culture—*great*. Her age, it seemed, was aging her faster and faster. The lines around her eyes increasing their creases, her eyelids growing extra lids. She sat down hard at the bar, averting the gaze of the mirror behind the bartender.

"Scotch, please. Neat. Make it a double."

Here, at least, she could drink without some shithead pawing at her or trying to kiss her or making some pathetic pass. This town was filled with men who had no game, just suits and questionable taste in footwear and ties.

When a woman in an alabaster pantsuit sat down, one stool away from Lilly, she tried to shoot cold daggers from her eyeballs. *Why can't people give other people space when they're clearly there to drink alone with their own rage and guilt? Isn't it motherfucking obvious? Isn't it all over me like porcupine quills?*

But when the stranger failed to move, and Lilly turned to make her feelings clearer, what arrested her attention was the woman's stern beauty. She looked to be sixty-something, maybe even pushing seventy. Her hair was silver, shoulder length, brushed back away from her face in waves. Her eyes were blue, or that kind of blue that fades with age. Even after Lilly turned away again, she could see her plainly in the mirror. The stranger noticed, but she didn't flinch.

The woman ordered vodka on the rocks with a lemon wedge. Lilly's relief that neither of them were drinking cocktails kindled a little warmth in her chest.

The infant bartender asked Lilly if she wanted another, and Lilly nodded. When the other woman received her vodka, she downed it and asked for another with her eyes and a slight nod to the child bartender.

Lilly's mind drifted away from the bar and the stranger, lighting on her work, her success rate as a mental health professional. Some of the boys she'd worked with had been saved, in a way; they'd found foster homes and counseling and mental health resources. At least that's what the data she entered said on the paperwork. But the follow-ups she'd conducted had been dismal. The truth was, no matter how hard she labored, nothing seemed to get much better.

She thought about her nightmares. Horror show.

She thought about her sex life. Ridiculous.

So when the woman moved to sit directly next to her at the bar, Lilly held as still as a statue. Anything was better than her life right now, wasn't it? Anything was better than drowning in your own mire.

"I don't mean to intrude," the woman began. "But I noticed your hand is bleeding."

Make the heart hard, like a baseball.

Lilly held her hand up and looked at it in the mirror in front of them. Sure enough. *She looks like Vanessa Redgrave.*

"Can I have a napkin, some water?" Lilly asked the bartender. She side-eyed the stranger. "I'm fine. Really. I must have brushed it against something—opened up a scab."

"Must be a story there," the woman next to Lilly said. "Not exactly a paper cut."

No, no it wasn't. Lilly knew where the wound had come from. She'd scraped her hand against a cinder-block wall after she left Mikael—done it intentionally, the pain the only thing she could give herself in the moment. He'd taken the umbilical cord, and she'd taken his story about some lost girl out in the world, and she had no idea what the fuck to do about any of it. Now he was gone. If they found him, he'd be truly fucked.

She felt the pang of her own uselessness. As always, she felt desperate to *do something*—to punch someone, to stage a breakout, to get that boy out of there, deliver him to freedom, even if it meant risking having his rage flare up again in the process—anything to avoid punishing him into becoming a permanently violent man. That's why she'd scraped her hand at the detention facility, to keep from feeling helpless and numb; maybe she'd scraped it again, on the brick wall outside the front door of the bar, just to keep things alive. But that was too long a story to tell an innocent stranger, wasn't it? That was the trouble with her entire existence.

"No. Not a paper cut."

As she blotted at her hand with the napkin, Lilly stole another glance at the woman. In some ways, she looked like an apparition, some artist's vision, with her light-gray suit and silver hair and eyes as transparent as water. Or else she'd been dispatched to override all Lilly's usual choices with an image of something she'd never imagined.

The woman placed her own clenched hand on the bar in front of

Lilly. Lilly stared at the woman's fist. She clearly was holding something. She felt a prickle of curiosity in her shoulders. They eyed each other.

The woman turned her hand over and opened it. In her palm was a coin. "I saw you drop this on the ground before you came into the bar," the woman said. "I thought you might want it back."

The fucking penny. Before Lilly could respond, the woman dropped it into the last half-inch of her vodka, swirled the clear liquid around, then fished it out. "This is worth quite a bit of money," she said. "It's a Flowing Hair cent. 1793. I don't think you want to ignore this object. I think you want to keep it." Now she dropped the coin into Lilly's drink. "I would know," the woman said, turning the collar up on her gray suit. "I have one exactly like it."

Oh god. A fucking geriatric coin collector. "So you collect coins?" Lilly kept her eyes on her drink. Vacant and transparent, like alcohol.

"No," the woman said. "I don't have any special interest in coins." She took a sip of her dirty vodka. "I do however have a collection of certain . . . *objects* I've procured over the years."

Lilly felt both attracted and repulsed. Wasn't there a word for that? She ordered them both another round. They drank in silence, adjacent.

"I love the way that third shot brings your shoulders down away from your ears, don't you?" the woman said finally, stepping down from her stool. "Opens your chest up to—well, almost anything. You know?" She made ready to leave. Slowly. Ran fingers through her silver hair.

Her magnificent mane of silver hair. Her goddamn beautiful height and broad shoulders when she stood. Lilly kept her eyes on the mirror image, steadying herself. If she looked at her, if she made eye contact . . .

"Have you ever had opium tea? I have some at my place—I live very near here. It'll turn the hurt on your hand into nothing." ·

Lilly had to admit it: in that moment, there was nothing on the planet she wanted more than this strange woman's opium tea. She didn't know why, and she didn't care. When would she ever be offered opium tea again? Besides, her hand was truly throbbing. So was her clit, a little.

The walls of the entryway to the woman's apartment were covered with images of snakes. Postcards, photographs, paintings, drawings, even some bright-colored snakeskin patches, hundreds of them, all pinned to the wall.

Aurora said nothing as they walked down the hall to the main room.

Lilly held her tongue too. It was as if an agreement had been forged between them in that narrow passage, the hallway spilling out into each of four rooms. Lilly felt the question softly tickling at her—*What's with the snakes?*—but she did not ask. She liked the snakes. Instantly. They were not your ordinary welcome.

She still didn't know the woman's name. She decided she didn't care.

The woman went to the kitchen to make the tea. "Have a seat," she said, gesturing toward the living room, where an enormous turquoise velvet couch took up most of the space. "Transformation," she said, running the sink water. "Snakes. I like creatures that know how to shed their skins."

Lilly sat on the plush couch and thought about how many skins a woman must shed in order to survive a lifetime. Something more than attraction spread across her chest. Something like a mutual recognition, which was nothing she'd ever felt in her entire life.

The tea was delicious. A warm slide down the throat, a hint of lavender the woman must have added, a numbing of the lips; then, within half an hour, a rush of endorphins and a giddy painlessness.

"Oh my god, I haven't felt this in so long," Lilly said. They'd both settled on the enormous couch, arranging their bodies more and more comfortably as time ticked by.

"What *this?*" the woman asked.

"This calm. This nothingness. This floating. I love it."

The older woman smiled. "Would you care to see a very interesting room?"

Lilly felt silly and seductive at the same time. She giggled. A snorting laugh came out. Ordinarily, that would have embarrassed her, but not when she'd been dipped in opium tea.

"Yes, I would love to. If it's anything like your entry hall, I'm all in." Lilly tried to get up from the couch, teetered a little, and snort-laughed again.

The woman opened the door to her bedroom. Or, not a bedroom, really, but something else: a room filled with intricately designed furniture and machines of some kind—the word *contraptions* came to mind. As Lilly stepped all the way into the room, her understanding grew. The furniture was all antique, and—a deeper truth—everything in the room was sexual in design. Lilly stopped in front of what looked like a vintage battery, with a wand attached.

"You've seen these before, I'm sure. A 'muscle relaxer' from the 1880s, marketed primarily to men. Until it emerged that doctors were using it on female patients to cure hysteria. In other words, the first vibrator."

Lilly chuckled, but she was distracted by an object in the center of the room: a square padded table that sprouted a black rubber ball about the size of an apple near the center. Lilly put her hand on the ball. It felt cool and smooth to the touch.

"This thing was supposed to be for treating pelvic disorders in women. From a medical standpoint, it was . . . medieval. From another point of view, something else entirely. When women figured out their own home uses for a table like this, doctors warned that they should be supervised so as not to . . . *overstimulate*. The engine that vibrated the ball was steam-powered."

Across the room, mounted on the far wall, was something that looked like a saddle.

"Obesity. Gout. And again, hysteria. But that's not why women used them." She smiled.

Ropes hung from the ceiling, silently coiled like beautiful thick snakes. On a small raised stage sat a crossbeam equipped with a set of leather wrist cuffs, and a second set of cuffs, for the ankles, spread far apart at the base. Lilly felt dizzy. Her mouth filled with spit.

"What's this?" Lilly gestured toward an elaborate machine near the door.

"A spanking machine." She released a low chuckle. "So you stood here, at one end, bent over this leather ledge, right? And when you turned the machine on, a great THWAP from behind!" The older woman demonstrated the action and they laughed at the force of the metal arm and paddle that shot up from the other end of the device.

On the wall, all manner of cock and cunt chastity cages, hanging like decorations.

But inside their shared laughter, their growing lust and intimacy, another object caught Lilly's eye: a shallow wooden box the size of a body, with thin metal bars across the top of it, something between a coffin and an ornate cage. Inside it, at the bottom, a blood-red velvet cushion. The metal bars seemed to have openings at chest level, at crotch level, at mouth level. Lilly could not stop staring.

"Ahhhh, I see what's caught your eye. That's a holding pen," the woman said.

"It looks like a coffin," Lilly said. An array of devices—toys, wands, spurs—was arranged on the box like a crown. As Lilly stood near the box, she felt the flesh in her body ache: Her arms. Her legs. The cleft between her hips and legs. Something in her life ached. That feeling, again, of something both improbable and unsettlingly familiar.

"Would you like to try it?" the woman said, opening the lid.

Would she like to try stepping into her own dream? Into a space that has haunted her body as long as her body's memory? Would she like to find out, at last, what happens next?

Her body suddenly broke into a heated sweat. *Is it possible to reenter your own past, your own dreams and grief and loss and trauma, if someone else is there to guide you through every moment of your experience? Was it possible that she could reach her own deepest pain through pleasure?*

"Do you think a person can . . . confront their own pain?" she asked.

"Yes," the older woman said, gently opening the box. "Pleasure and pain are a great deal bigger than the story we've been told. Like their own epoch."

Lilly shed her clothes quickly, her clitoris already erect, her desire uncovered—a desire not separate from guilt and fear and negation, but plunging straight into the mouth of it.

As the older woman closed the lid, she said, "Are you sure?"

Lilly nodded yes, but her steady eyes were the word for it.

"My name is Aurora. If you feel unsafe at any moment, say *water.*"

Lexicon

On the seventh day inside Aurora's apartment, Lilly rolls her tongue around an apple between Aurora's legs. Laughter. She can smell and taste the salt wet. Lilly bites into the apple, hard enough to hold it in her mouth, lifts her head, spits it to the floor, bites again into the pulp of Aurora with an ungodly hunger. Breathing. Kissing. Sucking. Tonguing.

Lilly's fingers inside, one-two-three-four-five—a sea creature entering a water cave until a rhythmic thrusting emerges from Aurora's hips a flip Aurora topping Lilly's back Lilly biting down into feathers Aurora eating Lilly's ass spreading her legs tendriling with her arm octopus up to cunt the other mouth of her has it been hours and hours or days and nights and days sun washes the room through the ceiling-to-floor curtains the color of alabaster the walls midnight blue the carpet bloodred sun washes the room night wave washes the room time moves between bodies the sheets wet smeared tangled necks legs a longing eating into a longing a life eating into a death the bloodbeat of it.

Days.

Nights.

> *I used to have one leg*
> *My beloved cousin made me another*
> *Then a girl came to me*
> *timeless*
> *I want to give you something*

From under a pillow Aurora pulls a coil of rope the colors of a corn snake Lilly the model on her belly anticipation lodged like the touch of dreams between each vertebrae Aurora the rigger pulling Lilly's arms behind her Aurora binding her hands tender gentle torque not then tender gentle torque a gasp please if there is a god or a universe let this time of binding pass slowly or let this language between bodies break time then on to ankles the knots are practiced the knots are loving the knots are tightening with any move Lilly makes Lilly wants to move the torque the gasp of it

Aurora stands

Lilly waits

A kind of death this waiting

Aurora standing

———

Aurora pulls Lilly's body up and up hoisting her lifting her off the bed into suspension *Seiu Ito painted his pregnant wife hanging from ropes* whispered into Lilly's ear *the art of it the wet of it the torque of it* the ropes taut between Lilly's knees dividing the lips of her labia up her belly crisscrossing her back arched her legs bent her arms bound behind her a kind of thick hard corset rope stitched across her back the little bulges of arm bitable the woman hanging from the ceiling carabiners glinting rope the color of corn snake caught bird arched swallow strained neck *eronawa* a whisper *semenawa* a whisper or a dare Lilly screaming yes except silent the language their bodies the language the tug of the ropes on skin their language eye to eye no one sees the girl enter the room with an object no one sees the girl leave there is just this language of desire this is only Lilly's suspended body there is only Aurora tonguing her limb by limb then nothing and into the nothing the everything suspended

Apple	Indigo	Theft
Tongue	Rope	Room
Aurora	Whale	Snake
Cunt	Wail	Vandens
Axolotl	Waves	Boat
Hips	Sapnuoti	Motherwaters
Thrust	Uu	Yakon:kwe
Days	Ohne:ka	Nights
Water	Suck	Leg
Sun	Blood	Turtle
Moon	Boy	Arm
Cave	Girl	Epistle
Brother	Liberty	Yakut
Torch	Treaty	Uol
Umbilical	Timir	Imaginal
Ehnita	Dream	Story
Father	Desire	Kus
History	Motina	Birth
Red	White	Blue

Hand over hand, her eyes locked on Lilly's body, Aurora slowly lowers Lilly to the ground; unties her lovingly; massages every line made from rope on her body; holds her like an infant; kisses her; coos to her; slips her sips of water warm blankets the subspace and afterwhere.

Entwined bodies.

I will hold you forever beyond time even just for now—though look, but just now, look there, look at the object in the corner of the room.

There: a bloody toddler boy, naked and wriggling and laughing, his fat little arms outstretched to the two women drenched in their own pleasurepain.

"What the fuck are we supposed to do with *that*?" Lilly hisses from inside Aurora's embrace.

"Use your instincts," Aurora says, petting Lilly's hair.

"I don't have any instincts for that kind of thing."

Aurora gets out of bed, walks over to the toddler, and picks it up. "Then use your imagination. Tell me a story about your brother."

Lilly pulls the bed covers up around her like a child might. "I loved him so much. It hurts."

"Then tell that story," Aurora says. And she nestles the child between them.

Aurora, my lost forever dawn. Where are you?

I can't remember if this is the third or fourth bottle I've thrown into the harbor with a letter to you inside it. It isn't hope, unless there really is such a thing as hope against hope. In my heart I believe that you would admire the act too. The care with which I roll each letter into a tube small enough to fit inside a bottle. The bottles themselves are in hues of green and blue and amber, sometimes with an ornate stopper. I watch them float away in the evenings at dusk. I imagine you finding them, beautiful reliquaries carrying what's left of our knowledge of each other.

I wouldn't say the harbor water is indifferent. Somehow it seems to me that the swirling eddies and soft currents receive the bottles and epistles gently. Like hands. So many things we put to water to try to give them meaning: Petals. Bodies. Wreaths for the departed. Coins for luck.

And my Big Daughter in the harbor. Standing tall. Still.

I do not know where you are.

I do know that, in your last letter, you told me to watch for a gift if I ever found you gone.

To say that I left my interlude with you the night of the apple feeling a snake coiled at the base of my spine—to say that would be an understatement. I never thought of it being perhaps the last night I would see you. I left with the lunge and swell of someone who can't wait until the next time, and the next, and the next, like an addict.

Why didn't you tell me? I just walked away like an idiot, hoping the night would never end.

I have thought many hours since your disappearance about that night: what I did, where I went.

The doors on your street all lead to a place where someone could slip from one reality into another. Two doors to the left and I could lose this ache with someone whose ram's-head-of-a-cock would bring me quite close to losing consciousness. Our dear friend Kate's well-traveled establishment around the corner. Four doors down and across the street and I could slip into my dreams through the pipe.

I can still hear you explaining your rules to the client through the door when I was leaving. "No sexual intercourse. In the strictest definition of that term, as you recognize it. If that's your game, you've come to the wrong Rooms. Go down the street with your shriveled"—and here a quick crotch-glance—"imagination." I know your aims well, my secular and singular angel. Cocks and cunts and anuses and mouths and hands and tongues and feet and breasts and ears and necks and torsos and legs and those muscular flabs that are the sweet thick truth of an ass are for something else than people have been trained to understand. You offered your differently bodied experiences to anyone who was willing to learn how to be in their body differently as well. You meant to push flesh against "the idiotic limits of the ridiculous reproductive impulse." From your point of view, we'd gotten the body all wrong.

In your Rooms, intense varieties of sensual sensation refigured everything. Nothing to do with immorality or morality. I understood that even in our youth. It was always your imagination at the helm, let loose, navigating us up and through uncharted channels. "Anyone can have sex," you'd quip. "I've been there. I've done all of that. What I want is . . . colossal. Unnamable. Something that might

*seem like ordinariness or nothingness on the surface until it reveals
itself to you as a universe. A going beyond the sexual. An evolution.
An odyssey into erotics—not a Homerian odyssey of all-conquering
might and war, which to me is duller than death, whole purblind
epochs have been built on that tyrannical and impotent thrust"—
and you would roll your eyes—"but in its place an odyssey that
carries humans past simple pleasure and through ecstatic pain unto
deeper pleasure, both a thrust and a devouring."*

*When I'd look at you without understanding, you'd speak to
me like a child. "Dearest, just picture two women joining their
miraculous angles with each other, thrusting endlessly, opening into
each other. That will give you a sense of the shape, the how of it.
Mouth to mouth in waves. You boys always just want to know where
to stick your appendage, where to aim, where to shoot. That's been
part of the problem all along—a formal problem at base. Not your
fault, however. You were made that way. The protuberance dulls your
wits. If you'd like, I can harness that thing so that your blood flows
more freely to feed your imagination."*

*An American woman and her two daughters ran the nearest
opium establishment. On this street, all people from everywhere bled
into one another without discrimination. People recently released
from the poorhouses and prisons, well-to-do businessmen and bankers
and lawyers and judges, whores and thieves and bar owners and
patrons, shopkeepers and laborers from mills and factories, all mixed
together—and children, children everywhere. Children who worked
the dens or the brothels, children who worked the streets and the
clients, children who had no homes to call their own except the streets.*

*For about eight dollars I could procure a ration of five ounces, then
go home to ready my smoker's kit—a lamp, a sponge, a shell with
opium, bowl cleaner, scissors, needle. But my pleasure would be better
cared for at the opium joint, where the mother and her daughters*

*could supply me with a reclining sleeping pad, a hookah, a pipe, and
tins, and constant soothing, partly domestic and familial attention.*

*That night, a girl of no more than seventeen, upper-class by the
look of her dress, was on the bed just above mine, unconscious, ahead
of me in her dream journey. To my right, a man who might have
been one hundred years old. I slept.*

Then, the detonation.

*It shook the beds, my body, the building. The light had come, so
it had to be morning. The people who had been near me were gone;
others stole in before my dreaming had ended. My head knocked the
headboard of the sleeping pad. I got up but not quickly; others were at
the window before me. I couldn't see beyond their heads, but I could
hear them.*

Fire.

*A building had exploded and now it was on fire. I could see the
flickering light above their heads.*

*I retrieved my coat and ran outside, hoping you were nowhere near
the blast. I ran past your building a ways, and when I looked up, I
thought I saw you—I did, with a hundred faces of children all
around you.*

But it must have been an opium haze.

Where are you? I am lost.

Frédéric

My beloved Aurora,

I did what you said.

I watched for a gift when I found you gone.

The day your gift arrived, I had risen from a dream in which I wrestled an arm that had no body. Just a giant arm, but the arm was winning. In the dream, the limb was much bigger than I. And yes, I was naked, of course. Though the dream ended without conclusion, it was clear that I had spent myself in every conceivable way.

The day of your delivery, I answered the door in my dressing robes. "What?" I called out with temper at the knock at my door.

When I opened the door, the delivery boy looked a little frightened. He carried a box of the type that usually housed a delivery of long-stemmed roses, and my heart warmed and I smiled a little, as I had just that night been with the ram's cock, and you know the funny thing about him was his sentimentality. The most sentimental brute I've ever known.

I gave the delivery boy more coins than he deserved, closed the door, and took the box to my bed. There was no marking on the box. I lifted the lid, ready to inhale the smell of roses.

Aurora, the box had no roses.

Inside, instead, your leg. The leg I designed for you.

That's when your words came rushing back to me. "If I am ever gone, look for a gift. An object of importance for us."

I wept. I felt the gift and the word gone as if they'd been soldered together. I knew I would likely never see you again.

And while I held—not your leg, but the leg I made for you—I noticed something. Paper. A slip of paper, tucked inside the leg. My hands began to shake.

I pulled from the leg your letter.

My cousin. My love—Oh, Frédéric, isn't there some other word we might use? What an overwrought and emptied thing that word is.

Love. I've something to share with you. This parting gift. Inside this beautiful leg is a story.

There are times when I feel my missing leg in my arm—almost always when I am writing to you. "Phantom limb," as it's known. Some amputees, I know, feel pain where the limb used to live; others just a sensation of the thing. Many of the children I have harbored for all these years have known the experience. (Yes, children. My wards. Don't act surprised, my cousin. Surely you can imagine something more surprising in Room 8 other than carnal pleasure.)

That sensation—so difficult to describe. Something like an itch, almost a gesture, in the part of the body nearest the sever. I have read of scientists who believe that the body may be harboring memories once carried in these damaged regions, that even after a given limb is gone, those memories may lurch forward now and again. One doctor of my acquaintance, Silas Weir Mitchell, has posited that the cause may be an irritation in the peripheral nervous system. But what of those who are born without limbs? I asked him once after a particularly intense session in the Room of Ropes. Such patients have been known to experience phantom limb as well. He admitted that such cases remain a mystery.

Sometimes I imagine a Room filled with all our missing limbs. Most people would consider such a vision grotesque, but in my mind's

*eye, the Room is unbearably beautiful. The limbs are ornate, like
jewelry or crowns or velvet gowns or feathered hats. The limbs are so
beautiful, away from their former bodies, that they take on their own
identities as objects.*

A hand stands in for a face.

*When I write to you, cousin, I can feel my leg. It does not feel like
a phantom, not like a phantasm; my leg feels present. Many times I
have stood up from my desk without my beloved prosthetic and fallen
on my face, forgetting that a one-legged woman must work for her
balance in the world.*

*I have chosen this moment to tell you about the depth of my love
for you.*

*When I was recovering in a hospital far away from the one where
my leg was murdered and stolen, I was delirious from pain and the
medications for pain—so you might say I was in a suspended state of
pleasurepain for weeks. My darling, I want you to understand, I
went to a real place. The regular world around me, the comings and
goings of doctors and nurses in the ward, the white of the sheets, the
blue and white of nurses' uniforms, I saw them as no more than
blurry and dreamlike. Sound too was muffled. It was almost like
being underwater. Then, one day as I was beginning to make my way
back to our shared reality, I looked down at the place where my leg
should be, and I saw—your hand.*

*I understood why this should be: in the muffled coo of their voices,
the nurses had told me that you visited me every day. But on this day,
I saw your hand resting where my leg should be on the bed. And so I
looked at you and said your name aloud and smiled.*

That night I dreamed of waves.

*The next day, I could hear you in a natural way, and I could see
you, and you came in with a long box. You sat down next to me, as
always, and you took an object out of the box. The object was a*

wooden leg with a foot, the wood oiled and glowing. All over the wood, intricate hand-carved roses. On the foot, perfect toes with painted toenails. So delicate. So beautiful.

That leg took my breath away. Took language away.

I wept an ocean after you left that evening. In place of language, all I had were tears of gratitude.

Was this love?

I am a childless unmarried woman whose pleasure and pain have traveled great distances. What do I know about love? It seemed as if it might be love. I have never felt anything like it, before or since.

I created the Room of Vibrations specifically for amputees or anyone who feels a phantom limb experience. There, for a moment, even someone who has lost a breast or a tooth or an eye—or an I, my love—can feel temporarily whole, the vibration standing in for what is missing. Perhaps, for some, standing in for love.

As I write this, I can feel my leg in my hands. But not just that. I feel my face—that idiotic obsessive surface filled with holes and lies and mistaken ideas about beauty and communication—in my hands. Which is to say, I think my entire identity lives in my hands. I thus renounce my face.

When you think of me (Will you think of me, my dove?), do not think of my face.

> *Ever yours into the everything (or nothing),*
> *Aurora*

Aurora, my dawn, my loss,

Had we seen each other, Aurora, in your Rooms? Did we see each other that very first time, as children, locked inside your moment of desire and blood and mouth and apple? Did that moment turn into our entire lives?

I have so much left to tell you.

I cannot stop stuffing bottles with letters. Throwing them into the river or sea. So many stories I should have shared! I throw them into the abyss as if they might yet reach you, or finish me. I want to write you a devotional, a confessional. I want to tell you my origin story, straight into the gaping mouth of your absence.

I was not the first boy born to my mother. There was a Frédéric before me.

He died when he was seven months old. My parents also had a daughter, I'm told, who died after a month. There were these floating siblings, a boy and a girl, the boy inhabiting a space in womb and world before me, the girl so small. Smaller than anything. Not even a word.

So, you see, I was the second Frédéric—born inside their grief and loss. My siblings floating away. Like you.

When I was nine, we moved to Paris. That first year, my mother made my remaining brother and me lunches, and we ate them on a park bench near l'Arc de Triomphe. That monument was my first

object of desire. I couldn't stop looking at it; I heard nothing my
mother or brother said to me when in its presence; often, distracted as I
listened, I bit my tongue or the inside of my cheek while chewing. The
arc was pure magnificence.

We lived on Rue d'Enfer, a fact I hope you find wonderful.

We lived near the Hospital of Found Children and Orphans and
the site of the famous guillotine. In the Place de la Concorde, a pillar
had been erected—a statue made as a gift from Egypt to Paris. The
obelisk erected itself inside my imagination as well. I began to dream
of Egypt without knowing more of that ancient land than I learned
in history books and lessons. You will no doubt accuse me of
exoticizing. I confess immediately. I request punishment.

I attended school at the same institution as Molière, Voltaire, and
Victor Hugo. I interacted with Chopin, Liszt. There is a dreamy
haze to this part of my life, the times before Napoleon III's rise to
power and his declaration as emperor.

On the outside, as you know, I am a man with a success story. A
prominent artist, sought-after, world-renowned. But my memories
arrange themselves differently from what my lineage and pedigree
might suggest. If anything, I would say I was carried to success on a
wave of infamy. But even that seems too simple. My memories do not
hold still inside a story.

When I worked on the now universally despised Rapp statue—
even now I can hear my critics asking about the confounding position
of the arm—I fell from the highest point of the scaffolding, near his
head. I lay on the floor at the statue's feet for an entire hour, or so my
mother told me later. My brother tried to revive me. I don't remember
much about being unconscious there at the feet of the statue. I do
remember that, when I regained consciousness, I saw my brother's face
first. I was covered in leeches.

Sometimes, if I close my eyes, I can still feel the leeches on my chest.

Perhaps that is why I was attracted so to the Room of Burning Cups. Or is that room perhaps a throwback to your nun desires?

Here is an admission that would end my career if anyone but you knew it: I have since then suffered from episodes of amnesia, sometimes including seizures. The seizures feel uncannily like a departure from reality, like traveling to some other time and place. The colors of life turn washed out or muted. People I know to be dead and gone reappear. Sometimes, fragments of previous experience play out before me, as if memories could be acted out on the stage of the brain. The seizures also give me gifts, Aurora—images and ideas to last a lifetime—or maybe time itself cleaving open enough for me to gently pull imagination forth from the slit before it sutures shut.

The seizures, Aurora. No one knows. Should anyone find out, my life's work would be over. I tell you this as a traded intimacy. The sustaining thrill of knowing you deeply is worth the risk. I tell you this as a spell, in the hope of conjuring you back.

My memories live scattered all over my body, in a way that my knowledge and training do not. I remember, for instance, the first time I made a small model out of wet bread. Before I learned how to use clay. To this day, when I cannot sleep, I will procure bread and knead it with water, using it to create small models—usually of breasts or cocks—in my off hours. It brings me a kind of calm.

But sometimes the forms that emerge from the bread are different: not lovers, but a boy and a girl. Lost, penniless, huddled together.

I am haunted by the dead boy who came before me, inside of whose name I stand.

I am haunted by the girl who lived so briefly.
Sometimes I call the colossus my Big Daughter.
Sometimes I call out to you across time and water. Sometimes I
think of following you, stepping off the edge, going to water.

> *Yours eternally, into the abyss,*
> *Frédéric*

My Dawn,

The sun is setting and the water is blue and orange-yellow, with little caps of white diamonds.

The hole you have left in my life is an unsuturable wound.

Inside this last bottle, I will let go of my letter of goodbye, Aurora.

I am leaving this strange and beautiful place called a country. My Big Daughter is done. The colossus is erected. She seems to grow from the very water itself, in certain light. I have a cough I cannot master either, and thus I return by ship tomorrow.

I hope against hope that my daughter, my brainchild, inspires this young nation to think of freedom as alive. Freedom is a living organism, the statue a symbol to carry the life forward. Perhaps presidents will speak at her feet and inspire the people. Perhaps the masses will gather courage from her. Perhaps she may be a beacon for those caught inside tempests.

But I also hope that this country respects and honors that the whole project of constructing and erecting this statue has been one of enormous generosity and self-sacrifice. Time, work, and money have been sacrificed. At risk of immodesty, I believe the colossus to be the most important statue in the world—and I am her father, her existence born of the toil of my imagination and the countless hands of laborers. Are you laughing yet?

I can hear you. "Ah, the male genius. Always spraying itself about."

I remember well the raps you so devotedly gave my cock in an effort to reroute both my blood and my imagination.

I meant to make you laugh—or to inspire one of your barbed retorts. Now I just feel ridiculous.

I miss you.

Aurora, if you ever meet Liberty, if you are out there somewhere and you have occasion to visit her, to enter her, please know: I have tried to infuse her form with a kind of power—that is, your power, your erotic power, recognized by Plato as the fundamental creative impulse, with its sensual element. Or, to put it differently—for you would never put it the way Plato did, would you; no, you'd call him someone who sublimated sensation so that he might ejaculate intellect—I have tried to invest Liberty with that profound power and unrelenting bliss you carry inside yourself. Your joy. Your command of pure sensation. Your ever-devouring and ever-generating body. The pure rush of you. If only a woman could be that: ungendered into her power. This is why I have rendered Liberty's masculine and feminine face and body as one. It is my understanding of you, beloved. No other woman like you exists, except in the form of Liberty. No virgin, no mother, no sister, daughter, wife, or whore. Only Liberty.

I can see your face in youth, bleeding and laughing, sutures ripped open, a bloody apple on the floor.

How we picked the apple back up and ate it with zeal. How you birthed desire and imagination in a boy forever.

My loss is eternal.

My love is likely lost with you—my deepest love—although, you are right, in the end you are always right, we need another word for it.

The bottle I pitch into the water is blue this time. A current catches the object, and then all is writ in water.

Ethnography 6

Underneath the massive Capitol building—with its external layers of pomp and authority, with its internal ceremonies and work conducted by elected officials as busy as bees, with its mighty facade of security and order, with its countless portals of ingress and egress, a whole underground city of laborers keeps things running. There are hundreds of us hidden in the bowels of the buildings. Painters and cleaners and plumbers and electricians, mechanics and sanitation workers and food preparation workers. Our bodies carry a different story from those that make the news. The mopping and waxing have given many of us—at least those of us who have worked more than thirty years—arthritis. The marble dusters sometimes break down. I dust the woodwork and clean the cigarette and cigar ash. There are thirty-nine buildings to clean and an underground subway and 1,400 restrooms. There are graveyard-shift architectural and engineering employees, as busy as invisible night creatures.

I like to bring a bag of apples and tangerines for the break room. My father before me, Othar, used to as well. My crew is ten people. One woman, Tisha. Sometimes we tease her, but Tisha is stronger than half the men and she insists on making the coffee. We need four or five pots a night. You can feel the ghost of all the workers before us—the people who labored under orders from others, the people who built the original structures. The battles over working conditions and wages that happened here, the New Deal, most of which didn't apply to us. Our well-being has not been part of any story. Some of our family members and fellow workers dug through contaminated trash for years without any protection. Contaminated with asbestos or blood or toxic materials, all of it falling like dust over our bodies, some of it surely taken within, contaminating us in turn.

The stories above us happen in dramatic, televised splashes with international weight. Who lives and who dies underneath the belly of things—well, that doesn't make the news.

I go to work around eleven at night and I finish around six in the morning. I guess you could say we keep the buildings clean so that others can achieve the great work of the nation . . . but we're the ones who take care of all the shit. It's almost like we're an entire undercity. No telling what goes on above us. Like another history. Another world.

Tisha's brother ascended, though. He worked for the Capitol Police. He no longer works there or anywhere. There's a cost to ascension.

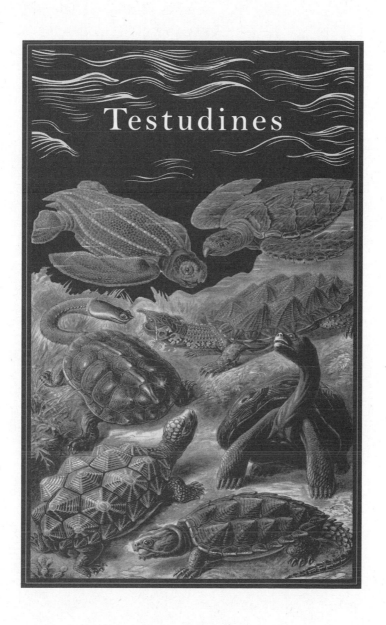

Testudines

Of Time and Water

Tell me the story again."

Indigo sits under the kitchen table turning an object over in her small hands. Outside the window of their floating habitat, the water sloshes against the platforms. The sky is gray today, the water gray, or she'd be outside helping to plant more rosemary and potatoes and tomatoes in the floating greenhouse nearest their pod.

Miles inland, what was once The Brook has taken a different shape again; buildings have either lost their bearings and collapsed or changed form, like bodies bending and leaning. London plane trees, Norway maples, and Callery pear trees originally from Asia thread through the former streets and alleys, or rest fallen and uprooted with broken limbs becoming detritus or food for worms and insects. Pin oaks, stuck stubbornly in concrete, stand steadfast. Vegetation rewilds everything urban. Animals make their homes.

On water, the floating habitats spread out across the surface, or dip under into the bellies of aquatic dwellings; some bamboo-framed cylindrical structures punch skyward like stubborn thumbs. Crabs, oysters, lobsters, shrimp, northern pipefish, pufferfish, jellyfish, and tiny seahorses thrive in the riverway and ocean. Whales and seals have conversations regarding the stamina of sturgeons.

Mikael unrolls several large sheaths of drafting paper out onto the table in the kitchen. The blue ink of the drawings is almost like a language to him. Rooftop farms. Parks with paths that soak up water and reduce heat. Healing gardens. Education centers powered by environmentally generated electricity. Hydropower stations. Terraced farms that recycle organic waste. Floodplains remade into villages with giant retention ponds to collect rainwater. Indigo emerges from under the table, stands up, and looks at the drawings with him.

"That looks like a starfish," she says of one.

"The habitats all have names that reflect their forms and inspirations—can you see?" He gently passes his hand over some of the forms. "The Sea Manta, gently undulating across the top of the water like the wings of manta rays, the belly of the structure dipping down into the ocean."

"Yes! And the same colors—black on top, white on the bottom."

He points to another. "The Tropos, a series of floating cities that turn and curl like seashells. Sea star habitats that radiate outward and turn. Marine nomad pods secured to shallow sea-floor areas in clusters like coral. Seascrapers diving down below the surface of the water and extending into the sky. Aquaponic hubs for floating food islands." Every drawing a piece of the emerging Species Cohabitation Project.

"I see," Indigo says, returning to her spot underneath the table. "Now can you tell me the story again?"

The desire of a child is everything.

He looks underneath the table. "You were pulled from the water by a magical water girl." He sits. He starts to draw, waits for a response. "Then you grew a mermaid tail in place of legs."

Indigo smiles beneath the weight of his drawing. "I don't have a mermaid tail. I'm twelve. I know there's no such thing as mermaids." She reaches around to touch the back of her neck, where her name is written in blue ink forever.

"I know. I just wanted to see if you were listening." He drops his head below the table to see her. "What's that in your hand?"

She scooches around so that her back is to him.

"You were delivered by a beautiful aquanaut."

"What's an aquanaut?" She puts the object into her mouth, rolls her tongue over it, around it: Salt. Copper.

Mikael holds his breath, then pulls a blue pen from his pocket, starts sketching another transportation feature to the bridge. "An aquanaut is any person who remains under the water breathing at the ambient pressure long enough for the concentration of inert components of the breath, as dissolved in the body tissues, to reach equilibrium."

"Saturation," Indigo says.

"Yes. From the Latin word *aqua* and the Greek *nautes*. Water sailor. Like an astronaut, only in water. Much more phenomenal than a mermaid."

"So Laisvė is . . . a water sailor?"

"Yes. Although that's not exactly accurate. It's just one translation. She thinks of herself as a carrier."

Indigo begins to hum between sentences. Some tune of her own design. "Does she always bring people back and forth?"

"No!" Mikael laughs. "It's kind of weird. Sometimes she brings old rusted things I can't even understand. She'll set something on the table, and I won't even know what it is. One time, she brought up this old object with barnacles and coral and mussels all over it. It was found in the remains of a Roman shipwreck off the coast of the Greek island Antikythera in 1901. The object dated to around 200 to 90 BC. The Antikythera Mechanism, they called it. It was a machine the ancient Greeks used to predict the positions of the stars and the motion of the sun and moon. It's the most sophisticated mechanism known from the ancient world; nothing as complex is known for the next thousand years. I used to wonder if she stole it from a museum."

"She's a thief?"

"No. Not really. She carries things. It's like she doesn't truly care about the difference between people and objects, animals and building materials—treasures, lost things. Like everything has the same value as everything else. Except children. She pulls children from waters all over time."

"Is something wrong with her?" Indigo's brows make small wave shapes.

"No," Mikael says a little too slowly.

"Is Laisvė my mother?" Indigo peers up at Mikael from the underneath of things, something in her mouth making her words a little off.

"That's a hard question," Mikael says. "In some ways, you were born of water. We all are, really. But it is true that Laisvė went to find you across time, she brought you here, and she lifted you up out of the water, into my arms." He crouches down to her level. "Now spit whatever is in your mouth out into my hand, please." *You are something like the broken chain. You are something like an umbilical cord. You are a connection between mothers and sons, fathers and daughters, the past and the present and the future. You are beautiful in a way language has not yet named.*

"But babies don't come from just water. I've read all about it. Babies come from their mother's bellies after a sperm and an egg love each other."

"We all came from water, if you think about it. We all move through water to get to the world," Mikael reminds her. "Now spit." He holds his hand out in front of her face.

"Am I an orphan?" Indigo's last word warbles as she spits the object—an old coin—into his hand.

"No," he says, his heartbeat loud in his ears. "There are many meanings to the word *mother*. Or *father*. Or *family*. Other kinds of stories. Other ways of coming into the world. We can learn to tell different stories to ourselves about who we are." He palms Indigo's cheek as softly as a whisper.

"Is my mother dead?" Indigo's eyes are the word for it—this feeling Mikael has, to be lost, to be found, to have to invent the story in between over and over again, to surrender to unnameableness so that new words and sentences and myths might get born. He remembers Vera dying in the street. He remembers the day Laisvė brought him Indigo. The memories live in his hands, his hands making designs for life.

The night before Laisvė delivered Indigo to him, Mikael wept an ocean.

He dreamed of the habitats rising from the sea, reaching for the cosmos where the sky platforms were being constructed, then diving back down to the floor of the ocean, where the seascapes were nearing completion. He dreamed a beautiful collection of habitats spreading in all directions. Or it wasn't a dream at all, it was his boyhood vision coming true in his life with Laisvė, his never-ending dream, turning into his life's labor. He saw the surface of the ocean and the swell of the sky and the seam of the horizon.

But in the middle of the dream, a great dark mass emerged from the ocean and swallowed all the water away. What seemed impossible changed instantly. Next there was no sky, just the black of space, without stars. He rolled around, naked, in the emptiness. No sound except a kind of rushing in his ears, like when your own blood becomes too loud in your own head. *This must be death*, he thought. *Something catastrophic must have occurred while I was sleeping.* Mikael wept. He wept so violently from his floating place in space that his tears became cosmic torrents, like the sky was now the ocean. And then he was back in his bed.

He woke up dreaming that he was in a pool of sweat, only the water was real, it was just lapping outside his window, pushing gently in rhythmic waves against the platforms that made up the habitats. The water the thing between sky living and sea living, between earth and the cosmos, between past and present, between dream and real.

He stepped out onto the platform, felt the night air raise the hairs on his arms and legs. A light rain fell.

The water below him stirred. A kind of green glow drew his attention to the surface. He kneeled down, tried to touch it, and before he could make contact with the wet world, a child was bawling up at him, raised from the waters by a hand, an arm, a shoulder, and then Laisvė's familiar face. A crying child, impossible to ignore. He dropped to his knees and scooped the infant up in his arms. He held it close to his chest. "Shhhhhhhhhhhh, little creature," he whispered, patting its back gently.

"Look at the back of her neck," Laisvė said, treading water, her voice filled with electricity. "I found her."

As if she'd recovered a sunken treasure.

At first, Mikael didn't know what Laisvė was talking about, but then the water and the baby and the word *neck* closed a circuit in his body. Could she . . . ? He gently turned the baby's head, just enough to see the tattoo.

"But how? How did you find her?" Mikael gasped, cradling the infant in his arms. The child was no longer crying.

"I thought of the color indigo," Laisvė said, hoisting herself up from the water onto the platform. "There was a dead woman with a flowered dress, and that opened a portal up in the water. You know how I've told you—the motherwaters carry me. I found her in your previous time and place, in an orphan house run by women. Artists or lesbians or nuns or something. I knew it was her because of the tattoo," she answered, as if any of that were possible.

And yet, with Laisvė, any story was possible.

"Look."

Mikael follows Indigo's outstretched arm all the way to her finger, pointing out the window. There he sees Laisvė, pulling herself up from the water onto the dock. He can't tell if she looks old or young or neither. More and more, she seems less human and more . . . something else.

They walk out together to greet her, help her up out of the water.

Laisvė emerges midsentence. "I'm sure you know the first designs for Proteus, don't you? They were pretty magnificent." She pulls long wet curls of black hair away from her eyes. "Around the year 2020, Fabien Cousteau and this industrial designer, Yves Béhar, created a four-thousand-square-foot modular lab sixty feet underwater, off the coast of Curaçao. Fabien took after his grandfather Jacques, whose early Conshelf projects were meant to be precursors to future underwater villages. But your creations are much more phenomenal, Mikael." She gazes out at the collection of habitats. "Look at the beauty. The vision." Then she continues. "Anyway, this French diver, Henri Cosquer, found prehistoric cave paintings a hundred and twenty feet underwater. Beautiful animals. Bisons, horses, antelope, ibex—and penguins, seals, even jellyfish. There's even an image that might be the first representation of murder! A human with a seal's head pierced by a spear."

Mikael hands Laisvė a towel. Indigo places a pair of sneakers near her feet. They know her stories don't necessarily have beginnings, middles, or ends. They fragment and accumulate, however they happen to appear in Laisvė's head. They've learned to listen differently.

Laisvė steps into the sneakers and dries her hair, her head tilted sideways, still talking. A few aquanauts in full gear emerge behind her, their oxygen tanks and wetsuits and masks making them look like odd sea creatures. Some are missing an arm or a leg or hand or a foot, but Mikael's aquaprosthetic designs make them look as if they are really a new species of water creatures.

Laisvė continues her narration, delivering information, objects, ideas: "The habitat power supplies all check out—ocean, sun, wind . . . But we need to talk about the underwater farms and the pods. The labs and medical bays are solid, but the dormitories are . . . well, they're kind of ugly. They can't be ugly. Living underwater should feel like the dreams children have. We can't have ugly." She dries her hair. "The moon pool is perfect, though."

"Why is it called a moon pool?" Indigo's question folds into Laisvė's monologue as they walk back into the habitat, painted indigo, cerulean, aquamarine, and midnight blue.

"Good question. Because, on very calm nights, the water under the rig reflects moonlight. Like the ocean is glowing open," Laisvė says, "like a perfect portal. You know, portals are everything. Even a single thought can be a portal. A single word. You know, the way poetry moves."

A Bedtime Story

Most people think the future is unbelievable, but that's only because they think the past, the present, and the future are like lines going in a single direction. What Laisvė knows in her heart is that everything that we might become at first sounds unbelievable, like a speculative story or a fairy tale, both in the world and lifted a little away from it. Imagination leaping from sea into sky and back, like a beautiful black orca.

When Laisvė tells bedtime stories to the children, they sound different from the stories other mothers or sisters or wives or daughters tell. They gather around her in all shapes and sizes, differently bodied, differently abled, untethered from their origins.

Today she brings a treasure in the form of a poem by Emma Lazarus:

The New Colossus

Not like the brazen giant of Greek fame,
With conquering limbs astride from land to land;
Here at our sea-washed, sunset gates shall stand
A mighty woman with a torch, whose flame
Is the imprisoned lightning, and her name
Mother of Exiles. From her beacon-hand
Glows world-wide welcome; her mild eyes command
The air-bridged harbor that twin cities frame.
"Keep, ancient lands, your storied pomp!" cries she
With silent lips. "Give me your tired, your poor,
Your huddled masses yearning to breathe free,
The wretched refuse of your teeming shore.
Send these, the homeless, tempest-tost to me,
I lift my lamp beside the golden door!"

The children clap or smile or make their faces into questions. A girl who stands up, in her bold curiosity, asks, "Are we the tempest-tossed? Tempest means storm."

"I think yes," Laisvė says. "And I think the ancient lands and storied pomp—well, all that kind of . . . *drowned*." The children laugh.

"Is there still a lamp?" a shy boy ventures.

"Yes. It's underwater sometimes. But we can go see it." She pulls something from her coat pocket—a clod of dirt. She pokes her finger around within it, turning up a few mycelia and a worm. "See these?"

The children get up and gather around her hand. "Are those roots?" asks one child with a wandering eye.

"Good guess," she answers. "But no. These are mycelia, from which grow mushrooms. Fungi are heterotrophs."

"What's a heteruff?"

"Hetero*trophs* get energy from their surroundings, just like humans. The largest living organism in the world is mycelium, a honey fungus in what used to be the Pacific Northwest. It might even be the oldest living mass on the planet. See that little creature?"

"A worm," a kid with glasses says.

"Not just 'a worm,'" another kid pipes up. "*Eisenia fetida*—tiger worm. *Dendrobaena veneta*—blue nose worm. *Lumbricus rubellus*—bloodworm. *Eisenia Andrei*—red tiger worm. *Lumbricus terrestris*—earthworm, Darwin's favorite . . ."

Laisvė smiles.

"Geologic time has caught up with the lifetime of a human being," she continues. "Look at the water." The children move like a single organism to gaze at the water around them. "The acid in the ocean and the glacial melts happened in my father's lifetime; in this way, time changed. Slipped forever. So geologic change has shrunk to the size of a story we can tell one another in a single sitting.

"But that means we have a hard job to do. We have to figure out the words to the story together."

A girl squats down and puts her hand in the water with reverence.

"Some of the first multicelled animals were worms. Sponges. Arthropods. Soft jelly creatures like beautiful bags, delicate disks. Then, after the Cambrian explosion, most of the modern animal forms emerged. Early corals, mollusks and clams, nautiloids and bryozoa and echinoderms. Early plankton. Then the first green plants and fungi on land. Almost like the land and water kissed, and that gave rise to life and color."

"The fish in the oceans. Coral," a boy says, beaming with belonging.

"Correct," Laisvė says. "Next, mosses and ferns. Seed-bearing plants making a break for it. Trees. The first land vertebrates. Frogs. Mice.

Salamanders. Mountains becoming mountains. Early sharks and winged insects radiating suddenly, like a flash, larger than your hand."

The children hold their hands up, mimicking her.

"Did life make the water happy in the beginning? Was the water lonely?" asks a girl with an amphibious extension on her prosthetic leg. *Is it lonely underwater?*

"I think life made the water very happy, yes," Laisvė says. Tears threaten to flood her eyes without her permission. "But then something like a planetary heart attack happened, maybe the Permian-Triassic extinction event. Nearly all life on the planet became extinct. Can you imagine this moment? All life disappears, just as things are really getting interesting?"

The children's eyes go wide. Some of their mouths drop open.

"Is that when the dinosaurs dropped dead?"

"No, that was a different extinction. Maybe the Chicxulub impact. A huge comet or asteroid, something between ten and eighty kilometers in diameter, blasts open a crater underneath the Yucatán peninsula. The K-Pg extinction event. Suddenly, three-quarters of animal and plant species on earth were wiped out. Extinctions are always happening, though. Death into life into death into life."

Laisvė senses a tendril of fear in the group of children. She kneels down with them. "But glorious things happen all the time too," she says. "Leatherback sea turtles and green sea turtles survived. Crocodiles. Birds survived. Such beautiful birds. Horseshoe crabs!" She makes fake pincers with her hands and the children laugh. "Sharks. Platypuses. Bees. So even though the K-Pg extinction may have devastated life on Earth, it also created an enormous evolutionary opportunity, radical adaptive radiation, sudden and prolific divergence into new species, shapes, sizes, forms. Bears. Horses. Bats. Birds. Fish. Whales. Primates . . ."

"Us," several children say.

"Eventually, yes. But listen. The time of recognizable human beings is so tiny—too small to be visible against geologic time. Our lives, our history, our species, haven't even come close to beginning. Your existence is not yet even recordable, not when you try to measure it against geologic time, against the Earth's story of herself. The tsunami that drowned the Sea Wall and The Brook was like a single raindrop."

The children hush and consider this.

Laisvė thinks of Aster and Svajonė.

She holds the handful of dirt out again as she tells the story. The worm wriggles.

"Fungi are six times heavier than the mass of all animals combined on the planet. Including human animals. Do they look like anything else to you?" The children gather around her hand.

"Dendrites?"

"Neurons?"

"Star systems?"

Laisvė smiles through tears. She then repeats the words she loves most from the language of geologic time. The children repeat them, creating a kind of chorus.

Cambrian
Proterozoic
Archean
Hadean
Anthropocene
Holocene
Pleistocene
Pliocene
Miocene
Oligocene

Eocene

Paleocene

Cretaceous

Jurassic

Triassic

Permian

Carboniferous

Devonian

Silurian

Ordovician

The words make a kind of poem, and when the children pull the words apart, stories of plants and animals emerge and fill their dreams. If their future is not to be made from nuclear families and cities and countries and governments and nations and wars, perhaps it will be made of stories connecting all forms of existence, a story in which even their humanity is just a thread, like the harmony of cosmic strings in space.

She wants to show the children how to memorize the story, to change it with their own tongue and breath and song. She wants to give them the words as if they were objects you could hold in your hand and use to turn time. She wants the words to become fluid in time and space, untethered from law and order and institutions that towered into collapse. She wants the words to rearrange, to locate differently, the way language itself could if you loosened it from human hubris and let it flow freely again as a sign system, as the land and water did, as species of plants and animals did, everything in existence suddenly again in flux, everything again possible.

Song of the Floating Boy
and the Water Girl

The statue has been drowned now for a long time. As the tides ebb and flow, the tips of the torch are the only things still visible from what was once the colossus, the beacon, the icon of a nation. Sometimes Laisvė and Mikael and Indigo take a boat out toward her; sometimes they bring some of the other habitat children with them.

One of the floating habitats they built for children without origins rests on the water, in the place where an immigrant hospital did many years ago. Sometimes Laisvė imagines the hospital's autopsy theater, or the contagious-disease area, or the laboratories. Sometimes she thinks about how, in an earlier epoch, her father would have been held there for his epilepsy—likely in the psychiatric holding area—tormented for something he never deserved.

Immigrant babies were born in the hospital. At the time, they automatically became citizens of a country. Within sight of a statue that was meant to signal to them their freedom. Whatever the word *freedom* meant, then, to them.

"The sick weren't the only ones shut out of the old hospitals," Laisvė once told Mikael, pausing to take a bite of kelp. "And the word *immigration* has been used as a cover story for bigotry and brutality since forever, all over the world. You know that. Even as the same nations were stocking their industries with an endless supply of human laborers." Then she'd remind him how xenophobic tendencies exist in all times, shutting out the same people no matter what lessons history has left us.

Anarchists
Murderers
Communists
Utopians
Radical socialists
Queer people
Mentally ill
Poor single mothers
Foreigners
Immigrants
Thieves
Orphans

And then she'd be off again, lost in her narrations of competing histories, opening long-lost times and places to him as if she were a human book.

When Mikael ushered Laisvė into the very first habitat he designed and built, she said, inexplicably, "The survivors of the *Titanic* were brought here, and allowed onto land. Except for six seamen from China . . . The people who took this land and called it their own were poisoned by their own bigotry from the start." She then returned to reciting the immigration histories she'd been telling him the entire time he'd known her, as if she were unable to stop.

Sometimes Mikael wondered if Laisvė suffered from mental illness. More often, he wept with relief that she existed in his life at all. Perhaps this is love: that space in between words, in between the meanings of words and things.

What Laisvė wanted, he finally decided, was to reverse pieces of history with her body. She wanted to create a real home for children who'd been orphaned or lost or abandoned or did not know where they came from, or children on the edge of danger. A place on water where a boy or a girl or anyone could float freely without fear of violence. Where children could educate one another outside the constraints of any institution or law meant to mold them into good citizens and laborers. This was a story he could bear.

It was easier, he realized, because there were no more Raids by then. There were no more nations, and so no more borders, and so no more immigrants, and so no more arrests or leaders or prisons. No more mass deportations. There were simply pockets of people all over the globe trying to exist alongside one another without a system of power to organize them. Like a new species.

Maybe a new system was coming. Maybe not. Here, in the place where they were, the people hadn't even wanted to gather together enough to make a name for their new existence. People stopped calling the area The Brook. They stopped caring where anyone was from. Maybe someday they'd want to gather, share resources, stories. For now, they existed in habitats connected by sky bridges and sea tunnels, or they were just floating, living, or learning to live.

At dusk, the habitats glow indigo, then black as the sun sets. From the windows of the surface habitats, depending on the tides, you can see the tips of the statue's torch poking up from the waves. At other times, the torch remains submerged. By now limpets and mussels, anemones and urchins, likely adorn her standard. Fish and octopuses make homes around her oxidized body. Who knows what other forms of life have emerged near her. Mikael has watched Laisvė stare out in that direction. But there is something more important to be seen.

Sometimes he watches her watch water for hours.

"Dolphins, sea turtles, seals, manatees, and whales all have an arc of bones in their front flippers," Laisvė says, staring at the fingers she has stretched in front of her.

When Laisvė steps from the ledge of the habitat back into the water, the motion no longer concerns Mikael. He knows she will carry an object with her, and he knows she'll bring a different object back. He knows she will bring other people back with her or take them to an otherwhere. He knows that the word *future* does not mean "away from us," but something more like "in us." Like everything that lives inside her imagination and dreams.

Once a month, a barge brings them supplies. The inhabitants of nearby habitats provide mutual aid in the form of food grown to share with inlanders, who are busy rewilding land from coast to coast, or sky folk, who feed all manner of birds. The man who steers the barge is an old old comma of a man. The old ship's bridge bears a blue letter *P* over the helm. When the old old comma of a man arrives, he always sits down for a visit with the water girl who has become a grown woman.

"Do you have a good trade in hand?"

"I believe I do," Laisvė says.

His eyes have receded into wrinkles and age. She thought he was old in the past, but that was because she was a child, she can see that now. She has her hair pulled back, woven into a braid as sturdy as a rope. They sit close together on crates on the barge. She holds her fisted hand toward him, then opens it. Inside her hand is an oxidized coin.

He carefully takes the coin into his hand, holds it up in front of him. "Ah. You are ready to part with it, are you?" The Flowing Hair cent.

"Yes, I believe I've carried this one long enough."

He nods his head. Closes his eyes. Then he reaches into his jacket and pulls out a box turtle.

"Bertrand?"

The turtle stretches his head out and nods. Makes a little croak, almost a burp.

The comma of a man says, "He's grown old enough for both of us, and he could use some extra care. One of his legs doesn't work quite right—" But before he can finish, Bertrand interrupts.

"Just hold on a minute here," he says. "I'm not here for pity. I'm here to make sure you two idiots from your species properly introduce yourselves! My god. The weirdness of you people. Your great, grand *humanity*! Your idiotic egos, all that individualism—what a crock! Now tell each other your names."

"Victor," the old man says quietly. "Isn't that a funny name? My mother was from what used to be Hong Kong China, but my father was Siberian! Apparently, my mother—who was a poet—wanted to name me Lìshĭ. But my father said, 'What kind of name is that? That's not a name! Not for a boy!' And so he gave me a boy's name, one that has never fit my face or my life. I'm no warrior!"

When he laughed, the crinkles around his eyes danced.

"In my heart, I carry Lìshĭ. I'm told it means 'history.'"

For just a moment, Laisvė looked at him in quiet wonder. Then she spoke. "I'm not Liza, the name you know. My mother chose my real name. My father wanted me to hide it to keep me safe. But I carry my real name in my heart too. My mother was a linguist. Mine is Laisvė. It means 'liberty.' But no one's name is Liberty."

Victor bowed. "History and Liberty sat on crates talking . . . while a cranky little turtle ordered them around." Victor's laugh filled the space between their bodies with light.

"Well, thank *oceans* that's done." Bertrand harrumphed. "Now show me where I can eat. You know—roots, mushrooms, flowers, berries, eggs, insects, that sort of thing. I've got all the drinking, soaking, and wading water I need around here. What I've got to do is burrow. You can't expect me not to burrow. Where is the nearest wild grass?"

"He's kind of bossy," Victor said.

Laisvė smiled and took Bertrand into her hands, held him close to her chest.

"Watch the leg, lady," Bertrand grumbled.

When Laisvė sings stories to children, it can take several hours. The stories have many layers; they're full of animals and natural elements as characters, like turtles and snakes and trees and worms, and always water. There is always a character named Aster, who pitches stars across the sky at night, and always a woman named Aurora, who brings the dawn, who spreads white lilies over any ground where war occurred, and always a man named Joseph, who brings the blanket of night gently around everyone and everything. There is always a beautiful man named Kem, who has a map of a new geography on his face and down his neck, like a human allegory of becoming and change, and a person named Endora, who welds the wounds between people, and a man named David, who sometimes turns into a swallow.

She asks the children who wants to play each role.

Who wants to be Aster, who marries the sea and changes the landforms?

Who wants to be Kem, whose body is a map of possibility?

Who can play the dawn?

David the swallow?

What about Endora? She likes to swear!

Who among you can be the beautiful lilies, like a hundred hands holding light?

And who can be Joseph, like a blanket at nighttime?

Who can be the *Tiktaalik*?

What it might feel like to pull oneself forward onto the ground from water an elbow at a time. She had done it herself. From the Narrows, from rivers, oceans, streams, a lake. Sometimes she also just felt compelled to drop to dirt and reinhabit the motion for no reason, just the pleasure of it. One elbow at a time.

Did the *Tiktaalik* take air in differently that first time, somehow longer; did she linger? Did she swivel her head around from that great neck, did her head want *more* even as her hind end and tail pulled her *back to water*? Did she open her mouth? Close it? Speak some sensation before language? Did she close her eyes in sensory delight or confusion as the air washed over her? Did her scales sing with eager curiosity, or cry for home? What pulled her? Hunger? Blind lunge? Accident of the stars? Did something call her? And when she finally made her S-body turn back to water, back to our shared, breathable blue past, was it relief or reserve that she felt swimming away?

Not only the moment that the *Tiktaalik* lingered on land, but the impossibility of ever telling the story—that is what Laisvė can't stop imagining.

The children spend the night inside the storytelling, their voices and heads raised up toward the night sky, naming new constellations.

Some say you can hear whales accompanying the story songs from the water, their wails threaded through her song stories. They say that if you throw a coin into water and make a wish, your wish might turn an entire epoch. These stories about stories are one way that stories survive.

But Mikael tends to think everything turns on imagination—the smile on a worker's face at the end of a day's labor building a future anyone might inhabit, or the face of a child who believes in something larger than themselves, a beauty held like a world, a marble, in your hand.

And liberty.

Coda

In the cages, we work to take care of one another. I stopped wondering when we could have showers, clean clothes, toothbrushes, or beds after two weeks. Children as young as two or three years old were with us without adult caregivers. A boy here, eleven years old, takes care of his three-year-old brother. He is so tired, he can barely stay awake. Another twelve-year-old girl cares for a four-year-old girl she does not know; she gives her extra food and protects her if someone is bullying her. The younger girl wears diapers. The older girl changes them. If you have the flu, you can sleep on a mattress on the floor in the flu cells. Sometimes we have fevers. Nobody puts their hands on our foreheads here. When I had the flu, if that's really what I had, there were twenty-seven other children in the cinder-block space, all with a fever, some shivering, all sharing mattresses on the floor. No one was looking after us. Sometimes they gave us pills, then not.

In the other Americas, where most of us began our lives, throwing rocks is a girl's first duty. You know you are choosing life over death. If you can be beaten for studying, raped for being in public, kidnapped on the street, why not fight? Fight to live. It's easy not to scream as a child. We all learn it. Before embarking on the journey, I witnessed a soldier dragging a girl. By her hair. He hit her, she fell, and then he kicked her while she was on the ground. With his boot. She didn't scream. Then she got up and ran. He followed her to a roof. He hit her again and told her that he would throw her off the roof. She said, *Do it*. Then she jumped up and stood on the ledge, daring him. Yesterday, the girl I sleep next to on the floor died in her sleep. I covered her face with the silver shock blanket. I said a silent prayer. Sometimes they leave the bright lights on all night.

Sometimes I picture the ocean where a window should be in this place, away from this all-too-human light and hard concrete floors. If I close my eyes, I can still smell the salt. I can still feel the rhythm of the waves. I think of all the people who have been carried by water, or lost to it, reaching for life. We are coming for you. Someday we will be enough. Children, I mean. And our imagination. We are relentless. Insurgent.

You can't kill the future in us.

Acknowledgments

How do you thank the idea that history is alive? This book simply would not exist if I had not read other books and encountered ideas in a kind of constant flux, a little like swimming in the ocean. The statue and story in *Thrust* is both real and imagined, or maybe in some liminal space in between. The idea of a "carrier" came from my mentor and friend, Ursula K. Le Guin, from her 1986 essay "The Carrier Bag Theory of Fiction." Of the many books and articles I used for research on the Statue of Liberty, I was most mesmerized by and I am forever in debt to the story that Elizabeth Mitchell told in *Liberty's Torch: The Great Adventure to Build the Statue of Liberty*, particularly in terms of the biographical material on Bartholdi, which inspired the character of Frédéric and served as a magical departure hub, while also helping me to conjure the details of a statue's journey. Mitchell's book contained many delightful (and sometimes troubling) firsthand accounts of the construction and reception of the colossus in America. Alongside her book and many others, I was drawn to an important article by Angela

Serratore in the May 28, 2019, issue of *Smithsonian* magazine, "The Americans Who Saw Lady Liberty as a False Idol of Broken Promises," the source of the quote from the early days of the *Cleveland Gazette,* as well as collected sentiments from suffragists, African Americans, and Chinese immigrants. This article prompted me to conjure the stories underneath a story. I also read a roomful of books on immigration, settler occupation, and early American labor ethnography. I am forever changed after learning to listen to the past differently from the way it was delivered to me.

Gratitude and Love to my dear friend J.M.L.B., who educated me mightily on the history, family, and social structure of the Haudenosaunee, and who gave me an incredible resource in the book *Mohawk Interruptus: Political Life across the Borders of Settler States* by Audra Simpson, as well as several articles on the Mohawk steelworker tradition (the Kahnawake Skywalkers). I was also inspired by an article by Lucie Levine posted on July 25, 2018, in *6SQFT,* "Men of Steel: How Brooklyn's Native American Ironworkers Built New York."

While reading ethnographies, I was also deeply inspired by the book *Decolonizing Ethnography: Undocumented Immigrants and New Directions in Social Science* by Carolina Alonso Bejarano, Lucia López Juárez, Mirian A. Mijangos García, and Daniel M. Goldstein, which brought me to many books and articles about the fluid nature of ethnography. The reimagined ethnographies in *Thrust* are my attempt to agitate the form of the novel by amplifying what M. M. Bakhtin so vividly described as heteroglossia. The closing ethnography in *Thrust* draws its inspiration from the direct interviews with children documented by Clara Long in her July 11, 2019, testimony before the U.S. House Committee on Oversight and Reform, Subcommittee on Civil Rights and Civil Liberties, transcripts of which appeared on the Human Rights Watch website. I am reminded how important it is to remember that unintentional distances exist in any human interaction that leads to bearing witness or representing the experiences of others. In particular, anyone interested in representing stories of oppression or repression—including a novelist—faces a hard and enduring challenge when liberty itself is under lock and key. It is my hope that the plurality of voice, body, and experience especially available in the form of the novel might serve to keep the tensions, contradictions, conflicts, and desires of the many rather than the one alive, noisy, unflinching.

My research on the history of sex work in 1800s America included two books that were of major influence in creating the character of Aurora: *City of Eros: New York City, Prostitution, and the Commercialization of Sex, 1790–1920* by Timothy J. Gilfoyle and *City of Women: Sex and Class in New York 1789–1860* by Christine Stansell. The material on Helen Jewett is drawn largely from Patricia Cline Cohen's excellent *The Murder of Helen Jewett.*

The story of the kidnapped child is extrapolated from the fascinating *Charley Ross the Kidnapped Child: The Father's Story*, by the boy's father, Christian K. Ross. Oceans of gratitude to Domi Shoemaker for finding and gifting me this book from 1876 (!!!).

The quoted material about Timothy McVeigh is documented in *American Terrorist: Timothy McVeigh and the Oklahoma City Bombing* by Lou Michel and Dan Herbeck. The authors spent more than forty hours interviewing McVeigh in prison, leading to the tapes that form the basis of their television special, *The McVeigh Tapes: Confessions of an American Terrorist.*

Books don't just materialize from an author's head, nor exclusively from research and creative labor. The making of books is a creative collaboration, and this book owes its very life to several radiant souls whose lives threaded through mine. I am forever grateful to Melanie Conroy-Goldman and everyone at Hobart and William Smith Colleges, where I spent a magical year as the Trias Writer. Put simply, the year changed my life forever. Most of the ground of *Thrust* emerged between long walks around Seneca Lake and deep creative engagement with the Trias Squad. (I remember every single one of you—Allison Palmer, Madeline

Herbert, Emma Honey, Max Romana, Christopher Costello, Bethany Kharrazi, Hanan Issa, Katie Kumta, Anna Flaherty, Lilly Shea, and Jackie Steinman—and I will forever.) All of us left winter term and traveled straight into the mouth of COVID; perhaps we are forever imprinted on one another from moving through our own creativity into the crucible that came next. I carry you all in my heart.

Endless gratitude to my Valkyrie agent, Rayhané Sanders, and my brilliant, patient, inspirational editor, Calvert Morgan. Without you two my imagination cannot find form or motion.

Full-throated love and thanks to my sister Brigid, who read early versions of this material, who helped me keep my passion light lit, and who reflected back to me that my ideas deserve to live.

And always to my north star, Andy Mingo, creative soulmate, love of my life. Thank you for helping me move this work from chaos to order (and for the whiteboard idea, even though I hated it at first). Thank you for believing in my stories and for keeping me on the planet in spite of myself. What a ride it's been. I love you into the everything.